Praise for *The G*

"*The Greatest Show on Dirt* is funny, fast-paced, and peopled with likable characters in a believable minor-league setting. In other words: manna for fans of sports fiction."

–JOSEPH WALLACE, author of *Diamond Ruby*

"In *The Greatest Show on Dirt*, James Bailey performs a double-play pivot worthy of Bill Mazeroski, deftly pairing a page-turning coming-of-age tale about the cluelessness and angst of the post-college years with a richly detailed tour behind the scenes at a minor league ballpark. Like protagonist Lane Hamilton, a young, low-level functionary with the Durham Bulls, many of us stumble through our early twenties waiting for a call-up to The Majors—that vague, personalized fantasy of a passionate, meaningful adult life—but Lane became for me the epitome of that waiting during a scene in which he literally stumbles while attempting to provide his uselessly inexpert help in pulling a tarp across a bush league field in a rainstorm. Even when it rains, *The Greatest Show on Dirt* delivers poignant and hilarious big league entertainment."

–JOSH WILKER, author of *Cardboard Gods*

"This coming-of-age story set against the ageless backdrop of minor league baseball is a fun and satisfying read. Bailey worked three years for the legendary Durham Bulls and his novel resonates with inside knowledge of both the game and business of baseball. The writing is lively, the cast of colorful characters drawn with care and compassion, and the flawed yet good-hearted protagonist, Lane Hamilton, proves to be as reliable a narrator as he is son, grandson, friend and lover. This is a fine first novel by a man whose love for baseball, and people, shines through."

–JEFF GILLENKIRK, author of *Home, Away*

"If you have ever been around the minor leagues—be it as a ballplayer, front office worker or sports writer—you cannot help but find a piece of yourself in one of the characters in James Bailey's *Greatest Show on Dirt*."

–ANDY LINKER, Longtime Harrisburg Senators beat writer

"A raucous, laugh-out-loud romp through the heartbeat of minor league baseball with an all-star front-office insider at the wheel. Bailey hits a homer that clears the cheap seats, all the characters in them, and all the hopeful romantics who work so hard to spin the turnstiles. Your minor league ballpark experience will never be the same."

–GENE SAPAKOFF, Sports columnist,
Charleston (S.C.) Post and Courier

"Nobody has a better feel for the sleepy rhythm of Durham life than James Bailey, nor can anyone give you a better guided tour of the fascinating subculture of minor league baseball. Give this man a steak. He's gone yard."

–MIKE BERARDINO, Sports columnist,
South Florida Sun Sentinel

"Bailey's knowledge of life in the minor leagues comes across in rich detail, making Greatest Show on Dirt an engaging and entertaining read of a young man finding himself during the daily grind of a season in Durham."

–JOHN MANUEL, Editor in chief,
Baseball America

The Greatest Show on Dirt

A Novel

James Bailey

Cover designed by Valerie Holbert. Front cover photo provided courtesy of D.L. Anderson. Back cover photo provided courtesy of Bill Miller.

Printed in the United States of America.

ISBN-13: 978-1-4611-1650-9
ISBN-10: 1-4611-1650-3

To Grant,
because I couldn't give up and ever tell you not to.

And to Jill,
for loving me back.

The Greatest Show on Dirt

SCORECARD

DURHAM BULLS FRONT OFFICE

DON SANDERS, GENERAL MANAGER
SONNY HIGGINS, ASST. GM/HEAD GROUNDSKEEPER
GRAY FRANCIS, SALES AND MARKETING
ASHANDRA BAKER, OFFICE MANAGER
JENNA PARSONS, GROUP SALES MANAGER
MIKE ADAMLEE, CONCESSIONS MANAGER
RICH FARRELL, STADIUM OPERATIONS/GROUNDS CREW
BLAKE MUNGO, GROUNDS CREW
LANE HAMILTON, OPERATIONS ASSISTANT
CARSON FOWLER, TICKET OFFICE ASSISTANT
SHANNON MILLER, INTERN, GROUP SALES
EMMA LEIGH WRIGHT, INTERN, PUBLIC RELATIONS
AARON LOVE, SOUVENIR SALES MANAGER
FAITH ANDREWS, SOUVENIR SALES
RON ANDERS, RADIO ANNOUNCER

GAME DAY STAFF

JOHNNY LAYNE, SPECIAL ASST. TO THE GM
NICK HENRY, PA ANNOUNCER
RONALD "PEANUT" WINTERS, GROUNDS CREW
WENDELL "SPANKY" PAUL, GROUNDS CREW
"VENDOR JOE" WHEELER, PROGRAM SALES
HARVEY MONK, TICKET TAKER
SHAUNA GALE, TICKET TAKER
EDDIE EDWARDS, BATBOY

SCORECARD

COACHES

GORDY MCNULTY	MANAGER
JIM PEAK	PITCHING COACH
GLEN BAGNALL	HITTING COACH

PLAYERS

FRANCISCO ACEVEDO	DH
MATT ACRES	P
CLEOTIS ANTHONY	OF
WILLIAM DURANTE	SS/2B
J.T. GAINES	P
ROGER GALE	C
PAUL GIORDANO	2B
GOOSE GRASCYK	P
DAIN GREGSON	SS
MARTIN HARCOURT	2B
LUTHER HUDSON	OF
CLYDE KNOWLES	3B/C
DEL KOLB	P
OSCAR LANTIGUA	P
ANDY MILLS	P
MIGUEL ORLANDO	OF
NELSON RAY	P
DOMINIC VEROTTO	3B
RABBIT WATERSON	OF
"WILD" EVAN WAYNE	P
WARREN YAUCH	P

CHAPTER ONE

I had a professor my junior year in college who told us that one day we'd each wake up and realize we hated our lives, and that this knowledge would set us free. Legend had it he had put in twenty-one years at Xerox and was pretty high up on the food chain when his epiphany struck. Within six months he was an academic, wearing corduroy sport jackets with patches on the elbows and a pipe stashed in the breast pocket. We never did coax his story out of him—what made him snap? He'd only smile and say, "Twenty-one years. How long will it take you?"

I got there a lot faster than he did.

My moment of clarity came, fittingly enough, on the john in the Cameron Village branch of First Carolina Bank. The Swedish meatballs I'd sampled from the office potluck stormed through my system like Sherman through Georgia. While the rest of the staff congregated for our weekly spirit breaking, I slunk off to the restroom to jettison what was left of my innards. So it was that I found myself at 5:03 with my gabardine slacks around my ankles debating which part of my job I hated the most. The productivity reports. The jacket and tie thing. The way Ed Collins, my fat bastard of a boss, revealed his gums when he flashed his phony smile. Nine months out of college I was dreaming about retirement.

I slid the door to the conference room open and tiptoed across the carpet to the last remaining open seat, at the far end of the table from where Ed stood, arms folded across his chest. The minute hand on the wall clock jerked forward with a dull *kah-lunk* as I sat down. I was exactly eight minutes late.

Ed cleared his throat and announced, "Glad you could join us, Hamilton. If we knew you were coming we would have waited."

This drew a faint chorus of laughter from the sycophants seated around the table. I scanned the room to register their faces.

"Sorry, sir," I mumbled.

"Did you have more important business to attend to?"

"I seem to have had a bad reaction to the meatballs."

Another round of tittering, only this time it was the corpulent bank manager glaring around the room logging names. He reached up and wiped the sweat off his forehead with the back of his shirtsleeve, revealing a spreading stain under his armpit.

"My wife made those meatballs," he seethed. "It must have been something else you ate, Hamilton. No one else has reported a problem."

I stared at the table top until he finally broke the uncomfortable silence and resumed his presentation where he'd left off before my entrance. After thirty seconds he hit his stride as though he'd never been interrupted. He lived for those meetings, an open forum every Thursday after closing time to ream out whoever had failed to reach quota over the past seven days. Ed Collins was a bully and he loved to play a crowd.

He tugged at his belt, as if there were some chance he could coax his pants up over his doughy belly. The effort stretched his broadcloth shirt nearly to the bursting point, and I silently prayed he'd pop a button. The ratio of skin to cloth was way off. His flabby white neck hung over his collar like a Thanksgiving turkey.

"Martin!" he barked, launching a bubble of spittle that splashed down on the conference room table a moment later. "No new mortgages this week? Did you give up?"

Jim Martin fidgeted in the chair next to mine, whistling faintly through his nose as he filtered air through his whisk-broom mustache. I averted my eyes toward the window, where a faint ray of sunlight fought its way through a break in the blinds.

"I've been, um, out most of the week, sir," Jim stammered. "Marie's on bedrest, and I—"

"Right, right," Ed grunted as he ran his fat fingers over his greasy, swirling combover. His hair appeared to be basted with some kind of honey glaze and the smoothing was unnecessary. "Allison here spent Monday night in ER with a broken ankle. She still met her targets."

At the end of the table, Allison Porto grinned and arched her back like a cat meeting a caress as she basked in the glow of her manager's praise. It was a weekly scene and it made me sick. I wanted to slam the chair supporting her elevated foot into the table. And it was sprained, not broken. She had slipped on an icy patch in the parking lot as we left work Monday night. Any of the rest of us would have walked it off.

I stared down at the seven-page printout on the table in front of me. Though my numbers were respectable this week, I was far from immune. Andy Quinn, the manager at my first branch over in Durham, had warned me about Ed the day my transfer came through. "Just watch your numbers, big guy," he said. "That cocksucker loves numbers."

Andy always called me "big guy." Corny, but it beat the hell out of "Hamilton!" Ed Collins reserved first names for his pets, like Allison. I'm not sure he even knew mine. He never called me Lane.

Kah-lunk. Five-twenty. The clock literally moved in reverse. Each jump the minute hand took was preceded by a distinct hitch, as though it needed to wind up before flushing away another sixty-second chunk of my life.

I clicked my pen and began doodling on Ed's spreadsheet, filling in the O's and other round letters. I sketched out a frosty mug, beer foaming over the rim. If I could just fast forward an hour I'd be holding a real one. Rich Farrell had called Monday morning and left a message on my voice mail. "Reunion. Mitch's. Thursday. Don't bring Becca."

Becca, a.k.a. Trina Overbay to the rest of the world, started in on her sighing routine the moment I mentioned I couldn't do dinner tonight. When she asked why, I panicked and said, "Paul asked me to help him with a youth clinic at his church." The words escaped so quickly I didn't have time to weigh plausibility until she'd already lowered her eyelids to half mast and tilted her head to the side. Her lie-detector pose. And what a whopper this was. Paul Giordano hadn't been to church since his great aunt died our senior year in high school. But he was my only friend who even attempted polite conversation with her, and that earned just enough reasonable doubt to avoid an on-the-spot conviction.

Rich's name was not to be uttered. And she didn't know half of what he said about her. He called her Becca after an old girlfriend of his. Rich met his Becca shortly after Christmas our junior year at North Carolina State University, right after she had broken up with her fiancé. He went from the shoulder she cried on to a whole lot more in just over a week. And then she called him. And called him. And called him. Three days after finals ended he boarded a flight to Europe to broaden his horizons for six weeks and escape his batshit girlfriend. His parents changed their number while he was gone because she kept calling. Eventually she latched onto some other poor, dumb bastard and he was off the hook.

So Rich and Trina didn't mix. As a result I hadn't seen him in over a month. Tonight was not to be missed, however. Cole Brunson, the last piece of our high school foursome, was in town, and tradition demanded we celebrate.

Kah-lunk. Five-twenty-six. I cross-checked it with my watch. Damn. Maybe the earth's gravitational pull had been altered and time was slowing down. I closed my eyes for a moment and the room grew eerily quiet. An elbow in my ribs confirmed I'd been caught napping.

"He asked 'what have you been doing?'" Jim whispered in my ear.

"Um," I stalled. "I've been working on new accounts."

Silence. Each tick of the clock marked off another second of my turn in the crosshairs of humiliation. I heard a bead of sweat rush past my ear as it streaked down the side of my face. Ed Collins goose-stepped around the table and I braced myself for the inevitable.

"Thin ice, Hamilton," he hissed over my left shoulder. "You're on some goddam thin ice."

With the exception of Allison, everyone in that branch was on thin ice. When the spring thaw struck he'd be plumb out of employees. After an awkward pause, he ran his stubby fingers across his combover and moved on to Marcia in home equity loans.

"He meant what have you been doing to help get the branch ready for the First Carolina Olympics," Jim whispered when the head sloth was out of range.

The First Carolina Olympics was Ed's stillborn brainchild, an interbranch competition to boost employee morale. The great irony being employee morale was down on account of him in the first place. We were supposed to "hurdle" certain levels in our loans and "sprint" our way to opening accounts for new customers. Had I been paying attention my answer wouldn't have been much better, because the whole thing was so stupid I was planning to call in sick the day of the competition. I might have checked my dignity at the door every morning, but it was always there on standby to prevent me from three-legged racing around the parking lot.

I followed Ed with my eyes for the next excruciating twenty minutes, determined not to get tripped up again. He excoriated nearly everyone, including all the tellers, but Jim and I were left alone, fuckup pariahs at the far end of the table. At last he went into his summation and the end was in sight. When he blubbered, "No meeting next week. I'm on vacation," a cheerful flame flickered in every eye in the room.

We filtered out into the chilly early evening, and I pointed my pickup truck toward Hillsborough Street. From the plaza where the bank sat to Mitch's Tavern was only a short drive. I found the campus lot on the opposite side of the street practically empty. I parked under a towering oak that predated the lot and all the buildings surrounding it and scrambled down to the sidewalk. After a couple of false starts I weaved across the four lanes of traffic on Hillsborough, the main drag along the northern edge of the university.

Seventies rock music and clinking glassware filled my ears when I pulled the door open. Ascending the worn wooden staircase, I recalled the night I "discovered" the place, thanks to the crowd of on-lookers lining the sidewalk outside as they filmed the movie *Bull Durham*. The scene where Crash Davis and Nuke LaLoosh first meet was set there. The movie leaves the impression that it's in Durham, though. It's not. There's only one Mitch's and there would be an empty hole in the heart of Hillsborough Street if it ever moved.

Tonight it bustled with the usual dinner rush. As I reached the top step I scanned the bar for familiar faces. Finding none, I turned left and spotted Cole bobbing his head along with the music in a booth by the wall. Just like high school. He would close his eyes so he could "really feel the music." When he started doing it a cappella in the dugout during baseball games we decided he was a total freak. Actually that was obvious long before. When we were freshmen he would chant in the dugout like the team cheerleader.

His favorite was, "Be the ball, Lane!" though I never figured out what that was supposed to mean. Sometimes he'd just scream your name when you were batting. "LAAAAY-NEEEEE! LAAAAY-NEEEEE!" He looked kind of disturbed in a way, but it really loosened everyone up.

When he didn't come out for baseball our senior year, we lost more than our center fielder and leadoff man. He was the unifying force on the team, the one guy who transcended all the cliques. We didn't play anywhere near as well without him that spring. But baseball had been surpassed by his love of music. He played guitar and formed a band with a couple of burnouts from our school. They rocked parties every weekend, anywhere they were invited. A couple of kids on the chess club realized they could use Cole's band to lure chicks to their house when their parents left town. Cole never questioned their motive. He just loved to play.

He dropped out of college midway through our sophomore year when his new band, Disingenuity, started to get gigs on a semi-regular basis. Real, paying gigs, too, not just nerd parties. Studying infringed upon their practice time, and because no self-respecting musician got up at six in the morning to go to class, he eventually found himself on academic probation. When his dad refused to pony up the tuition money for spring semester he quit school. He and his bandmates moved up to Washington, D.C., a short time later to gain exposure. I hadn't seen him but twice since.

"What's up?" I called as I approached his table.

Cole opened his eyes and sprang up to greet me. As we embraced I caught a faint whiff of patchouli.

"Damn, man, look at you," I said. His hair was straight and long, much longer than the last time I'd seen him a year earlier. He'd also grown a scrappy Van Dyke beard.

"You're not doing too bad yourself there, Lane." He reached out to grab my tie. "I'm feeling a little underdressed. Rich didn't say it was semi-formal."

I yanked at the knot at my Adam's apple. "Totally forgot I had this stupid thing on."

"You wear one every day?"

"Yeah," I confessed as I thrust it deep into the pocket of my wool pea jacket. "Sucks."

"Makes you look professional."

"I hate it."

"How's the job?"

I shrugged and turned to flag down our waitress, who had stopped two tables over. She nodded and I sat down.

"It's a steady paycheck."

"That's more than I can say sometimes," he laughed. "We definitely have our ebbs and flows."

"Who's aibbin' and flown'?" asked a voice behind me in the Brooklyn meets Mayberry twang that could only belong to Paul, whose family had migrated from New York to Raleigh when he was seven. "Ho, Cole? Get the hell outta here. 'S'that you?"

Paul slapped his right paw down on my back, and I turned to shake hands with him. He looked startled when Cole spread his arms to embrace him.

"You look awesome, buddy," Cole said. "You're totally ripped."

Paul tapped me on the leg and I slid down so he could sit next to me in the wooden booth.

"I been working out a ton," Paul said. "I'm at the warehouse from six to two every day, then off to the gym. I put on ten pounds of muscle this winter."

I playfully pinched his bicep. Rock solid. Paul had been a devoted weight lifter ever since a handful of baseball scouts started following him during his junior year of college. Of the four of us he was the only one to stick with the game beyond high school, and our paths had diverged when he headed for UNC-Pembroke to play while the rest of us stayed in Raleigh and went to State. He signed a minor league contract with the Atlanta Braves last June after they picked him in the forty-third round of the draft.

"When do you leave for spring training?" Cole asked.

"Monday. Don't worry none, I'll be there for your show tomorrow."

"Me too," I nodded.

"How's about your girl?" Paul asked.

"She said yes. So ... maybe. Just don't tell her Rich is coming."

Paul laughed. Rich had documented the feud well for him over the course of the winter.

"Where is Richard?" I glanced over at the stairs in search of our delinquent friend.

"He mentioned he might be late," Paul said. "Had to help his roommate pack."

"Who, that new guy at the Bulls?"

"Yeah. Ryan, the kid from Boston."

"Where's he going?" I asked.

"Home."

"Really? It took Rich forever to fill that room. What happened?"

"His mom's been diagnosed with an inoperable brain tumor. He's going home to, ya know, be with her before she ..."

"That sucks."

"You gotta grab life by the balls, man."

"Wow," I said. "Now Rich will start back on me. Watch. He bugged me for four months to take that room."

"You still staying with your folks?"

"Yup. Can't beat the price."

"What's his place like?"

"Big old colonial in the city, up on Markham Avenue. Kinda run down, but what do they care? I helped him move in. I was sure we'd fall through the porch with all the heavy crap we had to carry in there. He shares it with a couple of grad students at Duke. And this kid. Well, not anymore."

"You should see the shithole we're in," Cole said, reentering the conversation. "All four of us in a two bedroom apartment. The only reason it works is we're always on the road."

Our waitress stopped back with our drink order, sloshing beer on the table as she slid the pitcher off her tray. When she left, Paul took charge of filling our glasses.

"Big show tomorrow, eh?" he said.

"Yeah." Cole bobbed his head. "Should be awesome to play Raleigh again."

"You guys finish your new CD yet?" Paul asked.

Cole dug into his coat pocket and pulled out Disingenuity's new album, *Fashion Fugitives*. He and his bandmates had posed for the cover shot wearing nothing but boxers while out on the National Mall in D.C. In the corner of the picture you could see a park ranger running toward them waving a flashlight.

"Hot off the presses." Cole smiled proudly. "It's not even on the shelves yet. We just got these back on Tuesday."

"You guys record this yourself?" I asked.

"Yes and no. We hired a producer to work with us, but we had to rent the studio time and pay for everything."

"Wow," Paul said. "Must be kinda pricey."

"Ain't cheap." Cole took a long pull on his beer. "Sure ain't cheap. I think we might come back here to record next time. But I really like this one. I think we might get some decent radio play on a few of these. College radio, you know. We're making a few connections here and there."

"I heard you guys once in Pulaski, if you can believe that." Paul had spent his first summer in pro ball up in the mountains of Virginia, playing for the Pulaski Braves in the Appalachian League. "I think it was the Virginia Tech station from Blacksburg. We could get it sometimes."

"No shit? I'm gonna have to add them to my list. I have a boatload of calls to make tomorrow. Trying to get the word out on the new disc."

"You guys don't have a manager?" Paul asked.

"Nah, not at the moment." Cole lifted his right hand over his head and gave a quick wave. "Hey, look who's here."

Rich approached from the top of the stairs, rubbing his arms to chase away the remaining chill. Despite the brisk temperatures he had worn only a thin fleece jacket. Cole rose and doled out another hug. That must have been something he picked up on the road. We were never huggers growing up. Rich sat down opposite Paul and immediately grabbed the pitcher.

"Sorry guys," he said. "Ryan's U-Haul didn't get there until after three. I had to help him get everything loaded."

Our server swung by and we ordered another pitcher and some sandwiches. I didn't even need to look at the menu. Turkey Reuben. I must have eaten a hundred of them in college. When our waitress was gone Cole proposed a toast.

"To friends." He hoisted his mug. "That nothing should come between us. Not music, baseball—"

"Women," Rich interjected and gave me a quick wink.

"Sorry," I said, after we touched glasses. "I've been lame."

"A little. Sometimes I wonder if you've been castrated."

"I said I was sorry."

"Have we got some issues to discuss?" Cole asked with mock severity.

"Lane's just kind of whipped, is all. I never see the kid anymore."

"It's just easier sometimes to not make waves, you know. She lays such a huge guilt trip on me if I even want to spend a night at home with my parents."

"I try to invite my boy here to lunch," Rich said. "And Mr. Sackless kind of gives me 'well, you know, I don't know, I'll let you know.' I want to reach through the phone and choke the fucker. Grow a pair, dude."

"I know, I know. Won't happen again. I promise."

"Bullshit," Rich laughed. He drained the rest of his beer and reached for the pitcher.

"We're all here now," Paul said. "Let's enjoy ourselves. How's life with the Durham Bulls?"

"Pretty good, actually." Rich had latched on with the Bulls' grounds crew shortly before we graduated. "Though we've got an opening to fill now. Lane?"

"See?" I chuckled.

"What?" Rich demanded.

"I told them you were going to bug me to move in again."

"I'm talking about the job, dipshit. We're gonna need to bring someone in, pronto."

"Doing what?"

"Little of everything. Grounds crew, media relations, selling ads. Whatever needs doing."

"Eh," I shrugged.

"What's 'eh' mean? You lovin' life at the bank all of a sudden?"

"Hardly."

"You know people kill for these jobs, dude. We had more than a hundred and fifty applicants for two openings at the winter meetings."

"Why don't you call one of them, then?"

"No one wants to go through all that again. I could get you in. Seriously."

"I dunno, man. I can't take that kind of pay cut."

"Money isn't everything, dude," Rich said.

"They're buying away the best days of your life," agreed Paul, who had never complained about working in the warehouse all winter just to afford chasing his dream.

Across the table Cole nodded. Of course, he hadn't held a job since getting fired from Winn-Dixie for stealing beer when he was seventeen.

"It ain't that simple," I said, grateful the waitress had appeared with our dinner, allowing the subject to drop. The only justification I could find for my job was I made as much as the three of them combined. I hardly wanted to go there. They'd probably stick me with the dinner tab.

"So, where to now?" Rich asked, when our plates had been cleared.

"I don't know if I can, guys," I said.

"What? You finally get a free night and you're ready for bed?" Rich thrust his hand into his pants pocket and slapped a quarter on the table. "You need to call her? Here. Go check in."

"It's not that."

"Yeah."

"No, seriously. I have a major important meeting at work tomorrow morning. I absolutely can't be hung over."

"Whatever. Let's go."

I glanced from Cole to Paul and down at the table. They were free to go on without me. But I knew they wouldn't. Paul was just disciplined enough that he could use me as an excuse to go home and rest.

"Lane?" A squeaky, taffy pull of a voice from the stairway broke the tension. The four of us turned in unison to find a pudgy mass wrapped in a puffy, Pepto-Bismol pink coat. The rosy face curtained by a tightly coiled perm belonged to Fanny Dyer, one of the tellers from my old branch. She worked in the window next to Trina.

"Shit," I muttered.

Rich's face lit up. He was the only other one at the table who recognized my predicament.

"David," Fanny called to her husband, who was only two steps behind her. "Look, it's Lane."

He waved as his wife charged toward our table.

"How have you been?" she asked, unbuttoning her coat. "I'm

always hoping you'll stop back by and visit."

"I'd like to," I said, with more gusto than was realistic. "But I'm so busy at my branch I never get the chance."

"Andy still talks about you all the time. You know, I think he wishes you'd stayed on. How do you like working for Ed?"

I sucked in my breath. "Ah. It's all right. He's not so bad."

"Why do you call him 'the Nazi,' then?" Rich interrupted.

"I do not." I smiled at Fanny. "I don't. I don't call him that. Really."

Fanny giggled and winked at me. "It's okay if you do. I've heard worse."

"Really?"

"You forget I worked for him, too. I went the opposite way. I moved to Andy's branch four years ago. He's so much easier to work for."

"Yeah," I conceded.

"Well." Fanny glanced over her shoulder. "David's hungry. We've got to get a table."

"It was nice seeing you," I said.

"Yeah. I thought that was you when I got to the top of the stairs. Oh, I can't wait to tell Trina tomorrow. What a happy surprise."

Rich snickered as the Pepto-Bismol coat weaved away through the crowd.

"You're fucked, aren't you?" he laughed.

"Yup."

"You didn't tell her, did you?"

"Nope."

"How'd you get away?"

"Told her I was helping Paul with a baseball clinic at his church."

"Say what?" Paul asked, as Rich gasped for air. He was laughing too hard inside to emit sound.

Our waitress stopped by to scoop up the stack of bills piled at the end of the table. Rich tapped her on the hand and managed enough breath to say, "Hold on a second. I think we're gonna need another pitcher."

"I'm so fucked," I said when she had gone.

"I don't get it," Cole said. "What's the big deal? It's not like we went to a titty club. She's not going to care."

"You don't know Trina," Rich and I said in unison. Only he was laughing when he said it, and I was grinding my teeth.

CHAPTER TWO

Fanny and her husband sat kitty corner from us, three tables down. After the second time she waved at me I capitulated.

"Okay, let's go somewhere," I said. "Anywhere. Drink up."

"What's the rush?" Rich asked.

"Just drink up. It's bad enough already. Let's get out of here."

I tossed a ten-dollar bill on the table and nudged Paul, who was chugging the last of his beer.

"Awright, awright. I'm going," he said.

Ignoring Fanny's smile I weaved around the waitress and descended the stairs, not bothering to button my coat until I reached the sidewalk, where I waited for my friends.

"So now where to?" Cole asked, when we reunited. "Dance club?"

"Hell no," I said. "None of you guys can dance anyway."

"And you can?"

I shrugged. Trina loved to dance. I kept up with her all right. But I'd seen those guys through four years of high school mixers and a random frat party or two, and they were laughable. Especially Cole, which was the least forgivable, considering he'd devoted his life to music.

"I've got a plan," Rich said. "Everyone get their cars. Let's meet at Cole's and I'll drive from there."

"Why Cole's?"

"He's closest, and his dad won't care if your car's there all night."

"All night?" I moaned. "Dude, I wasn't kidding about work."

"Don't be such a pansy. You'll like this place."

"Where is it?"

"Devine's. It's a sports bar over in Durham."

"I'm out. It's already nine. There's no way we're there and back by eleven."

"Let's just shoot some pool at my house," Cole said. "Then Lane can go home whenever."

"That works," I said. "I'll meet you guys over there."

Cole's was the basement of choice during our teen years. It was like going to Ricky Schroder's house in *Silver Spoons*. He had the arcade-style video games, foosball, air hockey, and the pool table. When his parents split up the resultant arms race netted more toys than any kid could properly enjoy in one lifetime. It's a wonder we all stayed thin with the never-ending junk food buffet served up down there. I think they were on the Hostess delivery route. As we aged, so did the libations. Tonight the beer bottles, packed tight in the bar downstairs, rattled against each other as Mr. Brunson opened the fridge.

Cole's dad ruled the pool table for an hour before leaving it to the "junior leaguers," as he called us, when he retired upstairs for the night. Then I got hot and won a few games, beating each of my friends in succession.

"That's it for me," I declared, after knocking home the eight ball to finish off Cole. In his prime he killed me every game, but he was rusty from his time away.

"What's up with that?" Paul demanded. "You can't just leave. You own the table."

"Yeah," Rich said. "You don't get to walk away as king."

"Fine. One more game. This is for king. Who's up?"

"Me," Rich said. "And don't worry. I'll dethrone you this time."

"Whatever."

If there were two more competitive kids in all of Raleigh than me and Rich, I never met them. In grade school it wasn't uncommon for one, or both, of us to go home in tears. I can't count the number of wrestling matches that took place in my driveway under the guise of a basketball game. There was no such thing as an open shot, unless you happened to knock your defender to the ground first. My mom eventually gave up on playing nurse and would just leave a box of Band-Aids and a bottle of Bactine out on the counter when he came over. I was not about to lose the table to him.

"CRACK!" My break rattled balls off all four bumpers. With a satisfying double thump, two of them dropped home.

"What was that?" I asked.

"Stripe, and a … another stripe," Paul called from the far corner.

"Two down," I laughed. "I'll run this and be in bed in fifteen minutes."

At the far end of the room Rich leaned forward on his bar stool and smiled. "You'd better. You ain't gettin' a second turn."

I surveyed the table, envisioning successive shots, finally settling on the 14-ball, which sat just shy of the side pocket. A soft kiss would leave me with a clear path to the 12, down in the corner. I spun the cue between my fingers as I leaned over to line up the shot. Just as I wound up, the phone on the bar rang and broke my concentration.

"It's Becca," Rich kidded. "Time for you to go."

I released my shot and the 14 tipped into the pocket. "It ain't because of her I have to leave."

"Same difference."

"What's that mean?"

"Means you wouldn't be working for that Nazi if not for her."

He had a point. Andy had given me a choice when my training period expired. I could stick at the Durham branch and pretend Trina and I weren't dating, or transfer elsewhere. I opted for the breathing room.

"I don't get it," Cole said. "Why do you put up with her?"

"You've never seen her, have you?" I asked.

"No one's worth all this," Cole said.

"She's not as bad as Rich is making her out. She's just a little possessive. Can you blame her?" I pulled the pool cue down behind my back mimicking a lat pull at the gym.

"Yeah, beanpole like you must have to fight 'em off with a club," Paul kidded. He flexed and you could almost hear his rippling muscles laughing at my puny ones. Of course, I didn't work out for two hours every night.

"She is hot, though. Back me up, Paul."

He shrugged. "Yeah, she's pretty. And she's always been awright around me."

Rich snorted.

"What? Even you have to concede this one. Those long, tight

legs. Great body. Beautiful face. She's got these piercing green eyes that just heat me right up when she smiles."

"Stop fantasizing and hit your fucking shot."

I leaned back over the table and sized up the 12. Staring up at Rich as I hit it, I listened until I heard the satisfying plunk of the ball nestling into the pocket. "That's four. And here goes the ten."

I slammed the 10-ball into the corner, where it connected solidly with the back of the pocket, pinball rattled, and popped back onto the table.

"Heh-heh-heh," Rich chuckled. "You're done."

He broadcast his run, shot by shot, as he calmly sank the 2, 3, 5, and 1 balls.

"Getting nervous?" he asked.

"Nope."

"Check this shit out. Jump ball. Over the fifteen, onto the four, in down at the far corner."

I leaned over the opposite end of the table and analyzed his angle. "Not in a million years."

"Just watch."

He drew his stick back and stabbed at the cue ball, scraping hard against the felt as he drove the ball high into the air. My eyes crossed as it drew nearer, my brain jamming for a costly split second. By the time I ducked, the ball had already caromed off my forehead. I crumpled to the floor like a marionette.

Two concerned faces peered over me when at last I opened my eyes. A third appeared a moment later as Paul reached in with a towel full of ice.

"Thank God," Rich said. "Thought I killed you for a minute."

Paul gently pressed the ice to my head, blocking my vision from all but the corner of my left eye. I reached up to feel my wound and he lifted the towel away. A welt had risen just above the bridge of my nose.

"You're gonna want to keep this on there," Paul said. "Or it'll get bigger."

"Thanks." I sat up and the room spun. Objects continued to flash past for several seconds after I closed my eyes. "Help me get to the couch."

Paul and Rich each grabbed an arm as Cole cleared his guitar case off the sofa. He slid a pillow in under my head and I closed my eyes again.

"I'm not forfeiting."

"Fair enough," Rich laughed. "We'll start fresh when you feel better."

"I gotta go. Seriously."

"You can't drive home," Paul said. "You can't even sit up. Just rest. We'll getcha home in a little bit."

I heard Cole rack up the table again, and someone fired off a powerful break shot. I fell asleep before I ever figured out who was playing. Sometime later Paul shook me awake.

"You ready?"

"What time is it?" I mumbled.

"It's about one-thirty."

"Fuck."

"You were asleep already. Same as if you were home. You'll be fine tomorrow."

I reached up and rubbed my forehead and traced around the bump with my finger.

"Do I look like a unicorn?"

"Nah. You can barely see it."

"Liar."

"I'm gonna drive you home in your truck, and Cole's going to follow and bring me back here."

"Thanks."

"Can you stand?"

"I think so."

I teetered to my feet with his help. Once outside, the frosty air revitalized me, loosening the pressure in my head enough that I felt almost normal again. As long as I focused on far away objects my vision was clear. Paul drove me home and helped me into the house.

"See you tonight at Cole's show," he whispered.

"I'll be there."

I kicked my shoes off and tossed my pants aside and fell into bed. Within two minutes I was asleep again. A hard rain pelting the window woke me what felt like a short time later. I pushed the curtain open above my bed and the room lightened a shade. A low droning of static-laced music teased my ears and I strained to identify the song. *"I've got friends in low places, where the whiskey drowns and the beer chases my blues away."* It was Garth Brooks. I hummed along wondering where it was coming from.

When the song ended I lifted my head to check the clock on my dresser. It was gone. Through the grayness I made out a shadowy mound where the clock should have been. My pants, I decided at last. Must have landed there when I chucked them last night. With a deep breath I peeled myself up from the mattress and stood. My head felt clear and I started tentatively across the room, gaining confidence with each step. I snatched my pants from the dresser top and the music intensified as the digital readout seared my heart. 9:47. In thirteen minutes I was due to meet with the representatives from We Play, a new sporting goods chain, in the conference room at work.

Yanking the door open, I found the house still and silent. My parents were gone to work and my sister Kate was at school. I moved to the bathroom and splashed water on my face. A shiny red knot, planted square in the middle of my forehead, stared back at me from the mirror. I hadn't seen it until now. I tugged down on my bangs, but they were too short to hide the deformity. Without shaving or showering I returned to my room and dressed. I found my wallet in the back pocket of my pants and rummaged through the front for my keys. They weren't there. I patted my coat. No keys.

I leaped down the stairs, my head now light from stress and lack of food as much as the injury. Dashing from the living room through the dining room and into the kitchen I twisted and spun in every direction, scanning for my key ring. Then it hit me: Paul had let me in. I hadn't touched it. I grabbed the phone off the wall and dialed his number. His mom answered and said he had stayed at Cole's all night and never came home. The next call went there. Cole's dad reported they'd gone out to breakfast and ought to be home shortly.

"Dammit." I slammed the phone back into its cradle. It immediately rang and I thought I'd broken it. When it rang a second time I picked it up, praying Ed Collins wouldn't be on the other end.

"Hello?"

"Lane?"

"Mom?"

"I tried you at work and you weren't there. Why are you still home?"

"Long story. I'm late. And I can't find my keys."

"I wondered about that. They were hanging off the front door this morning. I set them on the hook next to the coat closet."

"I should'a looked there. Thanks, Mom. I gotta go."

The clock in my truck read 10:15 when I turned the engine over. It was too late. There was no point, but I channeled my inner Richard Petty anyway. Maybe they'd been delayed. Maybe they'd waited for me. Yellow lights, red lights, school zones, they were all the same as I careened across Raleigh, finally screeching to a halt outside the bank. Heads turned as I ran in through the front entrance. On the table next to the conference room sat a We Play duffel bag. Maybe I wasn't too late. I turned the handle and pulled the door open to find Ed Collins and Allison Porto shaking hands with the We Play reps. My reps.

"This should work out great for us," one rep was saying.

Ed flashed a gummy grin and nodded, his greasy head shining in the fluorescent light. Allison giggled as she leaned on her phony crutches, and they all turned toward me.

"Sorry I'm late."

"Never mind, Hamilton," Ed said as he waved our guests past me.

After they filed out, I made my way across the lobby to my cubicle. As I struggled to pull my jacket off a cardboard box crashed onto my desk. In the doorway Ed's turkey neck quivered as he glared at me, his arms folded across his chest.

"I'm sorry I missed the meeting, sir. I had a little mishap last night." I pointed up at my forehead. "Lost consciousness for a little bit."

"How nice. Suits you well, Hamilton."

"I tried to get here on time. I hope everything came out okay with We Play."

"Allison handled it. Certainly better than you would have, anyway. You can thank her on your way out."

"Hunh?"

"Pack your shit in that box. You're gone."

"What? You're firing me?"

"Very perceptive, Hamilton. And all this time I thought you

were slow."

It was hard to separate his disdain from his glee. The one fed the other. I tried telling myself it wasn't personal, because I'd seen him treat some of my co-workers pretty shabbily, but he was enjoying it too much to factor that out.

I tossed a couple of framed photos, my address book, dictionary, and a few other odds and ends into the box, all the while mindful of the evil eye monitoring my progress. Within two minutes all my workplace possessions—every bit of home I'd ever brought in to personalize my scant scrap of turf—were packed. I hoisted the box up under my arm and started the slow, ignominious march to the parking lot. As I passed Jim, I stopped to shake hands.

"Out, Hamilton, God damn you!" Ed bellowed. "This ain't no fucking retirement parade!"

"Best of luck," I mumbled to Jim. "If he ever throws a box on your desk—"

"GET OUT!" His gruff voice resonated off the walls and throughout the branch.

Not an employee stirred. They all stared on, as did the customers. I took one last look around and found Teri Weathers, a friend of Kate's, waving feebly from behind the velvet rope. I nodded, then shuffled to the door and slipped out into the frosty morning. After heaving the box into the bed of my truck, I ripped the door open and jumped into the cab. I made better time getting home than I had going to work.

The silence of the house echoed around me as I entered the kitchen, where I dropped into the chair at the head of the table. Holding my throbbing head in my hands, I contemplated how I'd tell my parents. And Trina. Wow, she was gonna be pissed. I suspected sometimes she only agreed to go out with me because she thought I was on the management track. All I really learned in First Carolina's corporate training program was that I hated bank management. Andy taught me apathy, the key to his ten-year career there and something eminently more useful than anything I learned at headquarters. It would be nice to find a job where I didn't need that.

I munched an apple from the fruit bowl on the counter and pondered the opening with the Bulls. If Rich could live on the salary, I could too. I had a little money saved up. If I could parse it out over the summer I'd be fine. We'd just have to scale back on our dinner dates. Maybe Trina could cook once in a while. Hah. Good one.

I pulled a scrap of paper with Rich's work number from my wallet and dialed his office.

"This is Rich Farrell," he said, all professional, like he wanted to sell me a mutual fund. He made a lot of sales calls during the offseason and had developed a polished phone persona.

"Rich, man, it's Lane."

"Laaa-nerrr, how you feeling, buddy?"

"Not great. Okay, I guess. Still hurts."

"I'm so sorry. I couldn't believe that ball would fly off like that. You sure you're all right?"

"Yeah. I'll be fine."

"How'd your big meeting go?"

"It didn't."

"What happened?"

"I overslept. Couldn't hear the alarm. I missed the whole damn thing."

"Oh, fuck."

"Yup."

"What'd your boss say?"

"Pack your shit, Hamilton!"

"He fired you?"

"Yup."

"Damn."

"Is that job still open?"

"Yeah, I think so. As far as I know. Let me think here. Let me think. Don's going to Charleston for the weekend, but he might still be around. Let me hunt him down and I'll call you right back."

I hung up and paced the length of the kitchen for what felt like an eternity. In actual time it was only about ten minutes. Rich had just caught Don Sanders, the general manager of the Bulls, as he was on his way out the door. He couldn't see me today, but I had an appointment to meet him Monday morning at nine. Relieved and exhausted, I went upstairs and passed out on my bed.

The phone woke me at three-thirty. I jogged down the hall to answer, still groggy with sleep, and picked up on the fifth ring.

"There you are," Trina said. "I tried you at work three times.

Why aren't you at the office?"

"Didn't feel well today."

"That's what happens when you ditch the church clinic to go out drinking with the guys."

I pulled the phone off the bookshelf and slumped into the deep-pile carpet. Digging my fingers into the coil of the phone cord, I debated where to take this conversation.

"It's not exactly like that," I said at last.

"No? Fanny told me she ran into you at Mitch's."

"Yeah, we saw her and Dave there."

"So, you admit you were there."

"Yeah. But that's not why I missed work. Rich hit me in the head with a cue ball."

"Ha. Serves you right for lying to me."

"It was pretty serious. I passed out. I've got a huge lump on my head. I might have had a concussion."

"Oh." The tiniest hint of compassion crept into her voice. "I'm sorry. You okay?"

"I'm feeling better. I've been sleeping most of the day. Now I'm just hungry."

"Maybe we should just take it easy tonight and rest. We could order in."

"No, I'll be fine. My grandpa will be disappointed if we don't stop in for their anniversary. And I'd really like to see Cole play tonight. They don't come to Raleigh often."

Deep sigh. "Okay. But you make sure you're feeling up to all that. We can reassess after we visit your grandparents."

"I'll be fine. I'll come get you at six."

"Okay. I'll be ready."

"Love you."

"See you later."

She always got stingy with the "I love you's" when she was mad. On the good days she worked them into every third sentence. Counting "I love you's" provided a barometric reading for our relationship. Low today, with a chance of stormy weather.

CHAPTER THREE

She wasn't ready when I got there. She rarely was. I never met anyone so meticulous about their appearance until we started dating. She must have kept a checklist: Undergarments, body lotion, hair, clothes, makeup, mouthwash. Each step in its turn, none to be rushed through or glossed over. Only when her eyes were lined and softly shadowed, cheeks rouged, hair teased, neck perfumed, and attire primped was she ready for inspection. She added sizzle tonight with a satiny, sequined black dress that didn't even reach the midpoint on her thigh.

My grandparents had been married forty-nine years, and numerous well-wishers had been and gone by the time we arrived. When my grandpa opened the door to greet us he was lit like a candle. He had this far away look in his eye, as though he couldn't quite focus without significant effort. He gave it his best shot, however, when Trina took off her coat. He winked at me and stole my date, leading her into the kitchen on his arm.

Grandpa was always amusing when he drank. The last time I'd seen him like that was the day I graduated from N.C. State. He went there himself, when it was better known as State College, on the G.I. Bill for a couple of years after World War II, though he never finished. From the stories I'd heard, Grandpa knew how to party back then. My grandma kept him on the right track as long as she could, but he never distinguished himself as a student and when she got pregnant with my dad he dropped out and took a factory job.

He could still throw down a little, and he did so in style at my graduation party. My grandma kept muttering about "that old jackass," but I thought it was hilarious and he had a grand time of it. I'd never seen him sock away so much beer. There were at least sixty people there and my grandpa outdrank them all. Even me. My dad was all set to make a toast right before dinner when Grandpa snagged the microphone and took over.

"Lane," Gramps said, staring up at the head of the table where my father had insisted I sit. "I'm so proud of you. Nice State College boy like you should do just all right for hisself. Work hard, but have fun. It's your own fault if you don't."

He fell asleep on our living room couch about an hour after his speech, and my grandma had to drive him home that night. He looked to be on a similar schedule today, which gave us a little while yet to celebrate with him. I followed him and Trina into the kitchen and found my grandma visiting with my parents and Kate, who was two years younger than me. Kate and my mom exchanged critical glances that dissipated when I entered and were immediately replaced by looks of horror.

"What happened to you?" my mom shrieked.

"Had a little mishap last night."

"You look terrible." She accosted me with a forceful hug, digging her arms into my lower back.

"I'm fine, Mom. Really."

She withdrew and stepped back to examine me again. When I pulled the refrigerator door open, she returned to sizing up Trina.

"You look like Goliath," Kate said. "What'd you do?"

"Rich hit me with a pool ball." I touched a beer bottle to my forehead and a cooling shiver pulsed down between my eyes. "I slept most of the day today. I'm all right now."

"Oh. Teri Weathers said she—" Kate started.

I shook my head and made a slashing motion across my throat as my eyes pleaded with Kate to shut up.

"Um, Teri, you remember her, right?" Kate stumbled. "She, uh, once got hit there with a softball."

"Is one of those for me?" Trina interrupted, tugging the beer out of my left hand. "Open, please."

I twisted the cap off and handed her the bottle. She kissed me on the cheek, then rubbed her thumb on the spot to erase the lipstick. My grandpa patted the seat next to him and she slipped away to join him at the table.

"Phoooooh," I sighed when she was out of immediate range.

"She doesn't know?" Kate asked.

"Not yet. Do Mom and Dad?"

"Nope."

"Let's keep it that way for now."

"What happened, big brother?"

"I'll tell you tomorrow."

"'Kay," Kate nodded. She grabbed my beer and took a quick pull, then handed it back "What took you guys so long? Grandpa kept asking about you."

"Had to wait for her to get ready." I nodded toward Trina.

"Kinda fancy for a little party like this, ain't it?"

I waved down at my black sweater and blue jeans and shrugged my shoulders. "Hey, I went casual myself."

"You guys going out after this or does she dress like that all the time?"

"Both. Cole's band is playing tonight at the Brewery."

"She's going to *the Brewery* dressed like that?"

"Hey, I tried to warn her."

"She's not going to want to touch anything in there."

"Not my problem."

"Wanna bet?"

I shook my head and walked over to the table.

"Beautiful girl you got here, Lane," Grandpa said. "Helluva catch."

I sat down next to her and she leaned her head on my shoulder. I could see straight down the front of her dress. I guessed Grandpa had caught an eyeful earlier. As Grandma led my parents into the family room I could have sworn I heard her drop another "jackass."

"Your grandpa was just telling me about how he met your grandma."

"Her daddy kept a shop down on Glenwood Avenue," Grandpa recounted, as he had a hundred times before. "I seen her in there every day at the lunch counter. After three weeks I told her she made the best egg salad I ever ate. She smiled an' told me I was her best customer."

"Oh, that's sweet," Trina cooed.

"She sure was. Next day I come in for lunch and she had my sandwich waitin' for me, only there's a slice of apple pie next to it. Next day, another slice of pie. Finally on Friday I asked her to the picture show."

"What'd she say?" Trina asked.

"Why she said yes, of course. She had her eye on me all

along. We saw *The Philadelphia Story*, with Katherine Hepburn and Cary Grant. I loved the way she laughed. When I drove her home that night I knew she was the one."

"Awww," Trina said. "What a great story."

Grandpa rested his chin on his hand. His eyes were blurred and I knew we were about to lose him for the night.

"Let's move to the other room with my parents," I suggested. "It's more comfortable."

Grandpa jerked his head up and silently followed us to the family room. He plunked down in his recliner and surveyed the scene. That chair was almost as old as I was. When I was small he would bounce me on his knee there. I would laugh and laugh, and so would he. Sometimes he'd tilt the chair back and I'd take a nap there with him. He was ready to catch a few winks now. He kicked up the leg rest and stretched out. Within a minute his eyes were closed.

We visited with my grandma for another hour, then headed over to Hillsborough Street. Trina curled her lip up a couple of times as we entered the Brewery. I ignored her until she made a show of sniffing disapprovingly.

"What?"

"What's that smell?"

"What smell?"

"That musty, B.O. smell."

Over the years the walls had absorbed the sweat of a hundred thousand concertgoers and taken on a flavor something akin to a poorly ventilated gym locker that had been recently sprayed down with aerosol deodorant.

"That's nothing. You'll get used to it. You won't notice it in five minutes."

"This place is gross."

"It's not so bad." I scanned the room and felt a little overdressed myself. My clothes were clean and untorn. I could only imagine how she felt.

She folded her arms across her chest and shuffled her feet like a depressed clog dancer. "My shoes are sticking to the floor."

"Look," I sighed. "This is where they're playing. It might be a little dingy in here, but it's a good place to hear a band, and they haven't played Raleigh in months. I promised Cole we'd be here for the show."

"I didn't say I wanted to leave."

Trina headed for the bar and ordered a margarita, carefully avoiding contact with the counter and bar stools. She inspected the glass when the bartender handed it to her and almost looked disappointed when she couldn't find anything wrong with it. I tipped the bartender and grabbed my beer and we made our way back toward the stage. Paul entered, followed by a petite redhead. He introduced us to Nicole and ran to the bar for a couple bottles of beer. I hoped like hell the girls would get along so I could enjoy the rest of the evening.

Paul pulled a chair out for Nicole and they sat down at a table with their beers. When I took a seat as well, Trina reluctantly slid out the last chair. Paul shot me a knowing look and I rolled my eyes. He initiated a conversation between Nicole and Trina and stoked it along until they were self-sufficient. He was good that way. If I had tried to get them talking, she would have resisted.

After thirty minutes Paul and I went for a second round.

"Everything okay?" he asked.

"Same old, same old. Next time Cole plays the Brewery I'm leaving her at home."

"What's wrong?"

"'It stinks in here.'" I mocked. "'The floor's all gross. The bouncer's staring at my breasts.'"

"What does she expect?" Paul laughed.

"I didn't dress her."

"Where's Rich?"

"He'll be here. I talked to him today. He's getting me an interview with the Bulls."

"Really? What changed your mind?"

"I missed that meeting this morning."

"And?"

I thrust my thumb above my head like an umpire.

"Damn," Paul said.

"Trina doesn't know, so don't say anything."

We ran into Cole on the way back and he sat at our table with us. Trina had a funny look for him, but it was nothing compared to the pained contortion that swept across her face when Rich strolled in. He smirked a little more than was necessary in response, and my head started to hurt all over again. On Cole's advice, we sat through the opening band. They were a sorry bunch, though loud and not easily ignored. When they wrapped up, he disappeared backstage to prepare for his set.

I had seen him play a lot during the first couple years of college, but this iteration of Disingenuity was new to me. Though Cole and the drummer had played together on and off since high school, I'd never seen the other guitarist or bass player. They played a couple of covers, including a rousing version of Cheap Trick's "Surrender," but for the most part they cranked out original stuff. The ovation when they were done playing shook the floor; even Trina whistled a couple times. Three margaritas had mellowed her out a little. After we applauded for a minute or so, the band came back on stage and retook their places.

"I guess we got time for a couple more," started Cole, as he distractedly picked at his guitar strings. He shared lead singing duties with Alex, the bass player. "We're gonna rock up an old country song tonight for a friend of mine, who's had a rough day. Lane, this is for you, buddy."

What came next sounded like Guns'n'Roses goes to Nashville, and it took me a few bars until I placed the song. When Cole belted out "Take this job and shove it," he confirmed my fears. Trina perked up when she recognized it, and after singing along for a line or two she stopped and looked up at me.

"What's this for?" she shouted.

I shrugged and stared hard at the stage, pretending I was lost in the music. It didn't work. She tugged on my sweater and I turned to find those green eyes boring through me.

"Did something happen at work?" she yelled.

"What?!"

Her nose flared a little when she got mad. Like it did then.

"What happened today?"

I pointed up toward the stage and yelled, "Can this wait a few minutes?"

"Did you get fired?"

When I nodded Trina turned and started pushing through the crowd. Rich nudged me from behind.

"What happened?" he asked.

"What do you think?"

Under different circumstances I expect he'd have been grinning ear to ear, but you didn't have to trace this all too far back to find his imprint and he just pointed after her. "You better go."

I snaked through the crowd toward the lobby and found Trina waiting at the coat check. "I'm ready," she said, when the guy handed up her jacket.

"Now? They're not done playing yet."

She spun and stomped off toward the door. I grabbed my coat and jogged after her.

"Hold on!"

"When were you going to tell me?" she demanded as she reached the exit.

"Tomorrow."

"Do you tell the truth about anything anymore?"

She pushed the door open and stepped out into the brisk early morning. After a few steps she glanced back, insinuating I was to follow. I caught up to her out on the sidewalk.

"What really happened?"

"I showed up late this morning and Ed fired me."

"But why, Lane?" She threw her hands up and the hem of her dress lifted over the top of her stockings. "What did you *do*?"

"I overslept this morning because of this," I pointed to the goose egg on my head. "And I missed my meeting with We Play. Then Ed hucked a box at me and told me to pack."

"So now what?" she asked, as if she were about to lose the roof over her head because I'd lost my position.

"I'll find another job. I have an interview on Monday with the Bulls."

"Oh, great. Rich again. Doesn't he make less than I do?"

"So fucking what? It's a job."

"Lane," she cried, her nostrils quivering. "How are we ever going to get married on that kind of salary?"

"Married? Who said anything about getting married?"

Trina turned her back toward me and shook some tears loose. I knew she expected me to console her, then tell her I'd get another low-level management job at some other shitty bank so I could keep taking her to dinner every night. I watched her cry for a minute, until I couldn't take it anymore. When I tried to put my arm around her she spun away from me.

"I thought you loved me," she said. "I thought we had a future."

"I do. I do love you." Though I wasn't too sure at that exact moment. "But we don't need to rush it. We've only been dating six months."

"How long will it take?"

"How long for what?"

"How long until you know?"

"About marriage?" I coughed. "I'm only twenty-two, Trina. You're only twenty-three. What's the rush?"

Wrong answer. We went around in circles for another ten minutes as our fellow concertgoers streamed out around us. Paul broke the awkward tension by slapping me on the back, while brave little Nicole put her arm around Trina. The girls walked down the sidewalk as I said good-bye to Paul and wished him luck in Florida. Rich didn't say anything until I turned to head for the car.

"See you Monday," he called.

"Yeah. I'll be there at nine."

They waved and turned to go back inside. I found Trina standing by my truck down the street, laughing with Nicole. But the levity wasn't for me. She didn't utter so much as a syllable all the way back to Durham.

CHAPTER FOUR

By Monday morning the tumor growing out of my forehead had almost disappeared. I examined it from several angles as I prepared for my interview and decided at last that it could pass for a giant zit. The advantage being no one was likely to ask what happened, they'd be too busy trying to look away. To help them out, I drew my baseball tie out of the back of the closet. Row upon row of tiny baseballs, smiling through crooked seam mouths. A conversation starter is what my mom called it when she bought it for my twentieth birthday. I'd never gotten as far as cutting the tags off until now, but it had just enough kitsch value to offset its being a tie, and I figured it might carry some karma.

After getting the knot centered, I worked a comb through my hair, debating whether I looked more trustworthy with the part in the middle or on the side, before deciding it was too short to warrant either. I applied a dollop of Kate's mousse and pushed it straight back. Satisfied, I grabbed my keys and headed for Durham Athletic Park.

Rich was waiting for me outside the stadium when I pulled up. He coached me through a couple of questions as we walked in together, then set off in pursuit of the general manager as I leaned against the fence just inside the front gate clutching my hard-sided notebook. The chain links grilled a diamond pattern into my back through my white Oxford shirt. It had warmed up considerably over the weekend, and the sparrows nesting in the O's of the HOT DOGS sign above the concession stand chattered out their welcome to the first spring-like day of the year. With every breath I inhaled the sweet scent of tobacco curing in the nearby warehouses. I would soon come to associate that aroma with the ballpark, and it always smelled best in the morning.

The door to the office trailer creaked open. A man with thinning blond hair, maybe late thirties or fortyish, descended the stoop. "Lane?" he inquired, striding toward me with a slightly bowlegged gait.

"Yes, sir."

He enveloped my hand in his strong grip and gave it a couple of pumps as he introduced himself. Don was a soft-spoken guy with a hint of a twinkle in his eye and dimples in his cheeks when he smiled. He led me into the bowl of the stadium and found a sunny spot behind the first-base dugout and motioned for me to sit down.

"So Lane," he started, as he leaned back in the stadium seat. "Have you ever worked in baseball before?"

"No, sir." I squinted against the bright sun hanging just over his head. "I've been working in a bank since graduation. But I've been around baseball most of my life. I played with Rich from Little League through high school."

Don said nothing. I didn't know if he was sizing me up or waiting for me to elaborate. My hands began to sweat against the vinyl finish of the notebook and I realized this would be an opportune time to give him a copy of my résumé. I fumbled with the cover for a moment, then slid the top sheet out and handed it to him. He looked it over for half a minute as I fussed over whether to stretch my legs out or keep my feet planted formally in front of me.

"Rich mentioned you're not still with First Carolina."

"No, sir. Not since last week."

"What happened there?"

I told him the story from the beaning to the canning, relieved to find him smiling when I finished.

"I suppose Rich owes you a job, then."

"You could draw that conclusion."

"Did he mention we put in some long hours during the season? Fourteen hours on a game day is pretty standard."

"Yeah. I'm okay with that."

"That's seven, eight days in a row sometimes."

"Okay." I nodded. "I can do that."

"Good." He glanced from me out to the field, where two seagulls were chasing each other behind the pitcher's mound. "Did you have any questions for me?"

I flipped open the cover of my portfolio and scanned the notes I had scratched out earlier on a sheet of lined paper.

"I have one. Is this opening permanent? I mean, would it end when the season ended or would I stay on?"

"That depends on a lot of different things. We only carry a small staff through the winter. But anything's possible. Let's see how things go and worry about that later."

"Fair enough."

"I wouldn't have figured we'd have room for Rich at this time last year. But things worked out."

"How long have you worked here?"

"This will be my fifth season in Durham," he said, after pausing for a moment as if he first had to count the years out in his head. "I came here from Florence."

"So is that where you started in minor league ball, Florence?"

"No. I did three years in Columbus and two seasons in Greenwood before that."

"You've been in baseball a long time already, then."

"Well." He shrugged uncomfortably and patted his knee. "I couldn't play. This was the next best thing."

"I couldn't either. Rich and I tried to walk on at State, but we didn't last the afternoon."

Don clutched the arm rests on either side of him and pushed himself up with moderate effort. "You want the job?"

"Yes, sir."

"Let's go inside and fill out some paperwork."

I started the next morning and Rich introduced me around. We shared an office with Sonny Higgins, the assistant general manager and head groundskeeper, and Gray Francis, who was in charge of sales and marketing. Night and day, they were. Sonny was a farm boy from Mecklenburg County, out towards Charlotte, and he never went further than the bathroom without his spit cup. Between his drawl and an ever-present wad of tobacco up against his gums I had to translate everything he said in my head before it made sense. But I loved his laugh. It came free and easy at the slightest provocation, rising from his expansive belly up to his cowboy hat. He'd tip his head back so you could see his tonsils as he shook and roared. Gray had a quick wit and impeccable timing and would set off Sonny's laugh at least twice a day. I never met anyone whose mind worked faster. He overcame the streets of inner-city Baltimore, earning a full scholarship to Georgetown by winning back-to-back state titles in DECA, a business club for high school students. He was a phenomenal salesman, and I shadowed him my first day on the job as he taught me how to sell ads for the souvenir program.

Rich and I were tasked with increasing the program by eight pages over the previous season. All of last year's advertisers had already been tapped, so we had to find new customers. I learned more about sales that first week than I'd learned in nine months at the bank. The key to our success came when we hit the streets and harassed people in person. It's so much easier for them to dismiss you over the phone. Show up with a sharp-looking program and a half-polished sales pitch and some folks will buy an ad just to get you to leave them alone. We hit our goal by Friday afternoon and Don sent us home early.

With a couple of hours to kill before meeting Trina for dinner I followed Rich to Markham Avenue. He'd started pestering me to move in again, and he began chirping about it the moment we were in the door.

"I'm still not clear on your objection," he said. "We're only two minutes from work. It's so much easier than driving in from Raleigh every day."

"I know," I acknowledged as I lounged on the couch hanging my legs over the tattered arm.

"Rent's cheap. With a fourth we'd each be in for about two-fifty a month. That includes utilities."

"Yeah?" I mulled the offer for a minute as he blitzed through the channels on the television. "That's not bad."

"So why not? You prefer living with your parents?"

"I don't know. It's not so—"

"It's not so what?" he interrupted. "Oh shit, I got it. It's Becca, ain't it?"

"No. No. She's got nothing—"

"Bullshit!" He spiked the remote so hard on the couch that it bounced up and struck him on the chin. "She said something, right? What'd she say?"

"She's never said anything against me moving in here."

Rich ripped the sun-bleached Braves cap off his head and raised it as if he meant to whip me in the face. I flinched and he menaced me with it a couple more times until I sat up so I could defend myself.

"Look," I said. "She's been dropping hints about wanting me to move in for months. She even gave me a key for Christmas. It's always 'If you lived here, you wouldn't have to drive home so late.' Or 'Isn't this a great apartment?' As long as I stay at home I avoid the meltdown. I'm just being frugal, right?"

"Wrong. You're just being a fucking wuss. Nut up and do what you want to do."

"Whatever."

"Yeah, whatever. Gimme a break. You'd have a blast living here."

I let out a defeated sigh. "Show me the room again."

He led me up the dusky staircase, brightened only by the tentacles of sunlight that pierced the monstrous bougainvillea outside the landing window. Ryan's old room was the first one at the top of the steps. Like the rest of the house, it contained hardwood floors that begged to be refinished and the plaster on the ceiling had cracked in several places. Rich had furnished the room with an old twin bed and a chest of drawers he'd found in the basement, abandoned by a previous renter.

The bathroom next door, which everyone shared, held a mammoth claw foot tub wrapped in a mildewed plastic shower curtain. At the far end you could see the sub-flooring where half a dozen tiles had popped loose over time. At some point someone had stacked them under the tub and they were still barely visible through a thick coat of cobwebs. Three towels hung over the back of a wooden chair next to the pedestal sink, which was encrusted with toothpaste and shaving gel.

Rich's room was around the corner at the other end of the hall. Through his open door I saw a neatly made queen bed, a small wooden desk, and a bean bag chair that had miraculously survived years of abuse down in his parents' rec room. The doors to the other two bedrooms were closed and he didn't open them. "Slobs," he said as we passed them on the way back down.

"Are they good guys?" I asked.

"Nice enough."

"Oh, what the hell. I'll take it."

CHAPTER FIVE

We scrambled the last couple of weeks before Opening Day to get everything ready for show time. Don huddled us all together for what I guess you'd call a pep talk, but he was so low key it was a good thing everyone was already motivated. His speech sure wouldn't have fired us up. The veteran hands all looked like they'd heard this one before.

Sonny started walking away at one point and I was stunned by his rudeness, until everyone else followed. He just knew what came next. Don walked us out in front of the park and pointed up to the El Toro Stadium sign on the roof. On the bottom, in script writing, it read, "The Greatest Show On Dirt." He stressed how he wanted that to be more than a slogan to us. Despite years of steady attendance growth we were never to take the fans for granted.

There was a new team moving into the neighborhood, and they'd be competing for our customers. When he talked about the Carolina Mudcats, he did so with an almost Hatfield and McCoy mentality, understated of course, being Don. There was a thirty-five-mile territorial rights limit in minor league baseball, and the Bulls had felt safe for a long time, because Raleigh and Chapel Hill were too close for someone to move in. But the Mudcats had cleverly measured it off and plunked down in the middle of a tobacco field out near Zebulon, about fifteen miles east of Raleigh. Thanks to construction delays their stadium wouldn't be ready until midseason, but that didn't lessen the disdain felt for them in these quarters.

Every day there were new faces at the park as preparations heated up. Mike Adamlee, the concessions manager, was training rookie hands and welcoming back veterans. It looked like the carnival had swept into town. I could swear I'd seen some of them working the midway at the State Fair the previous fall. They rattled into the parking lot in battered jalopies with the side-view mirrors dangling from the windows, piled out, and reported for duty. I never could figure out if this one couple was brother and sister, boyfriend and girlfriend, or both. They had the same pale, blond hair; thin, upturned noses; and sharp, rodent teeth that had been rotted away by a lifelong addiction to Coca-Cola. You never saw one without the other. I dubbed them Jughaid and Mary Beth, after the kids in Snuffy Smith, which Rich heartily commended.

He had nicknames for almost everyone in the park. Some of them stuck so well they virtually replaced the person's original name. Take Ronald Winters for example. Or Peanut as he was known around the DAP. He started on the grounds crew the previous season with Rich, though being in high school he was mostly game-time help until summer began. His family had held season tickets since the Bulls came back to Durham in 1980. Little Ronald had been coming to games with his parents and his older sister for so long it was only natural he'd graduate to employee once he was old enough to work. A lean, sinewy kid with close-cropped brown hair and beady brown eyes that peered out at you from deep in his skull, he flapped his gums from the moment he walked in the park each day until the moment he left. I figured there must be a great story behind his name, but Rich explained the etymology to me in simple terms: "The kid eats a lot of peanuts."

They didn't all have to be mind-benders to stick.

I spent way too much time trying to think up a good handle to pin on Blake Mungo, Rich's motivationally challenged compatriot on the grounds crew, who had the stones to call in the morning before the season opener and tell Sonny he needed to take his car in for service. I threw out Mullet, in honor of his hair, and Hard Core, on account of his porn-star mustache, but Rich had already given him a name: Asshole.

"He doesn't deserve a nickname," Rich said. "All he does is bitch. Doesn't contribute shit around here. How can he not show up the day before the season starts?"

In his absence that morning, I helped Sonny and Rich re-sod most of right field. We never figured out why, but it was turning brown like some root disease had set in. So barely twenty-four hours before the opener we were carving huge sections out and slapping new turf on the field. The bulk of my afternoon was occupied hauling boxes of t-shirts and hats down from the Ballpark Corner store to the main souvenir stand, under the direction of

Aaron Love, who spent most of his time manning our store out at the mall. Ever since *Bull Durham* came out in 1988, the Bulls had been one of the top merchandisers in minor league baseball. So we had not one, but two souvenir stores, and a mail-order business on the side.

The original Ballpark Corner sat across the street from the stadium in the former home of *Baseball America* magazine, which was operated by the owner of the Bulls. He moved the periodical's headquarters a couple miles away in the late '80s, freeing up the space for our store and warehouse. Someone had to be there every second of the day between nine and six in case the 800 number rang with an order. Don was adamant on that score. I spent many a lunch hour there, relieving Faith Andrews, our middle aged t-shirt agent. Her full-time job was sitting up there in that musty, brick building, selling a couple hundred bucks worth of souvenirs in an average day. When the games started she shifted down to the stadium and worked in the left field souvenir stand. She was friendly, almost overly so—especially to all the guys. Despite the chunky diamond on her finger, I think she fantasized of seducing a player, or anyone really, and trying her hand as Annie Savoy. She generally wore a jersey with the top three buttons open, leaning over frequently in hopes that someone might sneak a peek. Toss in a generous spritz of White Linen perfume and she was ready for business.

She must have been bored most of the time. The phone almost never rang when I sat in for her, and most lunch hours passed without more than a couple of customers. I wouldn't have traded jobs with her for nothing, though I did come to appreciate the quiet time. It grew awfully scarce by early April.

Rich and I camped out on our front porch the night before the opener, drinking a bottle of red wine one of our roommates had given us. Burt was something of a wine snob, at the tender age of twenty-three. A grad student at Duke's Fuqua School of Business, he harbored some crazy notion that he'd be a millionaire before he turned thirty. It was laughable, especially given we didn't have a state lottery. He was too lazy to put his dishes in the sink or move his tennis shoes out of the traffic flow in the living room. How was he going to make a million bucks without putting some effort into it? His only hope was finding someone to pay him to talk. The kid knew a little bit about everything and could play either side of any argument, which he often did for sport. One of his professors had offered up a bottle of cabernet sauvignon as top prize in a business management class earlier in the week and Burt had bullshitted his way into first place. But the wine wasn't up to his standards and he passed it off to us.

Maybe I shouldn't bash on Burt's laziness too much when I own up to literally sharing the bottle with Rich because neither of us could be troubled to go into the kitchen to fetch a glass. Like a pair of winos, we passed the bottle back and forth, not even bothering to wipe the mouth with our sweaty t-shirts.

"You are going to freak tomorrow, Laner." Rich handed me the wine, by that point two-thirds gone. "There will be a line up the hill of people who want to get in and five minutes after Don unlocks the gate there will be so many bodies in the park you won't know where to turn."

I took a long pull on the bottle, wiping my chin with the back of my hand. I'd gone to half a dozen contests the year before, but I'd never noticed much of what was going on outside of the game and what Rich was doing on the grounds crew. I'd waited in line for pizza and beer without paying the slightest attention to what else was occurring in the main concourse.

"You're lucky to start off with a four-game stand. Last year we had a seven-night opener."

"Brutal." I somewhat reluctantly forked the bottle over, knowing I might not get it back.

"Yeah. We were still in school then, too. I drove over every afternoon as soon as I was out of class and I wouldn't get to bed until almost one."

"How'd you ever line this job up?" All I knew was he'd stumbled into the position. I'd never heard the story of how it happened.

"My dad and Don golf at the same club. They lost a field guy last spring, right before the season …"

"Just like Ryan this year for me," I finished his sentence.

"Serendipity," Rich mused as he drained the last of the cabernet.

"We got any more?"

"What? Wine?"

"Yeah."

"Do yourself a favor." He tossed the bottle in the recycle bin next to the door. "Go to bed. Don't start the season with a red-wine hangover."

CHAPTER SIX

I had just enough of a buzz going that I fell asleep still dressed on top of my bed as I waited for Rich to finish in the bathroom. The next thing I knew he was pounding on my door.

"Rise and shine, Laner," he called. "Big day ahead."

It didn't seem possible I'd slept more than fifteen minutes, but it was already five to seven. I rolled out of bed and rifled through the laundry basket next to the dresser looking for a clean pair of khakis and my blue Bulls golf shirt. I shaved and showered and was rummaging through the pantry when Rich pushed me toward the door, claiming there would be plenty of goodies at the park.

He was right. Don brought in four dozen donuts, which disappeared at an astonishing pace. People I'd never seen before just walked on up and helped themselves. After fueling up they all got to work. A plumber inspected the aging restrooms, giving us false hope that the urine troughs wouldn't overflow under the pressure of a capacity crowd. There was a technician in working on Ron Anders' radio equipment following the failure of his test broadcast the previous afternoon. We had two separate painting crews doing some last minute touchups, one along the exterior of the stadium, the other on a couple of the older outfield fence signs.

I wasn't sure what to do with myself until Don introduced me to an old-timer in a Bulls jacket. His name was Johnny Layne, and he'd been in baseball for more than fifty years, first as a player, then as a long-time minor league general manager.

"I gave Don his first job out of college," he recollected in a high, breathy voice that sounded like he'd just taken a hit of helium off a balloon. "He didn't know nothin' from nothin' back then. Now look at him."

Johnny was fond of that story, and I'd hear it many times throughout the year. He came in every morning during the season and did little jobs, like stuffing the game-day flyers into the *Bulls*

Illustrated programs. He wasn't quick, but he took his tasks seriously, hunching over the table for long stretches at a time, whistling flat tunes as he whittled down the stack of inserts. When he got low he'd harangue me to hurry up with the next batch on the copy machine.

Old Johnny got a kick out of working with me, calling us the Lane and Layne Show. He quizzed me on every aspect of my life, starting with love interests. He lit up when I showed him a picture of Trina that I kept in my wallet.

"That's a keeper there, boy," he said. "She's a honey."

Johnny may have been seventy-two, but he still liked the ladies. Of course, he was quick to mention he'd been married for almost fifty years "to the *same* woman."

When the programs were stuffed and ready to go, I polished off the game notes for the newspaper guys who covered the team. Gray said we usually had two for each game, Matt Hamer from the *Durham Herald-Sun* and Red Phelps from the *Raleigh News & Observer*. But tonight being the first game of the year, he thought I should expect more. I printed up eight copies of notes on the history of Bulls home openers, a recap of last season, and some short bios of the players on this year's roster.

By four o'clock we'd done everything that could be done. I plopped down in a front-row seat and watched the Bulls take batting practice. Hulking designated hitter Francisco Acevedo pounded at least a dozen balls over the fence. Some of the guys were trying to yank it foul down the right field line so they could hit the big bull that says "Hit Bull Win Steak." In the movie that made a great target because it was a home run, but in real life it was off in foul territory, so all it earned you was a long, impressive strike and a big buzz from the crowd. We had a lot of fans from out of town and you could see the puzzled expressions on their faces when they saw the bull "in the wrong place." One guy actually used those words to me, like I could just go over and move it into fair ground.

It didn't carry the same cachet, but it was much more impressive to see a guy launch a ball onto the Brame building beyond center field. Now that was a shot. It was 410 feet to center field, so I guessed that made it about 440 to put one on the Brame roof. Acevedo did it that afternoon, on his last swing. He drew some high fives from his teammates with that cut. I couldn't imagine what it felt like to hit a ball that far. I put a couple over the fence in high school, but they didn't clear it by much, and they certainly didn't go out in deep center.

When the players came off the field Sonny, Rich, Blake, Peanut, and this twelve-year-old kid I'd never seen before rushed on to prep for the game, raking the dirt and laying down the baselines. Half of me wanted to be down there with them, but my job was to hang out in the concourse and help keep things running smoothly once the gates opened at five-thirty. I climbed the stairs and reported to the mobile office to see if there was anything I could do until then.

Our office manager, Ashandra Baker, waved a bottle of Doan's Pills at me. "Take these down to Gordy."

With all the new faces, it slipped my mind who Gordy was, and she could tell by my vacant expression.

"McNulty ... the man-a-ger," she said, drawing it out like I was a special ed kid in a spelling bee.

My ears burned as I tried to think of a comeback or at least some way to play it off, but nothing slick was forthcoming. I grabbed the bottle and headed down the ramp toward the clubhouse just glad to get away from her. The Bulls locker room was a dingy and antiquated painted-brick dungeon, a certain disappointment to anyone after the digs they must have had in spring training. Then again, it couldn't have been any worse than wherever they played last year. I sure didn't hear any complaints as I wandered through to the manager's office. Gordy was perched atop an overturned sunflower seed bucket in his underwear talking to his coaches. He got up when I entered.

"There's a good man," he sang when I handed over the Doan's. "My back feels like I been kicked in the spine by a Tennessee pack mule. Thank you …"

"Lane," I said, as we shook hands.

He introduced me to pitching coach Jim Peak and hitting coach Glen Bagnall, who nonchalantly extended their hands before resuming their debate on area strip clubs as if I weren't there. Gordy chuckled and shrugged apologetically, then rejoined the discussion as soon as I backed out the door.

I heard the crowd before I saw it as I made my way back up

to the main concourse. A throng of fans had gathered outside the entrance, some eagerly lining the fence, others casually milling on the lawn chatting with friends. Gaggles of people filed into the Ballpark Corner shop across the street. Queues formed at the three ticket windows, though reserved seats had been sold out since Monday. The turreted ticket tower gave the park a fairy-tale feel, despite the distressed condition of the red-shingle roof. Like everything else in the main concourse, this outbuilding, which housed the ticket office and souvenir stand at ground level and the game-night bank upstairs, was doused in burnt orange and royal blue. This color combination overwhelmed visitors, who were surrounded by it the moment they entered the park. Orange walls with blue trim, blue walls with orange trim, awnings with fat orange stripes and thin blue ones stretching out overhead—it wasn't exactly chocolate and peanut butter, but something about the pairing made the park beautiful in an ugly sort of way.

Don strode to the gate, key in hand, and it was like watching the seals at the zoo when the keeper comes to toss fish in. The fans in front all stood at attention, relishing the thrill of being among the very first to enter the park for the new season. Harvey and Shauna, the ticket takers, adjusted their orange vests and prepared for the onslaught as Don slid the key into the padlock and shook the chain loose. Captain DesJardins of the Durham police helped him swing the gate open, and the fans poured into the park.

"Programs! Lucky number scorecards!" bellowed a hawker standing behind a portable podium about twenty feet beyond the entrance. "Get your brand new *Bulls Illustrated.* One dollar!"

The veteran pitchman wore a tie-dyed Bulls t-shirt and a fishing hat decorated with buttons and lapel pins. Customers lined up, waving their dollars, which he stuffed into the canvas pouch strapped around his waist. His spiel was interrupted only when he mixed in a hurried "Thank you" for every program he handed out.

Gray sidled up next to me and we greeted fans as they entered the park. After the initial wave passed things quieted down for a few minutes and he walked over to the podium.

"Joe the Vendor!" he exclaimed. "Vendor Joe! Where you been all winter?"

Vendor Joe glanced briefly at Gray, then bent down to pull a handful of programs from a box resting under his stand.

"Oh, hi Gray," he said without making eye contact as he fanned the stack of magazines. "I've been around. Football games. Other big events."

"It's good to see you again," Gray said.

"Thanks," Joe mumbled, then switched back into megaphone mode. "Programs! Lucky number scorecards!"

Joe was a professional vendor, as Gray explained to me. Occasionally he sold plasma on the side to earn a little extra cash, but peddling was his profession, and he was well suited to it. He was loud and had just the right cadence to be heard above the roar of the crowd. He worked any sporting event within a fifty-mile radius, earning enough for gas, food, and sometimes shelter. In good times he stayed at the Y. In bad, he slept in the back seat of his car.

By six the stream of fans had become a river. The turnstiles cranked just as fast as people could flow through. The line out front never completely abated, though it would thin out every ten minutes or so. The fans were universally in elevated spirits, making my job an easy one. I monitored talk on the radio while greeting folks, but there wasn't much required other than steering people in the right direction when they asked where the office was or how to find the restroom.

I was leaning into the souvenir stand to see how things were progressing on Aaron's turf when I felt a tap on my shoulder. My parents, who hadn't been to a Bulls game in three years, had made a last-minute decision to drive over from Raleigh. I led them into the stands and pointed them toward the best general admission seats in the house. They were right across the aisle from the boxes up behind the screen, and most people didn't realize they weren't reserved. Even with the overflow crowd there were open spots available. After promising to visit with them when things slowed down a little, I returned to the main concourse. Johnny Layne was standing with Gray, watching the crowd swell.

"What d'ya say there, Lane?" Johnny corralled me by the neck with his right hand. He still had a heck of a grip for an old guy, and he shook me gently with his meaty paw.

"This is a great crowd," I said. "I can't believe all these people."

"Let's see Frederick top this," Johnny challenged.

"What do you mean?"

"They pad." Johnny grimaced and waved his hand dismissively. "You tell me they really had four thousand fannies a night last year? Hah."

Gray chuckled and welcomed me into one of the newest yet keenest rivalries in the Carolina League. The Bulls and the upstart Frederick Keys had lobbied for top attendance honors the previous season, with neither team accepting the other's figures at face value. Somewhere up in Maryland there was probably an old Keys employee bashing our numbers. Not knowing much about the controversy I shrugged it off.

"Think I saw your girl," Johnny said with a wink.

"Trina?" It was a dubious report considering he'd never met her and had only seen her photo once, earlier that morning.

"She looked so sweet it hadda be her."

"Hmmm. She never mentioned she was coming. Who was she with?"

"'Nother beautiful gal." Johnny's eyes lit up when he talked about women. He tilted his head as if he were dreaming of a far off land where grass-skirted maidens fanned him with palm fronds. Suddenly he perked up and nodded behind me in the direction of the program peddler. "'S'that her?"

I wheeled around and found Trina leading her sister Janie through the crowd by the arm.

"Hey," I said. "Why didn't you tell me you were coming? I could have gotten you in."

"I wasn't sure we'd come out." She grabbed my right hand and wrapped it around her waist, then kissed me quickly, as though she were self-conscious with Johnny and Gray there. "Janie didn't call me back until after work."

"I *said* I'd come on Tuesday," Janie shrieked, confidentially adding, "We were coming all along, Lane."

"You're just as pretty as your picture," Johnny interrupted. "Lane's got a good eye."

Most girls would probably blush at such a remark. Trina just gave him half a smile, as if she heard that twenty times a day from every geezer in Durham County. Her sister, neither as stunning nor as cold, took immediately to Mr. Layne, who responded to her friendly flirtation by working his arm around her shoulder. Never satisfied, Johnny kept trying to rope Trina into the conversation. Her contributions amounted to a handful of sighs and several comments about how long the lines were getting at the concession stand. My offer to grab them something to eat was silenced with a glare. It wasn't food she wanted, but escape. Mine came in the form of a call on the radio, when Don needed someone to lead the singer onto the field for the national anthem.

I found a heavyset black woman with tightly shorn hair and gold hoop earrings the size of coffee can lids leaning against the gate by the dugout. We made small talk while waiting for her cue, and she told me she had sung the anthem there twice before. Her smile exposed a gap between her front teeth, where tiny spit bubbles snuck out as she spoke. When she started to sing the droplets got bigger, spraying in an arch every time she hit an "s." I had to look away midway through to keep from laughing. Instead I watched the home plate umpire, who was standing about ten feet the other side of her, to see if he noticed. Though he couldn't have been much older than me, he stared straight ahead at the flag, his cheeks slightly sucked in and lips pursed. His scowl dared every man on the field to even think about questioning his authority. When she finished singing he pulled his cap low over his forehead and glared at me as though he wished he could start the year by throwing me out of the game.

After leading the singer to her seat, I moved into the sardine-can press box, located at field level just behind home plate. There were seven guys crammed in there, including Nick Henry, the PA announcer. The fast-talking Virginian was the de facto czar of that 8-by-20 space. I found him a little intimidating, to be honest, but if he weren't so assertive someone would have had to spend a lot more time in there during games, probably me. Aside from Nick the press box occupants were the aforementioned Matt Hamer and Red Phelps; Frankie Glick, a second guy from the *Durham Herald-Sun*; Evan Story, from the *Duke Chronicle*; Porter Mason, who covered the Carolina League for *Baseball America* and was also stringing tonight for the Frederick paper; and Merrit Melvin, the official scorer. Aimee Lynn, a reporter from WRAL-TV, also popped in and hung around just long enough to get some opening shots for the eleven o'clock news. I introduced myself around and asked if anyone needed anything. Nick told me to bring them a couple of pizzas. Too bad if anyone wanted anything different, because Nick wanted pizza every night, and that's what I brought them every game from that point forth.

I made the rounds of the park after that, wandering from the left-field picnic area, where I visited for a little while with Jenna Parsons, our group sales manager, all the way around to right field. In the bottom of the fourth I kept my promise to my parents, stopping back by to see how they were enjoying the game. I never expected to find Trina and Janie sitting next to them.

For a girl who wanted to get married so bad Trina had never shown a tremendous interest in visiting with her future in-laws. My parents had taken us out to dinner one night in early December and she'd seen them at my grandparents' anniversary party. That was the grand total of her interaction with my family up until tonight. Somehow she recognized my mother in the line for the ladies room.

Mom's eyes roamed uncomfortably over Trina's thighs and exposed navel. She talked to her through the fully dressed Janie, who solicited embarrassing tales of my childhood as fast as Mom could tell them. My visit had interrupted the one about how I used to sing the ABC's while sitting on the can when I was in kindergarten. At least they weren't getting much from my dad, who wore an expression of mild annoyance. I think he had some ridiculous idea he'd actually be able to concentrate on the game. I crouched down on the steps next to their seats for a couple of outs until I heard Rich calling for me on the radio, at which point I made my excuses and hustled down to the tunnel under the stands where the grounds crew hung out.

Rich and Sonny were moving bags of Diamond Dry field treatment from a pallet into one of three storage bays under the grandstand with the assistance of the youth I'd seen on the field with them prior to the game. He was swimming in an overlarge Bulls t-shirt and constantly pushing his bangs out of his eyes. Peanut and Blake leaned over the fence at the mouth of the tunnel, watching the game and scanning the crowd.

"Where you been, Laner?" Rich asked.

"Little bit of everywhere. Press box, left field, sat with my parents for a few minutes."

"Where they sitting?" he grunted, hefting two bags onto his

shoulder.

"Up in the GA behind the screen. Trina's with them."

Rich stopped and wrinkled his face at me, raising one eyebrow. "Interesting."

"Hey there, Lane," Sonny cut in. "Y'all wanna make yourself useful an' grab a bag or two?"

"Figured you guys had it under control," I said. "Who's this? Rich's illegitimate son?"

The twelve-year-old narrowed his eyes and offered me a sarcastic head shake, clearly borrowed from Rich's repertoire of mannerisms.

"Lane, meet Spanky," Rich huffed, dropping his load with a thud that shook the ground under our feet. "Spanky, Lane."

Spanky ran his hand up across his brow to clear his bowl cut out of his eyes yet again and casually nodded hello at me. He looked like a seventh grader physically, but he acted ten years older.

"What's your story, Spanky?" I asked. "They violating some child labor laws here? I can help you escape."

"Look, you gonna help or not?" Spanky shot back.

Rich dropped the bag he had started lifting and nearly hit the ground laughing.

"Easy there, Spank," Sonny chuckled. "We're most done."

"What are you guys doing this for now anyway? And what's with Peanut and Blake over there? Spanky scare them off?"

Spanky pointed to the two other grounds crew members and shook his head. "Lazy fuckers."

Rich was nearly in tears. If he were a few years older this could have been his kid. He talked just like him.

"I like you, Spanky," I said. "You're hilarious."

"That's one hard-workin' kid, there, boy," Sonny said. "Poun' for poun'—"

"Shit, forget pound for pound," Rich said. "He's worth two of Blake any night. And we had to move this shit because three of our drag mats were buried under the pallet when it was delivered this afternoon."

Spanky wrestled the final bag free and Rich lifted the pallet up, revealing three tightly rolled mesh mats, about five or six feet long.

"I still say Blake's the dumbfuck who told the guy to drop it here," Rich said, stooping to pull up a mat.

Curious, I crouched down to examine one. The thing had to weigh fifty pounds. Rich unrolled his and stepped on it to smooth out the kinks where the links were bunched together.

Carson Fowler, the assistant in the ticket office, rushed into the tunnel, red faced and gasping as if he'd just sprinted all the way down the hill. "It's almost time," he said, when he found enough air to talk. "One more out."

The grounds crew dragged the infield every night in the middle of the fifth inning, wiping out the cleat marks and giving it a clean look for the second half of the game. Sonny, Peanut, Blake, and Carson hauled their mats over near the gate, while Rich and Spanky hung back with me for a moment.

"So the ticket kid gets to drag and I don't?" I said.

"That's what I said," Spanky squealed. "B-period. S-period."

"I put in a word for you," Rich said. "Sonny said Carson asked first. What was he gonna do?"

He stepped past, towing his mat, and I followed as far as the fence. Second baseman Martin Harcourt scooped up a weak grounder and fired to first, ending the visitor's half of the inning. Nick Henry cued up the William Tell Overture and the grounds crew started across the infield, dragging their heavy-duty mats behind. Two batboys rushed from the dugout to replace the bases with clean bags, and a couple minutes later we had a fresh, new infield.

I walked with Carson back up the ramp to the main concourse. He was giddy and babbling about how much fun it was down on the field after being stuck in the ticket office all game. They were doing brisk business on future game sales tonight, and he was thrown right back into it after his brief recess.

I repeated my rounds throughout the remainder of the game and was about to return for a final stop to say good-night to my parents and Trina when Don intercepted me and sent me across the street to help Faith with the post-game rush at Ballpark Corner, which reopened in the late innings so fans could stop in on their way home. Her line was seven deep when I entered. We must have sold a thousand bucks worth of stuff over the next forty minutes. By the time the crowd filtered out the game was long over. I walked back into the concourse to find a growing cluster of game-day workers huddled around the stand where they sold the nachos and barbecue.

Trina marched up the ramp from left field, trailed by her sister, a scowl marring her face.

"Hey," I called. "You're still here?"

"Where have you been? We've been looking everywhere for you. I was ready to go twenty minutes ago."

"I was across the street. Had to help in the store."

"That would have been nice to know."

Janie looked irritated as well, but I sensed she was more pissed off at her sister than at me.

"I was on my way to say good-night when Don sent me over there." I tried to filter the defensive tone out of my voice, but I'm not that good an actor and most of it seeped through. "What was I supposed to do?"

"Well, whatever. Are you ready to go?"

"I'm not done yet. I still have to fax out the game reports."

"How long will that take?"

"Dunno. Never done it before. Probably half an hour, forty minutes."

I figured it could be accomplished in closer to five, but I rounded up, hoping she'd call it a night. It worked. She stormed off, Janie lingering behind for a moment, offering an apologetic look to show someone in the family had some manners. I turned toward the mobile office and saw Rich leaning against the concession stand sipping on a plastic cup of beer. He nodded at me with a knowing smirk that told me he'd witnessed the whole thing.

My struggles with the automatic dialer on the fax machine stretched the task into a twenty-minute ordeal, proving me more prophetic than I'd hoped. Ashandra watched for a good long while before finally offering to show me what I was doing wrong. I think she felt smart when she knew something one of the rest of us didn't.

Job finally accomplished, I found Rich at the nacho stand. He led me behind the counter and poured us each a beer. The crowd had dwindled to about a dozen people by now, with Nick the PA announcer holding court, unmercifully roasting the kid from the Duke paper. Nick needed to make people laugh, and to meet that objective he had to find someone for everyone to laugh at. It was a skill he acquired over the years to keep people from making fun of him, which we generally did only behind his back. Rich and I drifted to the perimeter, where we were joined a moment later by Peanut.

"Heard your girl was here." Peanut's face lit up, as if he expected some juicy details to flow forth and tickle his funny bone.

"Yeah," I sighed. "You missed the show."

"You gotta introduce me next time she comes."

"Don't hold your breath, boy. I wouldn't count on a return visit any time soon."

CHAPTER SEVEN

Every time the phone rang Friday morning a new wave of moths fluttered through my stomach. I was ninety-nine percent sure Trina wouldn't call, but that last one percent was rooting for her to make the effort. My line finally buzzed at five past eleven and I took a deep breath before answering.

"Lane Hamilton."

"Lane, it's Faith."

"Am I late? Oh, crap. Sorry, I'll be right up."

I had promised her I'd babysit the store when she went to lunch, but in my wallowing I had lost track of time. I jogged across the street and took my watch, seated atop her desk. As I flipped through radio stations on the boombox under the counter, I wrestled with the urge to call Trina myself. Twice I picked up the phone only to set it back in its cradle. The third time I dialed. Just as the first ring sounded, the bell on the door of the shop clanged against the glass and Martin Harcourt stepped in.

I hung the phone up and pushed it back to where I'd found it on Faith's desk as I acknowledged the Bulls second baseman. He nodded a greeting at me and glanced around to gather his bearings. A moment later he moved to a table of Bulls t-shirts.

"Do you have this one in a small?" he asked, holding up a burnt orange tee with the team name in small, bold letters on the left breast and a large Bulls D logo on the back. "I need something for my little sister."

I skirted the edge of the battered wooden counter and passed through the curtain that separated the sales floor from the storage room in the rear. There had to be 5,000 shirts back there, as we'd just stocked up for the season. Plywood shelves climbed from floor almost literally to ceiling, arrayed in rows like a supermarket. It took me a minute to find the style he wanted. After scaling the shelf, I pulled a stack of a dozen smalls from the pile and leapt to the floor. When I emerged from the back room, I found Martin perusing the Bulls caps with a couple of t-shirts draped over his left shoulder.

"Found one." I peeled a shirt off the stack and handed it to him.

"Thank you. I didn't mean for you to have to go to any trouble."

"No problem," I said. "Just took me a minute to find it. I don't usually work up here. But we've got tons of stuff back there. Let me know if you need anything else you don't see."

He thanked me again and pulled a couple of caps from the table.

"I can set that stuff on the counter so you don't have to carry it around."

"Thank you." He made a point of looking me in the eye when he spoke, as if the habit had been drilled into him from the time he was young. "I've got quite a list of people back in Missouri to buy for."

"Whereabouts?" I knew nothing about Missouri, beyond seeing the arch in St. Louis on TV every time they showed a Cardinals game, but I faked it a little in hopes of starting a halfway intelligent conversation.

"Kirksville."

"Kirksville, hunh. Is that the one near, uh …"

"Probably not," he laughed. "It's not near anything. Nothing you'd have heard of here, anyway. Hey, how do I get to the mall from here? I'd like to get something for my host family, too."

Instead of staying in the team apartments in North Durham, a couple of the players opted for the wholesome environment of a good Christian family home. He was one of them, the God squadders. I later learned that Andy Mills, a relief pitcher, was the other. I grabbed a blank phone-order form off of Faith's desk and drew him a map on the back of it, and he was on his way.

Faith returned shortly and we chatted for a little while. I told her about Martin's purchases and she mentioned Roger Gale had been in earlier. She spun that into a whole new conversation about how nice he was and how glad she was he was back this season. Roger was a backup catcher who would have had a better chance to climb the ladder if he retired from playing and became a coach. It's no great harbinger of success to spend three years in the

Carolina League, especially when you only get to play twice a week. You won't find a better-liked guy in the community, though. Roger was the guy on the team that spent his days visiting hospitals and schools and youth centers instead of lounging around the apartment pool recovering from a nightly bout of binge drinking like other players I won't mention.

As Faith talked she did the counter lean thing a couple of times. I averted my eyes the first time, out of politeness, but the second time I admit I looked. It was obvious she wanted me to, so maybe that was really the more courteous route to take. She gave me a little smile when I lifted my glance back up to eye level and I felt like I'd done my good deed for the day. The view was nice enough that I'd do it again under the right circumstances, but honestly it was more for her benefit than mine. She had to be closing in on forty, judging by the faint crows feet around her eyes, and you'd guess about that if you saw her. Fifteen years ago—maybe even ten—I bet she caught a lot of second looks, but now you had to hit her on a good day at just the right angle. Still, she was probably deserving of more attention than her husband was giving her. If I could help keep her confidence from sagging with such a minor degree of effort on my part then I'd have been a real jerk not to.

After lunch I set to work finishing the game notes, both for the *Bulls Illustrated* inserts and the newspaper guys. By two-thirty I was stuffing programs with Johnny Layne. He blathered on about how beautiful Trina was, and I halfheartedly held up my side of the conversation until I was able to turn it back on him and get him to talk about his wife, Dolores. He's probably told the story of meeting her at a USO dance in Fayetteville back in 1941 a hundred thousand times in his life, but he told it to me with such enthusiasm that I was almost jealous. Not that I'd have traded places with a senior citizen, but I wondered sometimes if I'd have stories like that to share fifty years down the road.

An hour before the gates opened Don handed me a key and told me to go fetch the magnet schedules for tonight's giveaway out of the tower. Of course I had no clue what he was talking about, so as soon as he left I raced down to the field and asked Rich to translate. He pointed across the street to a five-story brick building that looked like it was overdue for the wrecking ball. In a prior life it was used by the fire department for training exercises. I asked him to come with me, but he still had a lot of mowing to do. Instead he assigned Spanky to accompany me on my first tour of the storage facility.

The fire tower didn't look much better up close. I stood at the base of it, contemplating the paneless windows on the top couple of floors, and wondered how this could possibly be a good place to keep stuff. Spanky, who had trailed after me hauling a hand cart, got impatient and snatched the key from my hand and unbolted the padlock hanging from the latch. He struggled to pull the door open until I pitched in. Between us we swung it out from the threshold, revealing a chaotic mess of boxes, bags, and random pieces of equipment. I detected high-pitched squeals above and shuddered as I debated whether they came from rats or bats.

"Flashlight?" Spanky demanded, holding his palm out.

"Hunh?"

"You didn't bring a flashlight? Jesus. It's gonna take us an hour to find anything in here."

Suddenly I felt as if I were the twelve-year-old. But Rich hadn't told me I'd need a light. How was I supposed to know? I propped the front entrance open and between that and the sunshine filtering down the stairwell from the second floor it was bright enough for us to track down the schedules. It didn't take an hour, either. More like five minutes. I kept one eye trained on the stairs in case whatever was making the squealing noise came down for a bite, but we escaped unmolested. After loading the five boxes onto the cart, I trucked them up the sidewalk into the main concourse. Gray helped me rip the cartons open and we were ready with almost fifteen minutes to spare.

We had another beauty of a crowd. The weather was dry and warm, for April anyway, and Friday was generally a good draw. If anything I'd guess it was slightly bigger than our opening crowd, though the carnival atmosphere couldn't be replicated. The Bulls had the lead going into the ninth, until shortstop Dain Gregson, Atlanta's first-round bonus baby from a couple years back, tossed a sure double-play ball into right field and Frederick tied it up. He atoned in the bottom of the frame, lining a double into the corner to score Luther Hudson for the winning run. I got through the faxes in less than ten minutes and was out in the concourse by the time

Rich came up from the field.

Girls and ballplayers share a strange, symbiotic relationship. They each offer something the other wants—sex or status—which they exchange nightly at ballpark bazaars around the country. Luther had boosted his stock with a 2-for-3 performance, including his first home run of the year in the fourth inning. The bidding began with the tawdry blonde in the leather jacket and painted-on Levi's. Not to be upstaged, the light-skinned black girl with the straightened hair and curvy body sweetened her offer. Luther bantered with them, loudly enough to draw not-so-covert glances from the stragglers and hangers-on in the concourse. He was playing the crowd as well as the girls, glancing around as we shook our heads and tried to pretend we were above such amoral and despicable acts. By the time Rich and I started on our second beer we'd seen both girls stretch their shirt collars forward to grant Luther a preview of their wares. That was a move Faith hadn't tried yet. The battle apparently wound up a tie, as Durham's left fielder departed with a friend on each arm.

"Hope he catches syphilis," Rich cracked as Luther pulled out of the lot, spinning the tires on his Ford Explorer.

"Jealous?" I asked. "No love for the grounds crew?"

"Yeah, that'll be the fucking day."

He tilted his head back and sucked down the warm remains of his beer, wistfully staring at the empty vessel before setting it down on the counter.

"You're getting another, right?" I was nearly done with mine and figured I'd refill it if he planned to stick around for a bit.

"In a minute." He glared over at the carnies congregating around the entrance to the nacho stand. "I wish they'd leave. They're gonna ruin it for everyone."

"Wha'd'ya mean? There's plenty left in the keg, isn't there?"

"This is supposed to be a perk for us, not free beer night for every inbred fucker who sets foot in the park. We get too many people draining the line, Don'll shut the whole thing down."

"Tell 'em all to leave." He outranked anyone in an orange shirt. Maybe it was time to flex some muscle.

"I ain't tellin' no one nothing. You think I want a loogie in my burger tomorrow night?"

I started to laugh, but I realized he wasn't joking. That's one of the first lessons to be learned in the ballpark. Don't piss off the people who give you free food. The concessions staff was well represented in the concourse at the moment. If Rich or I told them to beat it the word would spread before the gates opened Saturday. We'd be forced to enlist Spanky as our personal food taster. And I wasn't too sure he wouldn't spit in my dinner himself.

Jughaid was cutting the rug to some Alan Jackson that one of his cronies had cranked in a pickup pulled just outside the front entrance. Mary Beth joined in and the hillbilly hoedown was on. I drained the dregs of my beer and was contemplating calling it a night when Don shuffled out of the main office, slowly making his way into the ring of rednecks.

"Un-unh," he said firmly. "I think it's time for everyone to go home and get ready for tomorrow's game."

It was hard to hear him over the music, but his expression said it all. He could have mimed it and they would have packed it in. I started for the gate until Don arrested me with a subtle glance. He blinked his eyes and shook his head once, nonverbally assuring me we were exempt from his eviction notice.

Don supervised the retreat of the riff-raff, then slipped into the nacho stand to grab a cold one for himself. He emerged to find a quiet core of me, Rich, Carson, Mike, and Matt Hamer from the *Herald-Sun*. I thought he'd take his beer back into the office, but he leaned against the counter and took a sip as we all looked on. As I came to learn, Don didn't drink with the crew very often after a game. He'd occasionally send for a beer and drink it at his desk while poring over the night's figures, but it was a rare evening that found him lounging late in the concourse. He broke what had grown into an awkward silence.

"Can't have them getting out of hand," he said. "Too much liability at risk."

Mike mumbled an apology on behalf of his concessions crew, but Don shrugged it off and the conversation reignited. I talked more with Don that night than I had since the day he hired me. He was a nice enough guy, but rigid as a butler most of the time, so I never approached him unless there was some official work issue I needed to discuss. Maybe that was why Matt seemed the most comfortable chatting with him. He didn't work there.

The conversation skidded to an abrupt halt shortly before

twelve-thirty, breaking up the party almost instantly. We moved en masse to the parking lot and headed home. I expected to find a message from Trina when we got back to the house, but Burt reported no one had called all evening. Alone in my bed, I wondered what she'd done all night. Had she tried not to think about me as much as I'd fought to keep her from barging into my thoughts?

I left two messages for her Saturday, sneaking a couple of calls in during opportune quiet moments. I hated to do that, because it only built anticipation for the return call—which never came. All afternoon an ongoing debate raged in my head arguing the case for and against her. I strongly suspected she was screening her calls, but maybe she was out. She could have been shopping or visiting her mom or doing charity work with shut-ins.

I didn't hear from her all weekend. By Sunday evening I was irritable and distracted. There was a good little crowd tapping the keg after the game, our first afternoon affair of the season, including a couple of the girls who worked the beer stand down in right field, Sue and Stacy. Technically they were concessions workers, but they were grad students at UNC and didn't act like idiots so they were excepted from Don's ban. Matt Hamer was there, as were Porter Mason from *Baseball America*, Carson, Mike, Blake, Nick, and a couple other guys I didn't know. Even Sonny stuck around for a little while. He usually took off as soon as Don didn't need him and went home to his wife.

We'd been hanging out for about twenty minutes when Rich demanded my keys.

"You wanna leave *already*?" I asked. He'd rhapsodized incessantly about sticking around last year until the wee hours of the morning on the final game of a homestand. It wasn't even dinnertime yet.

"No-o-o-o. But when we do go, I'll drive."

"Why?"

"Because I'm sick of seeing you all mopey. Either you're going to drink this mess out of your system or I'm gonna knock the shit out of you."

If it came down to it, I was pretty sure I could take Rich. It would have been close, but my reach would have given me the edge. I didn't want to resort to violence, however, so I handed over my pickup keys and drank. And drank. And drank. And he was right. I felt better after a while. I think he was hoping I'd run off behind the bleachers with Sue or Stacy and really flush Trina out of my system, but I settled for blasting my skull in with a dozen free beers. I wasn't alone. Rich forced Blake into my truck after he deemed him too intoxicated to drive home when we left at nine-thirty, and we carted his sorry ass all the way out to Cary. Shortly after we hit the Durham Freeway, Blake broke into some kind of drunken country rap, initiating a vicious cycle of Rich boosting the radio volume, Blake singing louder, Rich cranking the stereo again, ad infinitum. Finally, my friend cut the music off altogether.

"Shut the fuck up, man."

I wobbled my head to the right and saw Blake halt midsong.

"Hey, I'm just having fun," he laughed. "For a thousand bucks a month you gotta get your free beer's worth."

"Damn straight." I raised an imaginary toasting glass. "Here's to a thousand bucks a month."

Blake scowled down at me, the headlights from oncoming cars glistening off the diamond stud in his left ear. "You getting a thousand a month, too?"

Rich shook his head disgustedly and I simply shrugged.

"It took me two years to move up to that," Blake seethed. "What the hell?"

His drunken breath steamed the side of my face. I tried not to inhale because I was dangerously close to getting sick already and his alcoholic halitosis wasn't helping. He said nothing the rest of the ride, not even a thank you when we dropped him off. I slid over and poked my head out the window, sucking in fresh air as houses and mail boxes whipped past. By the time we reached the interstate I was pretty sure I could make it home without puking. I pulled my face back inside to find Rich fuming as he fumbled with the radio.

"Don't ever talk about your salary with him or anyone else," he lectured.

"It's so little. It's a, um, what's the word … it's a pittance. How could I know anyone ever started at less than that?"

"Well, some people do. And Blake bitched about it all last year. Don't ever talk money with him."

"Sorry. I didn't know."

"And now you do."

CHAPTER EIGHT

I was three planets away Monday morning when an alarm sounded mere inches from my head, setting off a series of red and yellow fireworks in my brain. Then grayness, as all went still and silent, before another firestorm of noise and color erupted. The pattern repeated, a little louder each time. Before I could place it, I was awake, clutching the phone in my outstretched hand.

"Mmm'lo," I mumbled.

"Rich?" a girl inquired.

"Uh. No. It's Lane. Let me get him."

The phone cord, kinked up worse than an old Slinky, knotted itself as I stretched the handset toward the nightstand. When I let go it sprang back into my ribs and clattered to the hardwood floor. I was next to crash land, rolling farther off the edge of the twin mattress than I'd projected. I could hear the voice squawking through the phone. Rich must have pissed someone off pretty good. Maybe Sue. Or Stacy. Which one was which, I wondered as I picked myself up. I pulled the door open and staggered down the hall to his room.

"Dude!" I screamed. "Phone's for you!"

Rich, not having anyone to talk to on a regular basis, didn't keep a phone in his room. He came out a moment later and grabbed the one on the shelf at the end of the hall.

"This is Rich … Hunh? … Who? … Shit."

He hung the phone up and turned to me with his eyes barely cracked open.

"It's for you, douchebag. It's Becca. Thanks for waking me up."

A moment later I lifted the phone off my floor, took a deep breath, and closed my eyes. That last part was just because my head hurt so badly. It didn't help much.

"Hello."

"Lane?" It really was her, though she sounded like she was

talking through a baby rattle.

"Hey. Where you been all weekend?"

"I was busy," she rattled. "I figured you were working so I went out with my sisters … and some friends."

"Oh." Interesting. She didn't have any friends. At least not girls. "Did you guys have fun?"

"Yeah," she said unconvincingly. "Apparently not as much as you did."

"I was working. Can't help it my job's fun."

"Sound hungover to me."

"Just tired. I was up late."

"Yeah." This sarcastically, like she didn't believe me. Then silence.

"You wanna get some dinner tonight?" I asked after about thirty seconds of no one saying anything.

"Can't. I'm going to my mom's for my brother's birthday."

I considered raising the legitimate question of why I wouldn't be included in such festivities but chose to let it go.

"Maybe tomorrow then?"

"Okay. Maybe Kyoto." She knew I hated Asian food. I'd told her at least twenty times. She only ever floated it when she wanted to antagonize me.

"Sure. I'll pick you up at six."

"It's a date." This is the first thing she'd said the whole time in a pleasant tone, like she just remembered she didn't hate my guts.

The drive to Trina's apartment took about ten minutes if I hit the lights just right. That didn't buy enough time Tuesday night to settle my stomach, which felt like it was hosting a mixed martial arts tournament. I parked my truck two spots down from her car and sat there nibbling the inside of my cheek while the song on the radio finished. The evening could unfold in a couple of very different ways. I couldn't say if I was more upset about not knowing what awaited up in her apartment or that I had so little influence over it.

I hadn't been this nervous since our first date. She'd just broken up with Vince, the heavily cologned, overly polished, Jaguar salesman who picked her up from the bank almost every night. He never deemed me worthy of a spoken word, just a silent head nod or an occasional wink as he passed by. Man, did I laugh the day I learned she dumped him. Then Andy goaded me into asking her out. "She wants to start over," he said. "Might as well be you as anyone else." He knew I'd been fantasizing about her since the day I started at his branch. I got lost trying to find her place that night, but the route was so familiar now my truck could have gotten there without me.

It was just shy of six when I knocked on her door, and it took a minute before I heard the deadbolt slide back. She pulled the door open wearing a white terrycloth robe, her hair wrapped in a towel and her face yet free of makeup.

"You're early," she said in lieu of an enthusiastic greeting. "I still need a few minutes."

I'd seen her get ready before. She didn't go from robe to ready in *a few minutes*. I was looking at an hour wait, easy. But instead of flopping on the couch I followed her back into the steamy bathroom. She turned around and raised a neatly trimmed eyebrow at me, but said nothing as she unwrapped her hair. Her counter extended the full length of the wall and I pushed myself up onto the open part beyond the sink and sat with my legs dangling a few inches above the floor.

"This could take a while," she said, shaking her head. She wasn't angry, though. More amused that I'd come sit there instead of watching TV like I usually did.

"No rush. I just want to see you. I missed you."

I hadn't planned to say that, though it was true. I missed hanging out, horsing around. Actually seeing her. The bullshit phone tag wasn't doing much for me.

"I missed you, too." She brushed her hair in quick strokes in preparation for blow-drying, and barely glanced up when she said it, though I detected the corners of her mouth curl up just a smidgen. Watching her was such a turn on for some reason. We'd been apart too long.

"You have fun last night?" I asked.

She set her brush down and tilted her head, as if she had water in her ear. Heavy, damp curls hung down to her elbow.

"It was okay. Nothing special."

"I'd have gone, you know."

"I know," she said softly, as she fumbled with the cord to her hair dryer. She plugged it in and turned it on, and any hope of further conversation was blown away by 1,800 watts of noise.

When her curls were nearly dry, she misted them with water from a pump dispenser and fogged her entire head in a cloud of hair spray. It was a lot of effort for someone who couldn't be troubled to microwave a frozen dinner. Another quick blast with the hair dryer, then at long last she began lining the tools of her trade back along the mirror.

"Almost ready." That was her equivalent of the two-minute warning in football. The timeouts and commercials could drag it out for a while yet, even without overtime.

"No rush. I'm having fun just watching you."

"You're not one of those guys who peeps on girls in the bathroom, are you?"

"Just you."

Trina smirked and cast me one of her ultra-sexy sideways glances, where nothing moved but her deep green eyes. I pounced, almost literally, jumping down from the counter and wrapping her in my arms. She resisted for a split second as though she were determined to start in on her makeup. A moment later we were on her bed. It felt so good, and not just physically. She became someone different when we had sex. The chip on her shoulder came off with her blouse or robe. As she shimmied on top of me, the sweat glistening on her breasts and arms and upturned neck, I realized this was the only time she ever buried her insecurities. She didn't have to be hip or on guard against saying the wrong thing. There were no other pretty girls from the bank, no gawking bouncers, no Andy, no Rich. Just me and her. These individual, amazing moments were the foundation of our entire relationship. This was why I loved her, and these episodes had enough of a carryover effect—at least when she wasn't withholding them for an extended period—to make up for a lot of attitude in between.

We both had a lot of energy to work off, and we went at it until well past our normal dinnertime. When we had satiated ourselves she told me to forget about Kyoto because she didn't want to get ready again. We ordered a pizza instead and sat around talking until almost eleven. She danced around the important stuff, but I picked at the edges until she finally admitted getting frustrated with me for not having time to spend with her last week. I told her that we'd face that every homestand, and I'd try to meet her for lunch some game days and maybe stay overnight occasionally so we wouldn't be reduced to missed messages and misunderstandings. She laughed and cried and showed me more genuine emotion than I'd seen from her all spring. I drew on her back with my fingertip and she reciprocated by tracing hearts on my chest with just enough pressure to leave a faint red outline where her fingernail had traveled. I fell asleep pressed tight against her naked back, feeling comfortable for the first time in a week.

While I regained balance in my world, the Bulls wobbled to a 2-5 mark on their road trip, putting them three games under .500 for the year. They returned to kick off a seven-game homestand on Monday against the Prince William Cannons. The pitching was definitely ahead of the hitting, with half the lineup batting under .200. Clyde Knowles, who platooned at third base, had gone hitless in eighteen at-bats since the team left town. He entered Monday's action with an .077 mark to his name. I felt so bad for the guy that I left him out of the media notes to preserve his anonymity.

I had worked out a swap with the assistant GM in Macon whereby I would fax him our game stories and boxes and he would do the same for us. It was the only way I could get stats from Paul's games, and the first thing I did each morning was read over Macon's results from the previous night of South Atlantic League action. Rich pointed out that if I got the same stuff for Double-A Greenville and Triple-A Richmond I could work them all into my game notes to highlight what was going on throughout the rest of the Braves farm system. The newspaper guys loved the idea. Not to bash on them, but like a lot of people they were lazy when it came to certain things—like their jobs. Here I was giving them gift-wrapped notes to throw at the end of their stories. At first they were grateful; eventually they came to expect it.

If Paul's first two weeks were any indication, he'd be in Durham before long. He got off to a .333 start with five doubles and four stolen bases in his first twelve games. I kept a daily tally on a notepad I stored in the top drawer of the desk I shared with Rich. Space was so tight Don was the only one with his own room, and he was over in the old office inside the stadium. The rest of us holed up in the portable trailer just outside the front gate.

Sonny came in around ten followed by Blake and asked us to leave so they could talk privately. They should have stayed down on the field. That mobile unit was anything but soundproof. We hung out in the lobby for a few minutes, but when their voices rose we went down to the tunnel to straighten out the equipment that had been tossed aside the previous homestand. We were distracted enough by our task I didn't notice Sonny walk up.

"Guys," he said, pulling down on the brim of his cowboy hat. "Got a minute?"

"What's up?" Rich asked.

"I hadda send Blake home for the day."

"Why?" I asked. "What happened?"

"Wull, he was angry about his paycheck. Said new guys like you were making as much as he was. He wanted more money, or he threatened to go work for the Mudcats."

"Good," Rich said. "Good riddance."

"I tol' him we wouldn't do that and he got all steamed and said a few things, an' I figured it was best if he cleared out for the day and cooled off."

"He thinks he can get more money out of the Mudcats?" I asked.

"I reckon so."

"Joke's on them," Rich said. "If they hire him they'll find out how fucking lazy he is."

"Maybe so," Sonny agreed. I'd never heard him cut on Blake before, though he couldn't have helped but notice he did the least amount of work of anyone on the grounds crew.

"What did Blake say?" I asked.

"He just kinda stormed off an' left. If he ain't back tomorrow I guess we'll know his decision."

"Addition by subtraction," Rich said. "I'll keep my fingers crossed he doesn't come back."

"Guess this means I might get to drag tonight," I said. "Unless there's someone ahead of me on the waiting list."

"Limber up," Sonny laughed. "Tonight's your night."

I left the press box after the opening frame ended and slipped down to the first-base line to see what the guys were up to. It was a typical early-season Monday and there wasn't much of a crowd. The stadium was so quiet we could hear Vendor Joe yelling from all the way up in the main concourse. After killing twenty minutes there, I took off and circulated around the park for a couple innings, checking in with the groups in the picnic areas and hanging out in the concourse with Gray watching the stragglers file in.

I cruised back down to the tunnel in the top of the fifth inning and peppered Rich with questions about dragging the field. When he realized how excited I was he started calling me the Drag Virgin and made me practice pulling my mat. The guys offered a sarcastic golf clap in time with my stride as I paraded the length of the tunnel, gripping the rope handle so tight the nylon cut into my fingers.

"Wild" Evan Wayne was on the hill for the Bulls, and he delayed my debut by walking the bases full. Jim Peak, the pitching coach, came out to calm him down. He must have said the right thing because the next three pitches were in the zone and Wayne recorded his fifth strikeout of the game to end the visitors' ups.

"Go, go, go," Rich egged me on. I sprinted out to the foul line lugging my mat and turned around to see the other four guys hanging back by the gate laughing. Finally they jogged out and we lined up as Nick cued the music. The infield drag was staggered, with one guy going first, then the next guy leaving, then the third guy, et cetera. Rich lined me up on the far left and told me to hit it. So I did. I started running with the mat, just like I had in the tunnel. I had gone about thirty feet when I heard him yelling at me.

"Whoa, Laner. Slow down."

I slackened my pace and peered over my right shoulder to find he was well behind me. He was just walking. When he'd gone about ten feet, Peanut started in, also just walking. Then Carson, and finally Sonny. I waited for a minute until Rich caught up and continued on my way.

"Nice and slow, dude, nice and slow." I heard that over and over until we returned to the first-base line and picked up our mats. "See what happens if you run with it?" Rich pointed to the dirt where I had started. "You get those waves from the mat popping up and down."

"Should I fix it?" The bottom of the fifth was about to start.

Prince William's pitcher had completed his warmups and was waiting to get the ball back from his third baseman.

"Just leave it. There's no time."

I jogged off the field burning with embarrassment, feeling like the entire stadium was laughing at me. The only ones who were, however, were in the tunnel. That punk Spanky was the worst. He kept tossing out little barbs about how even he knew you weren't supposed to run. Sonny threw his arm around my shoulder and told me not to worry about it.

I leaned against the fence and watched the game, trying to forget about my Drag Virgin moment. The Bulls advanced runners to second and third on a grounder, bringing ice-cold Clyde Knowles to the plate with two down. A strikeout in the third had dropped him to 2-for-27 on the year. As he walked from the dugout he crossed himself twice and kissed the pendant hanging around his neck. The desperate third baseman then drew something in the dirt with his bat before finally stepping into the left-handed batter's box. He took a ball low and outside, then stared at a changeup right over the heart of the plate. With the count 1-and-1, Cannons starter Aaron Key fired a slider toward the inside corner. Clyde turned on it, ripping a two-hopper to first. It should have been a routine play, an easy third out to end the inning. Instead, it hit a ridge in the dirt and spun beyond the reach of Prince William's stunned first baseman. The ball kicked into foul ground and Clyde dug out a two-run double.

"Holy shit," Rich laughed. "Did you see that bounce?"

"He owes you a dinner, Lane," Peanut said. "That one was all you."

Then they started the chant. "Vir-gin! Vir-gin! Vir-gin!"

The Bulls went on to win, 5-4, with Evan Wayne recording his first victory of the season. Clyde Knowles, fired up by his gift double, lined a clean single up the middle in the eighth inning to officially end his slump. We were hanging out in the concourse after the game when he walked through on his way out. Rich stopped him and told him the Drag Virgin story.

"I thought that ball kicked off awful funny," he admitted. "I'll take whatever I can get at this point, though."

We talked with him for a few minutes and he invited us to join him and Matt Acres, one of the team's starting pitchers, up at

Devine's for a beer. I was all gung ho, because it sounded like more fun than enduring the inevitable roasting from Nick. But Rich seemed almost reluctant as we walked to the truck.

"Dude," he started. "Lesson number two for the night: Don't be a jock sniffer."

"What in the hell are you talking about?"

"Just be cool, okay. Don't act like you want their autographs and don't tell them how good they are or anything like that."

"Why would I do that?" I argued as I turned the key and fired up the engine.

"I'm not saying you would. I'm just saying, don't."

For the record, I didn't jock sniff. I was even going to let them pay for our beers until Rich made me throw ten bucks down to cover our half of the tab. Clyde and Matt were pretty cool. As we walked back out to the parking lot, we negotiated with them to have Spanky dropped in a trash can before the following night's game. I had reason to hope the kid would take my place as the primary butt of jokes less than twenty-four hours after I'd seemingly locked the role up for the foreseeable future.

Rich radioed me when Spanky was apprehended Tuesday afternoon. I was all the way down in the left-field picnic area when he called, but I could hear the runt's screams over my walkie-talkie as I sprinted across the diamond, ducking batting-practice line drives. I arrived just in time to see him crawl out of the overturned can. It quickly became a tradition, however, so there would be plenty more opportunities to witness him getting lifted off the ground and deposited unceremoniously in the garbage. Secretly I think he liked the attention, though he'd kick his legs and curse like a prepubescent sailor all the same.

I was mildly surprised to spot Blake among the crowd sharing a hearty laugh at Spanky's expense. He ignored my greeting, walking coolly past as I righted the trash barrel and Rich dusted Spanky off.

"Guess the Mudcats didn't want him either," Rich said.

Blake didn't give me three words the rest of the homestand. After a couple of nights I didn't even look at him when he passed. If Sonny hadn't generously ceded me his drag spot I would have avoided the tunnel during the games just to escape the tension. The only joy I derived from dragging the field came in knowing my participation boosted Blake's misery index.

CHAPTER NINE

The far-flung layout of the South Atlantic League had thus far deprived us of an opportunity to see Paul play. Macon's schedule included no stops in Greensboro and its first visit to Fayetteville coincided with a Bulls homestand. So Rich and I had targeted Macon's series at Sumter as our first legitimate chance to catch Paul in action. When the Bulls hit the road we did likewise, taking Rich's Civic down to South Carolina, reaching Sumter in a little over three hours. We checked into the Ramada Inn, the visiting club's hotel, just after two and harassed the girl at the front desk until she broke down and told us which room was Paul's. We announced our arrival by pounding our fists on his door.

"Hold on a second," Paul said to someone. Then louder to us, "Who is it?"

"Cleaning lady," Rich sang in best migrant woman's voice.

"Who?"

"Cleaning lady. Open up. Me so horny for you."

"Enough, guys," Paul yelled. I heard him talking lower into the telephone again.

We caught snatches of his conversation as we loitered outside his room, ignoring the inquiring glances of a legitimate maid pushing her cart down the walkway. When she turned the corner we pounded on his door once more, just to let him know we hadn't left.

"I'm gonna have to call back, Ma," he said. "These guys must be bored."

"Murph!" he called after he hung up the phone. "If that's you I'm'a piss in your Gatorade again."

Rich and I leaned against the door, laughing so hard now our eyes teared up. When Paul pulled it open I fell across the threshold and tripped over his leg. He scampered out of the way as I hit the carpet.

"Gotcha." Rich fired a soft, playful punch into our buddy's

chest.

"No freakin' way." Paul reached down to help me up. "When'd you guys get here?"

"Half hour ago," I said. "Took a little while to track you down."

"It's so awesome to see you guys." His suntan was deeper, but otherwise he looked the same as he had the night of Cole's gig. "I had no idea you were coming."

"Didn't want to overpromise," Rich said. "In case Becca didn't let him go."

Paul ushered us into his room, where we hung out and caught up for half an hour until he had to get ready to go to the park. There was a hint of homesickness in the way he spoke about his parents and his girlfriend Nicole back in Raleigh. Like us, they had found opportunities to visit scarce.

When the Braves filed onto the team bus, we followed it to Riley Park, home of the Sumter Flyers. To call it a stadium was stretching it. If it were your high school field, you'd be playing your prep ball in style. But for the professional level, well, Paul should have been glad he wasn't in the Sally League a year earlier, because the Braves low Class A farm team played there for six seasons until they switched their affiliation to Macon over the winter. Now it was the Expos farmhands who toiled in obscurity each night.

That's no exaggeration. There weren't 200 people there that evening. We could have drawn a bigger crowd in Durham for batting practice. There's an old joke floating around baseball where a fan calls and inquires what time the game starts. The GM then asks, "What time can you be here?" That one probably originated in Sumter.

We watched both teams take BP, then cruised down the road for some dinner, arriving back with plenty of time yet to kill before the game. When we flashed our National Association passes at the gate the attendant examined them suspiciously, turning them over and attempting to read the fine print on the back. I doubt his eyes were strong enough for that, though. He was older than Johnny Layne by at least five years and kind of frail looking, with a bulky hearing aid protruding from his left ear. An NA pass entitled the bearer to entry at any minor league park. They were distributed to employees of the teams, media members, and others affiliated with the game. I was starting to doubt their legitimacy myself, having never actually used mine before. He made it out like we were trying to talk our way in on expired McDonald's coupons. If Rich hadn't been so insistent I might have caved and bought a ticket. Finally a younger gentleman sporting a Sumter Flyers golf shirt approached and expedited the process. He introduced himself as Kevin Klopak, the general manager of the team. When we told him we worked for the Bulls he got way too chummy, giving us a tour of their facilities, humble though they were. I felt a little embarrassed, but Rich soaked it up. He switched into networking mode, exchanging cards with the guy and everything.

"You never can tell," he pontificated as we picked out our seats over the visitors' dugout. "Someday he might be a useful contact."

Rich was funny that way. He clowned around as much as anyone during games, but underneath he obsessed about climbing the minor league ladder. Unless Don or Sonny moved on there wouldn't be room for him to continue growing in Durham, so he constantly scoped out opportunities to lay some groundwork for the future.

When the Flyers trotted onto the field we rose for a pre-recorded version of the national anthem. Paul was in his usual No. 2 hole, and we gave him a hearty ovation when he was announced, pounding our heels against the dugout from our front-row seats. Rich must have been channeling Cole, because he started yelling stuff like "Enloe High, baby!" and "Let's go, Giordano!" as Paul approached the plate. With the count 1-and-1, Paul stepped out of the box and went through his routine, yanking on his batting gloves, tapping his cleats with the bat, and adjusting his helmet. He had just lined himself back up—left foot aligned with the front of the plate, elbow out, bat head back at a perfect forty-five degree angle—when Rich let loose with, "Be the ball, Paul!" Paul threw up his right hand to ask for time from the plate umpire, but Saul Santovenia, the Sumter hurler, was already into his windup and he didn't get it. He stepped back anyway, chuckling to himself as the ump called strike two.

"Shut up, dude," I said. "You're breaking his concentration."

"I'm just loosening him up a little."

"If he K's it's your fault."

Rich held his tongue as Santovenia spun a slow, tight curve. Paul hitched his right elbow once and unloaded, a crisp crack of bat meeting ball echoing off the nearly empty bleachers. As the ball soared toward deep left center he lowered his head and charged out of the batter's box. The center fielder sprinted back into the gap, eyes trained on the white blur streaking through the cloudless sky. He strode onto the warning track, planted his right foot and leapt hard, crashing into the fence just as the ball arrived. I thought he'd made an incredible catch until I saw the ball ricochet forward. Sumter's left fielder, backing up on the play, hastily changed direction to track it down as his teammate examined his glove in disbelief.

As Paul cut a sharp corner around second, Macon's base coach motioned his hands downward to indicate there would be a play at third. Paul took off from about twelve feet away, propelling himself forward in a beautiful headfirst slide. Sumter's third baseman slapped the tag down on his back a split-second after his fingers reached the bag. The umpire threw his hands out, signaling him safe, and the Braves dugout erupted in cheers. Paul requested time and paced around the bag for a minute, brushing the red-clay dust from the front of his uniform. He stepped back onto the base and pointed to where we sat, as if to say that one was for us.

He was fired up. When Santovenia toed the rubber he danced off third base like we'd always do in Little League, where the odds were good every other pitch was going to the backstop. If he was playing mind games, it worked. The first pitch to Mike McNeely, Macon's first baseman, was high and outside, and when Sumter's starter got the ball back from his catcher he glared toward third base. He dispensed with the windup, working from the stretch instead, but Paul simply delayed his move toward the plate, darting forward as the pitch was released and slamming on the brakes when the catcher blocked the curveball in the dirt. McNeely was up in the count 2-0 and he grinned down at Paul appreciatively. Paul took a sizeable lead off third, diving back into the bag just ahead of a hasty pickoff throw. He drew another before the next pitch was sent plateward, this a fastball down the heart that McNeely should have punished. Instead he just missed it and the ball screamed straight back into the screen. As the 2-1 pitch was delivered, Paul stomped his feet and bluffed a move home with such disconcerting effect that the ball sailed past a diving catcher all the way to the wall. He scooted home easily, tallying the first run of the game.

It was 3-1 Braves when Paul came to the plate to lead off the top of the third. Santovenia obviously harbored some ill feelings for his base-running antics, because he started Paul off with a fastball throat high and in, landing him on the seat of his pants. Paul bantered with Sumter's catcher as he dusted himself off, then took an aggressive practice swing. Santovenia dialed up another heater a hair inside and Paul returned it with interest, scorching a blazing liner over the mound, forcing the Sumter right-hander to flatten himself against the turf. When we played in high school Paul would regularly astonish me with his bat control. He could push bunt seven balls out of ten into a cap set fifty feet from the plate. If a team ever shifted on him, or slid their second baseman over to take a pickoff throw, he was money to find the hole that was created. But I'd never seen him drive one through the box like that.

He stood on first, looking for a sign from his third-base coach, who simply shrugged and smiled as if to say, do whatever you want. Paul did. He stretched his lead out, diving back easily ahead of the throw. Longer lead, same result. Maximum lead, and this time he took off. Sumter pitched out, but the throw down was late and Paul was ninety feet closer to scoring his second run of the game, which he did on the next pitch, as McNeely lined a single into left field.

He batted three more times, adding a bunt single to his résumé to wind up 3-for-5 in the Braves' 9-4 victory. What did he fixate on after the game? The 3-2 curveball that buckled his knees for a called third strike in the ninth inning. It's hard for a perfectionist to enjoy life. We pulled him back on top by talking up his triple and his base-running heroics while downing a couple of pitchers at a nightspot near the hotel. He was so happy we'd come down it made me sorry I couldn't see him play more frequently. Rich and I were back on the road Tuesday morning, leaving him and his .371 average behind, though we figured the Braves might just as well bump him up to Durham now and present him with a new challenge.

To pay for my transgression of leaving town and having fun without Trina, I sentenced myself to forty-eight hours of confinement. At five-thirty Friday night I placed myself in her custody. The next two days were a blur of shopping, food, movies, and a couple of conjugal visits. The only thing even remotely resembling an argument was our discussion of where to eat dinner Sunday night. I tossed Devine's on the table just out of habit, but quickly caved when Trina begged for Red Lobster.

The crowd was spilling out of the restaurant lobby when we pulled up and I circled the parking lot twice before settling on a tight space in the last row.

"This doesn't look so good," I said as we approached the entrance. Half a dozen patrons milled about on the front sidewalk smoking cigarettes as they waited for a table.

"You just don't want to eat here," Trina said.

"No, I just don't want to wait forever. I'm hungry."

She slipped through the entrance and I followed in her wake as we forced our way through the crowd. "How long's the wait?" I asked the hostess.

"How many?" she inquired without looking up from her clipboard.

"Just the two of us."

"Probably about an hour right now." She jammed her pen behind her ear and gave me a crooked smile that said she couldn't care less if that estimate sent us racing for the door.

"What's going on tonight?"

"Graduation weekend. There are a lot of parents in town. Can I get a name, please?"

"Do we want to wait an hour?" I asked Trina. "I'm starving."

"It won't take that long." She pushed me aside and said, "We'll wait. Put us down for two under Trina."

The hostess scratched her name down at the bottom of the list and waved us away, leaving us to stake our claim to a few feet of real estate among the jumbled masses. When the McMasters party of four was called we inherited their turf by the gumball machines.

"You sure you want to wait this out?" I asked as I leaned uncomfortably across the top of the candy dispenser.

"We're already here. We might as well stay. We haven't

eaten here in months."

"Whatever. I've got to use the bathroom. I think this is going to be a long wait."

I gave her a quick kiss and left her to guard our territory. The men's room was over capacity as well and there were several guys ahead of me in line for a urinal. Ten minutes later I emerged to find an Asian couple had jumped our claim on the candy machine. I scanned the room, finally spotting Trina conversing with a couple of guys in the bar. They were neatly dressed in shiny t-shirts and pressed pants, maybe thirty-ish, curly hair perfectly gelled into place. I fought my way toward the bar, passing the hostess stand just as she leaned into her microphone and announced, "Landon, party of two. Table for Landon." One of Trina's acquaintances raised his hand and gave a quick salute in my direction. I responded with a casual head nod and pushed on, only to realize he'd been waving at the hostess. He gave me a cursory once-over as he and his buddy passed by, and I denounced him under my breath as they followed the hostess into the seating area.

"Who are *they?*" I asked when Trina had rejoined me.

"Who?"

"Those two Dapper Dans you were talking with."

"Oh, them." She shrugged and glanced at her feet. "They know my sister. I think she went to school with them."

"Small world."

"Yep."

"That one guy, with the gray shirt, kind of looked familiar to me."

"Really?" Trina forced a smile and her nostrils flared involuntarily.

"Yeah. Did he play ball anywhere around here?"

"I don't know. Maybe. Like I said, Janie knows him better than me."

"I got it. I think I saw him in the bank once or twice. You ever see him in there?"

"I don't think so. You know, maybe we should go to Devine's. You were right about the wait."

"Are you sure? It looks like it's starting to clear out a little."

"No. We can go. I know you'd rather eat there anyway."

I took her hand and led her outside. Free of the crowd she

stopped and pulled me toward her and planted an unscripted kiss on my chin. I tried to kiss her back, but she started for the truck. We got a table on the patio at Devine's and sat outside in the fading sunlight for an hour after our plates had been cleared away. I killed most of the pitcher we ordered as she alternated between rapid-fire discourse and distracted quiet.

"Everything okay?" I asked after a lull in the conversation. "You seem half a mile away."

"Yep," she said. "I'm just tired. I had a great weekend, but I'm exhausted."

CHAPTER TEN

Don called everyone together for a quick staff meeting in the lobby of the trailer Monday morning, primarily to introduce two new interns. Both were fresh out of class, having just completed their junior year of college. Shannon Miller, who was going to assist Jenna with group sales, attended Appalachian State. She was borderline anorexic, with a bony face and straight, brown hair that drooped limply away from the part in the center of her scalp. Conversely, Emily Wright, who went to UNC Wilmington, notched in at a belt size beyond her ideal weight. Her close-cropped blonde hair had a mind of its own, defiantly jutting out in several directions at once as though someone had just rubbed a balloon on her head. She wore no makeup, though a tasteful hint of lilac—just enough to know it was there, not enough to gag me—teased my nostrils as she stood next to me in the lobby. She was my heir as public relations contact, and my first duty following the meeting was leading her through the compilation of the media notes for tonight's game.

"Okay, Emily," I said, as I pulled a second chair up to the staff computer. "Would you rather watch or do you want to put today's notes together?"

"It's Emma," she corrected politely. "Leigh's my middle name. Only my family calls me Emma Leigh. At school I just use Emma."

"Sorry. I thought it was all one."

"Everyone does. I guess my parents were being clever when they named me."

"It's nice, though. Emma Leigh. At least it goes well together."

"It's too formal." She wrinkled her nose and crinkled her eyes in a measured display of distaste. "It sounds like a diploma or a wedding invitation."

"There you go. Maybe someday your husband will call you

that."

"Dag, he better not. I might have to slap him."

As she hadn't answered my original question, I opened last week's file and began clicking the mouse, wiping out a few items I knew were no longer relevant. I leafed through the faxes that had arrived to my attention, pointing out some of the highlights I might include from other teams in the Braves system. We then combed through the stats from the Bulls' 3-4 road trip, looking for interesting tidbits. Rabbit Waterson swiped five bases on the week, Dain Gregson connected for his first homer of the season at Kinston, and Warren Yauch recorded saves in two of the team's wins. Emma caught on quickly. She had been a student assistant in the sports information office at Wilmington the past two years, making her at least as qualified as I was to mine nuggets from the box scores.

Johnny Layne ate up his new program-stuffing assistant, dubbing her a "ray of sunshine." He hung on every word that rolled off her tongue, his eyes dancing to the lilting rhythm of her voice. She adopted him as her Durham grandfather and regaled him with news from back home, as if he had some sudden connection to her faraway cast of characters. The Lane and Layne Show was cancelled. He had found a new partner.

I broke up their act late in the afternoon, figuring she should get a full tour of the park before the gates opened. Starting across the street in Ballpark Corner, I introduced her to everyone I knew, and a couple of people I didn't. Gordy McNulty, the manager, made a crack about what an upgrade she was over the previous media guy, chucking me on the shoulder in case I thought he was serious. The only unenthusiastic greetings we got came from Nick Henry, who seemed unsure of what to say with a "female" in the press box, and the other new intern. Shannon's words were polite enough, but they were contrasted by disinterested body language and furtive glances cast toward Jenna, as if she were looking to share an inside joke with her new boss.

I checked into the press box so frequently during the game that Matt Hamer kidded they never saw me half that much before Emma took over my job. I laughed along with the media guys as my mind raced for a comeback. I was mortified she'd think A) I didn't trust her, or B) I was infatuated with her. Or C) both. But she was more riled up about his comment than I was.

"He's just lookin' out for me, y'all," Emma said in her coastal accent, shaking her forefinger at Matt. "Don't y'all be startin' any rumors."

All the same I departed when the inning ended. I hung out with Rich in the tunnel until the ninth inning, when I decided I'd exiled myself from the press box so long my absence itself raised suspicion. When I returned I took the chair next to Matt, who was tapping away on his portable computer, the heap of curly hair atop his head jiggling like a Jell-O mold as he typed.

"What's that?" I asked.

He contorted his face at me and lifted his palms, as if to indicate it was damn obvious what it was. "It's my game story."

"Who won?" I inquired. Red Phelps of the rival newspaper chuckled softly into his hand. Kinston trailed 4-2 but had runners on first and second with no one down. I didn't feel confident enough in the lead to start sending out my faxes yet.

"Durham," he mumbled, wrapping his arm around the edge of his machine like we used to do in school when we didn't want someone to cheat off our exam.

Warren Yauch was sweating on the mound, trying to wriggle out of a self-made mess. He seduced Tribe catcher Ernie Jennings into a two-strike count with consecutive major league fastballs, both up above the letters on his jersey.

"See, he'll K, Thompson will ground into a DP, and we'll all go home," claimed the clairvoyant Matt.

But it didn't work out that way. The Bulls closer delivered another predictable fastball, this one a hair lower, and Jennings deposited it over the left-field wall to give Kinston a 5-4 lead.

"Goddammit." Matt jammed a fat finger on his keyboard to backspace over the first three paragraphs of his recap as Nick and Red erupted in laughter.

Yauch settled down and retired the next three Indians hitters on two grounders and a popup. But the damage was done. He'd pissed away a sterling start by Matt Acres, who had worked into the eighth before turning things over to the pen. The Bulls still had three outs to play with as they faced Eric West, Kinston's soft-tossing relief ace. Slow, slower, slowest, then suddenly 80 mph looked like Nolan Ryan. West had already racked up eight saves on the young season by lulling batters to sleep.

Martin Harcourt led off the Bulls' half of the inning. The frustration dripped down his face after he opened up way too early on a West changeup, waving helplessly to fall behind in the count 0-2. He slapped the barrel of his bat with his right hand, muttering to himself as he took a few steps out of the batter's box. I read his lips say, "Stay back, dummy." As he eyed the next offering he exaggeratedly held his hands behind him and tapped his front foot against the ground midstride to slow his forward motion. West's curveball broke outside. I'd already chalked it up as a beautiful waste pitch until Martin flipped his bat out and floated the ball into shallow left field for a leadoff single.

With no one out and a man on first, there are plenty of scenarios that could push a runner across the plate. Gordy eliminated a couple of them with Luther Hudson, his best power hitter, due up. Kinston's infielders didn't even bother cheating up for the bunt, because they knew Luther wouldn't drop one. Bunts don't impress the chicks. Instead he stole the collective breath of the 1,500 or so fans left on hand with a long drive down the left-field line that hooked foul just in front of the fence. West won the battle, however, taming Durham's No. 3 hitter on a backdoor curve. Martin stared across the diamond for a series of signs, nodding confidently as Francisco Acevedo stepped to the plate. The Bulls were well aware of West's weakness holding runners and Martin bolted on the first pitch, sliding in safely ahead of the throw. Acevedo then brought the crowd to its feet by ripping the second pitch he saw into center field for a single, tying the game. They slumped back into their seats moments later when Dain Gregson grounded a tailor-made double-play ball to his counterpart at shortstop, sending the contest to extra innings.

It looked like the Bulls were going to hand the game away, as reliever Nelson Ray opened the tenth by walking the first three Kinston batters. Standard operating procedure for him. At 6-foot-3 and a loose, lanky 190 pounds, he looked like the prototypical pitcher until you saw him in action. He had no command whatsoever, and this was hardly the first time he'd juiced the bases on freebies. That should have earned the next Indian batter the take sign, but he popped out on the first pitch and Nelson induced a pinch-hitter to ground meekly back to him for a home-to-first double play. Matt Hamer's groans became increasingly tortured as the tenth inning disappeared with no further scoring. I slipped out just before the eleventh inning started, fearing he would find some creative manner in which to martyr himself. Don was standing in the concourse chatting with Captain DesJardins when I walked up, trying to get away from the game that wouldn't end. We made some brief small talk until he tasked me with thanking the departees and retreated into his office.

A steady trickle of deserters swelled as each half inning concluded. I could have guessed by their expressions what the status of the game was had Ron Anders' account not been piped into the concourse. Half-listening to his play-by-play, I sat balanced atop the railing near the exit, sipping on a plastic cup of Cheerwine soda until a white meteorite hurtled downward not six inches in front of my eyes. "The 1-2 pitch is fouled straight back over everything ..." Ron announced. I processed the event and turned to see a ball bouncing off the cement and out the gate. Had it happened two hours earlier an army of kids would have upended me, but it was past their bedtimes and they were long gone. I set my drink down and jogged after the foul ball, catching up to it as it lost steam halfway up the hill.

As I examined my souvenir, the popping of gravel in the parking lot broadcast the arrival of a dilapidated sedan. With a rusty grunt the driver's door swung open and a full-figured, middle-aged woman climbed out. She wore a waitress uniform with a Honey's Restaurant logo embroidered on the left breast pocket, a pencil protruding from the bun tightly twisted against the back of her head.

"Good evening," I greeted as she shuffled toward the gate.

"Howdy," she returned. "Is my Wendell here?"

"Wendell?" Perplexed, I glanced over at Aaron in the souvenir stand. He wore just as vacant an expression as I did. I turned back to the waitress and she closed her eyes for a moment as if deep in thought.

"Spanky," she corrected herself. "He go by Spanky here."

"Ohhhhhh. Yeah, he should be around."

I pulled the radio from my back pocket and depressed the talk button.

"Rich?"

After a momentary pause he responded. "S'up Laner?"

"Can you tell Wendell his mom's here?" I tried to suppress my grin, but it was impossible. Fortunately Spanky's mom had wandered toward the seating area and didn't notice my expression or the muffled laughter emanating from my walkie-talkie.

"He's on his way," Rich reported.

A minute later Spanky appeared in the concourse. His mother leaned down to give him a hug, which he returned with some degree of embarrassment. He casually waved good-night as he followed her out the gate.

"Why are you still here?" I asked Aaron. It was nearly eleven-thirty and no one had bought anything from his stand since I'd come up from the press box.

"Good question," he replied. "I figured Don would shut me down before now."

"Yeah, that's the first thing on his mind."

"Mind watching it for me a minute? I'm gonna go ask if I can close up."

He pushed the door at the base of the ticket tower open and I stepped in after he scampered out. I planted myself on the barstool behind the counter and rested my feet on the top shelf, careful not to touch the merchandise with my shoes. Aaron returned a minute later, smiling like a man who was about to go home. I helped him board up the stand and he took off for the night.

Seeing no reason to remain in the concourse I slipped down to the tunnel, where I participated in a group prayer. Like so many others it went unanswered and the scoring drought continued unabated into Tuesday morning. Fewer than 100 fans remained to witness the Indians push a run across in the top of the sixteenth to take a 6-5 lead. Fortunately the Bulls didn't rally and the game came to a merciful end just after twelve-thirty.

It was past one by the time Emma and I finished sending out the faxes, and I sensed anxiety on her part as we lingered in the concourse.

"You okay driving home?" I asked.

"I think so." She sounded as nervous as you'd expect a small-town girl from tiny Shallotte, N.C., to be at the prospect of an after-hours drive through some sketchy neighborhoods.

"We can follow you, if you'd like."

"Oh, thank you, Lane. That's sweet of you to offer. But my aunt said Martin would make sure I got home okay."

"Martin? You mean Martin Harcourt?"

"Yes. He's staying with my aunt and uncle. Didn't you know?"

"I knew he lived with a host family. That's all."

"I don't even know what he looks like out of uniform," Emma laughed. "They were on the road when I got in Saturday, and I was here by the time he got home this morning. I hope he hasn't left yet."

"If your aunt told him, he won't forget," I assured her. "He's a pretty conscientious guy. In fact, here he is now."

The weary second baseman was the last player to straggle up the hill from the clubhouse, glancing around for a girl he didn't know. I introduced him to his new housemate and they drove off into the night. The keg went untouched for the first time all season, as the rest of us were too exhausted to bother. Too much free baseball trumps free beer.

CHAPTER ELEVEN

Tuesday morning we got word from Don that the Braves were sending some of their top brass to town later in the week. Arnie Landers, the director of player development, and Jack Mortensen, a special assistant to the general manager, were making the rounds and were slated to be in Durham on Thursday and Friday. Paul's dad used to tell us stories about life in the Army and how they had to "paint the rocks" to spruce things up when a general visited their base. The same principle applied in the minor leagues. Affiliations between minor league teams and their major league partners are up for renewal every two years. A bad impression could leave a club standing in the next round of musical chairs.

You wouldn't figure Durham had much to worry about, unless you got a close peek at the decaying infrastructure of Durham Athletic Park. There were spots in the walls of both clubhouses where gravel crumbled loose on contact. The only thing holding the mortar firm in many places was paint. I applied a fresh dab of royal blue to walls, railings, stairs, and just about anything else that wasn't moving that afternoon. Rich and I rearranged the equipment in the tunnel Wednesday morning, literally mopping the concrete that you generally didn't see because it was crusted over with a thin layer of dirt. And we kept right on going into the home clubhouse. I mopped the showers out with bleach solution so strong I could barely breathe. But I wasn't going to scrub the tile for anyone short of the President, so we drew the line there.

Mike had his crew working overtime to shine up the concession stands, Sonny and Blake took a blow torch to the weeds that had begun to grow around the rim of the infield dirt, and anyone else who wasn't otherwise occupied was wise to look busy before they found themselves tasked with some stripe of hellish cleanup duty. By the time the high muckety-mucks arrived

Thursday the DAP was as pristine as a Depression-era park could be.

Rich and I pulled into the parking lot behind a shiny new Lincoln Town Car when we returned from a quick lunch up at the mall. Rich recognized Jack Mortensen from last year's visit, and while Jack played chummy when he climbed out of the rental, I'm sure he didn't remember Rich. He probably met a thousand people a year at ballparks all over the country. It would have been a waste of brain cells to stow away the name of every groundskeeper he encountered. Arnie Landers was more reserved, to the point he didn't even bother pretending he remembered anyone but Don. He reminded me of a robot that hadn't been programmed to laugh or even understand jokes, and I felt uncomfortable around him. Naturally we all gravitated toward Jack.

They sat together in the owner's box just behind the plate, watching Wild Evan Wayne's shotgun approach to pitching. I was assigned to check in on them periodically throughout the game to extend whatever hospitality was suitable. I fetched soda, beer, peanuts, a barbeque sandwich, and two slices of pizza. I felt like a stewardess. But Jack was gracious, trading one-liners for food, and I'm sure I could have found a worse way to spend a ballgame.

Friday morning Sonny bustled into the office and dropped a stack of clean laundry on the corner of his desk. He went through shirts like no one else I'd ever known. Twice a homestand he'd restock after his wife washed the sweat stains of out the batch that had accumulated on the passenger's side floor of his pickup.

"Y'all comin' to lunch?" he asked.

"Where?" I inquired.

"Bullock's. Jack's treatin'. Everyone's invited."

"Family style," Rich exclaimed. "I'm all in."

"Lane?"

"Hell, yeah." You learn pretty quick when surviving on a thousand bucks a month to never turn down a free meal. Especially Bullock's. Comfort food. I always overdid it there, but never once regretted it. My daydreaming of hush puppies, chopped barbecue, Brunswick stew, and tea was interrupted when I remembered a prior engagement. "Aw, dammit. I'm supposed to go to lunch with Trina today."

"Sucks to be you, dude," Rich laughed.

"Can't ya call her?" Sonny asked. "Everyone else'll be goin' for sure."

"Guess I can try." I pulled the phone towards me as though it were a pinless grenade.

"Try?" Rich heckled. "Don't be such a pussy."

He peppered me with verbal abuse as I waited on hold, Fleetwood Mac piping through the line to agonize me further still. Finally Trina picked up.

"Hey," I started, trying to sound chipper. "How's your morning?"

"Good so far. Why?"

"Well, uh, we've all been, uhm, invited to lunch by the general manager of the Braves." A little white exaggeration never hurt anyone. "But I wanted to check with you first, because, uh, well, we were supposed to go out."

Silence. A deep sigh. A few more seconds of peeved silence. "You know I never get to see you anymore, Lane. Once a week for lunch. Would it kill you?"

"Well, uhm, it's just ... maybe we could go tomorrow instead."

"I'm going to my mom's tomorrow."

"Oh." I laid my head down on my arm, which was stretched forth across the desk, and closed my eyes. My nose rested on the desktop and I could practically taste the faux-wooden finish as I forced air deep into the back of my lungs.

"Or maybe you just don't want to have lunch with me. Maybe I'm not as much fun as the manager of the Braves."

"General manager," I corrected her, to no good purpose. "And you're just as fun. I just wanted to ask because they're only here today ... but ... I'll just tell them they can go without me."

"Don't let me hold you back."

"No, no. It's okay. We'll have fun. I'll come get you at a quarter to twelve just like we planned."

"All right."

"See you then, o—."

Click. She hung up before I finished. I lifted my eyes to see Rich shaking his head at me.

"Fucking pathetic, dude," he said. "Just check your nuts at the door. You ain't using them."

"It's not that simple." I dropped the handset back into place on the phone. "She won't talk to me for three days if I blow her off for lunch."

"Maybe that would be a good thing." He smirked, then rose and walked out of the office.

I dropped my head again in meditation. Maybe he was right.

As the rest of the crew piled into their cars at eleven-thirty, I spied through the office window like Ted Lundt, the Jehovah's Witness kid in fifth grade who had to watch from the hall during class holiday parties. Ted never had to eat lunch with Bitchy Trina, though, so I had him there. We forced the conversation at times, but dined in silence for the most part, I picturing my co-workers enjoying their hearty family meal, she equally far away in a different direction.

It took sixteen games, but Rich finally tagged me with a DAP nickname. I didn't realize it was my new moniker when he used it, because it had rolled off his tongue so frequently since we were first old enough to know what the word meant. But when Spanky greeted me with, "Hey, Pussy, how was lunch?" I figured something was up. I heard it from Peanut as well, and Blake finally found an excuse to talk to me so he could work it in. Sonny didn't use language like that, and wouldn't abuse a guy just to make points with Rich, so he still called me Lane.

Conversely, one crazy character went out of his way to find me, just to call me Pussy. Eddie Edwards had been a fixture as team batboy for longer than anyone else had worked with the club. At twenty-three, chronologically speaking, he was a bat*man*. Mentally, however, he was all boy. Sonny assured me he wasn't retarded in the clinical sense, but the kid was dumber than the lumber he carted back from the batter's box. Our best guess was he'd been burdened from birth by fetal alcohol syndrome. I had no idea how far he actually made it in school, though I couldn't imagine he'd perform at a sixth-grade level in any subject.

He was a DAP institution, Batboy Eddie. He'd look at you with eyes that never seemed to focus on anything, mumbling some jive you'd never understand. The only words I ever positively ID'd out of his mouth were, "Tha's kangaroo!" Everything was kangaroo, i.e. messed up, in his world. Outside of Rich and Sonny no one could translate anything else Eddie ever said. Until Friday.

I saw those big, crooked, yellow teeth gnashing and his pink tongue wagging and I knew he was into something, because he didn't generally single me out for his unintelligible rants. But when I wandered down to the tunnel late that afternoon he came strutting up grinning so broadly he could barely keep his eyes open. "S'up Pussy! Hahahahahahahaha. Pussy! Hahahahahaha." He bent over exaggeratedly, hitting himself on the leg as he laughed.

"Shut up, Coño," I said. "Coño" was what the Latin players called him. The nice translation was roughly "crazy" in Spanish, but there were others.

"HEH!" He belched out a guttural laugh, glancing from me to Rich and back again. "Pussy!"

"Thanks," I said to Rich, and I quit the tunnel. Finding somewhere else to hang out until the gates opened seemed like a good idea. I drifted up the ramp into the concourse, where I found Emma leaning into the souvenir stand, talking with Aaron. To them I was still Lane, and we chatted until Don appeared with the key and unlocked the gates.

The first fans into the park always fell into two distinct camps: season-ticket holders and first-timers. Even a relative newbie like me could spot them. Randy Munn, a bronze medalist in the 1974 Special Olympics who lived with his mom about half a mile from the park, was almost always the first in line. Tonight he roared through, greeting Don with a spasmodic high five and rushing up to Vendor Joe's stand to purchase a program, his saintly mother following in his wake. The Ryans, who were in their seventies, never missed a game. Mr. Ryan clutched a cane carved to resemble a Louisville Slugger, though I never saw him put much weight on it. It was more conversation piece than crutch. I'm sure they didn't know my name yet, but they made a point of greeting me every night nonetheless.

The out-of-towners were just as easy pick out. Starry-eyed tourists in freshly minted Bulls t-shirts, snapping photos of the park and anyone or anything associated with the team. When the mood struck me I'd offer to take group pictures for them, and they'd shower me with gratitude and a tale of their pilgrimage from Iowa or New Hampshire. There are more people out there touring the nation in conversion vans chasing the purity offered by minor league baseball than you'd think. And Durham was their

Mecca.

Despite threatening skies the early walkup crowd was strong, with lines ten deep at all three ticket windows. I conducted an informal poll and the general consensus was the rain would move around us. Only Captain DesJardins was willing to guarantee we'd get wet. He closed one eye and stared into the horizon, nodding sagely. When the sky darkened further he winked at me and pointed to the heavens. The first drops were big and sporadic, and a familiar trace of dusty, wet cement reached my nostrils as the concourse became speckled with rain.

Within a minute the pattern of drop marks filled in. As guests scurried for cover under the awnings I trotted down the hill to the field, where Sonny was marshaling the troops for the first tarp pull of the season. Orange-shirted concessions workers followed me, rushing to find a place in line as we unrolled the cover. There were a dozen of us altogether, and we made quick work of getting the infield protected. The wind kicked up just as we pulled the tarp across the third-base line, and a loud boom resonated through the stadium a split second after a jagged bolt of lightning parted the dusky sky. We rushed off the field into the deserted Bulls dugout to wait out the storm, which passed quickly. When Don radioed Sonny to inform him the radar looked clear to the west, we swarmed the diamond once again, running with the heavy tarp into the outfield to dump the water in the grass before rolling it up and stowing it next to the first-base railing.

As we tended to the mound and home plate area, the players returned to the field to loosen up. The umpire called "Play ball" just twelve minutes later than scheduled. The lineup had a distinct flavor tonight, with several regulars getting the day off. Miguel Orlando, a little-used reserve who had made a few appearances in right field, got the nod in center. And third baseman Clyde Knowles strapped on the shin guards and started behind the plate. Rich told me later he had heard Gordy griping about it, but Jack and Arnie had had a couple of special requests and they called the shots. I didn't see much of the game, but Clyde showed me more than I would have expected for a converted infielder in the two-plus innings I watched. He blocked a couple of pitches in the dirt and made a beautiful pickoff throw down to first base to nail a Winston-Salem base runner who had strayed too far off the bag.

Miguel was lithe and athletic but looked lost at the plate during his at-bat in the fourth inning. He waved at a couple of curveballs in grandmotherly fashion, missing so bad I actually pitied him. That was all I saw of his at-bats, so I was surprised to learn he went 2-for-4 when I checked the box score later.

A sizeable crowd congregated outside the nacho stand after the game, and someone started a buzz about going out for a change. I think it was Carson, the ticket office assistant. He proposed He's Not Here down in Chapel Hill, but I was exhausted and wanted something closer to home. With some intense lobbying on my part Devine's carried the vote.

Emma was psyched to be going out with the gang for the first time, which surprised me even more than her going to begin with. Within moments after we'd decided on a destination she was bouncing around inviting everyone she saw to join us. We watched with horror as she approached Vendor Joe, who was mopping his sweaty face with a yellowed towel, perspiration stains spreading from the armpits of his tie-dyed shirt. He looked at her blankly and shook his head, thanking her politely for asking, and we exhaled. Nothing against Joe, but it would have changed the entire dynamic of the outing if he'd come along. I wasn't sure if he was on medication or needed medication, but his globe seemed to rotate slightly off its optimal axis.

Emma skipped over to where Rich, Carson, and I were waiting and shrugged her shoulders.

"I asked everyone. I guess it's just us," she reported.

"This is fine," Rich said. "Good group. We don't want it too big."

"Hey, what about Jenna and Shannon?" Emma asked, having apparently just remembered them.

"Ehhh," Rich grunted. He'd shared his impressions of Shannon with me earlier in the week. He said she looked like a heroin addict, I guess on account of her scrawny figure and limp, stringy hair. Somehow that evolved into Crack Whore Girl, one of my all-time favorite DAP nicknames.

"It's not nice to leave them out," Emma scolded. "We should at least ask."

She darted off to find the girls without waiting for someone to overrule her. A minute later she was back, rosy cheeked and breathless.

"They might meet us there. Jenna's waiting on her boyfriend."

I didn't care either way as long as the beer was cold. We caravanned the few blocks over to Main Street and grabbed a table inside. The four of us split a couple baskets of cheese fries and ordered a pitcher of beer. We speculated whether the group sales girls would show and dissected Shannon's unique brand of sarcasm. Carson nonchalantly pressed his forefinger to his lips at one point and I redirected the conversation to the game, which the Bulls had dropped 7-4.

"Hey guys," Jenna called as she led her pack through the entrance. "Sorry we're late."

I got up to pull a couple of chairs over from the next table and froze momentarily when Blake strutted in.

"Thanks for the invite," he snarled.

I exchanged a puzzled look with Rich and replied, "No problem."

Blake stepped forward so we were standing toe-to-toe and glared at me. I had two inches of height on him but gave away about seventy pounds.

"I was being sarcastic, Pussy."

"So was I."

A nervous chuckle flared through the group and Blake rolled his shoulders as if to puff himself up. I followed his eyes as they swept from me to the table and back, wondering if he were dumb enough to hit me in a crowded bar. Which hand would he strike with if he were?

Jenna's boyfriend broke the tension, slapping his thick hand on Blake's back. "You gonna shoot some stick with us?"

Blake curled his mustache menacingly at me before taking a step back. "Yeah. I'll meet you in there. I gotta take a piss first." As he brushed past me he whispered, "Fucking smartmouth."

I just smiled and watched him go.

"Okay, then," Jenna laughed. "Guys, this is Kyle." She waved a hand toward her boyfriend, a stocky fellow in wire-rimmed spectacles and a Gap baseball cap. "And this is his frat brother Charlie." He was of a similar build, no glasses, no cap, and a two-inch port-wine birthmark in the shape of a comma on his right cheek. I fixated on his scar like a young child staring at a cripple in the grocery store. Rich, who later referred to the guy as Gorbachev, was similarly fascinated.

"We can move to that big table over there," I offered, when I regained my manners.

"That's okay," Jenna said. "We're going to play pool. Join us?"

A collective shrug indicated they were on their own, and they migrated to the side room to wait for the table to open.

"Sorry, y'all," Emma said. "I forgot to invite Blake."

"Don't apologize." I retook my seat. "We didn't *overlook* him."

"Oh come on, he's not so bad," Carson said. "Maybe I'll play with them later."

"Have fun," Rich said. We hadn't played since the night he brained me at Cole's house, though he loved to shoot pool. Right now, however, he looked comfortable where he was. I felt the same way myself, Blake or no Blake.

"You check your voice mail tonight?" Rich asked me.

"No. I don't usually bother until morning."

"I had a message from Cole. He's going to be back in Raleigh the end of next week."

"He's a friend of ours from high school," I explained as a means of not excluding the others. "He plays in a band called Disingenuity and they've been touring since March."

"I've seen them," Emma chipped in. "They were in Wilmington last fall."

"What'd ya think?" I asked.

She shrugged. "They were good. I didn't know their songs, though, so it was hard to really get into it."

"How'd you hear about them?"

"My boyfriend—well, this *guy* I went out with—he liked them. So I went with him."

"And what happened to the guy?" I pried. "If you don't mind telling us all your life story."

"Oh, I don't care," she laughed. "As if anyone would find it interesting. He dumped me a week later."

"What? Why?"

"Yeah, what's up with that?" Rich echoed. I was surprised he was so interested. But he wasn't alone. Carson leaned forward, straining to hear her over the conversation at the table behind ours.

"Oh, it's the usual thing," Emma tittered, nervously playing with her earring. Her hazel eyes darted from face to face then down to the table top, resting finally on me. "Guys lose interest when they realize there won't be a conquest."

"Not all guys," Carson interjected, as if making a case for himself.

I slipped my hand through the handle of the pitcher and refilled my glass. Rich nodded at me and I hit him as well, then set the empty container back on the table.

"Well," Emma paused. "The guys I've dated have. You should see their faces when I tell them I'm saving myself." She laughed nervously again, as if she couldn't believe she were spilling intimate secrets to co-workers she hadn't even known for a week.

"There's nothing wrong with that," Rich stated. This, the same guy who had bragged about deflowering a virgin the first week of our freshman year at State.

Carson nodded in agreement like a bobblehead doll.

"There's only one guy I've ever known who wasn't run off by that, and he's got other issues. The last guy I dated, this spring, well, he acted like he was okay with waiting. Even though his hands were roaming *constantly*." We all laughed as she mimed slapping hands away from her breast. "I think the last straw for him was when I got my hair cut."

"So, you don't always wear it that short?" I asked. "I mean, not that there's anything wrong with it like it is."

She rolled her eyes and ran her hand through the stubborn tuft atop her head, lifting her fingers through the muss of strands, none more than two inches long.

"It was for a good cause. But I admit it looked pretty bad when I was first scalped. It was only about half an inch long. I looked like a butch, y'all."

"Why'd you do it?" Carson asked.

"There's this sweet girl at my church, she's only eleven. She's my little Sunday school buddy. Well, anyway, she had cancer and hadda have chemotherapy, and, poor thing, her hair started falling out. So I cut mine off to give her some moral support. She had such beautiful brown hair before, I felt so horrible for her."

"No way," I said. "You did that? You know you're making the rest of us look bad to God, right?"

"That's very selfless," Carson said. "I admire your courage."

He looked like he was admiring more than that from where I was sitting. It was almost embarrassing watching him fawn over Emma. Not that she wasn't deserving. But his technique was so, I don't know, Eagle Scout.

"I saw her two weeks ago, and her hair is longer than mine now. Mine grows so slow, y'all. I didn't think it would take so long."

"How long was it before?" I asked.

"About to here." She tapped her back a couple of inches below shoulder level. "It's gonna take a year to get back there at this pace."

"I like it the way it is." I could imagine she looked nice with longer hair, but the tamed wildness was becoming on her somehow.

"Thank you, Lane." A faint blush rose in her cheeks. "But enough about my hair. What's going on with you guys? Where are your girlfriends?"

Rich chuckled, as if she should know he was too wily to be ensnared by a woman. Carson held his tongue, having no one special to mention. That left me.

"Who knows? After my lunch today I'm not really interested in finding her tonight."

"So you didn't even have a good time, Pussy?" Rich jabbed.

"Don't call him that," Emma entreated. "That's terrible. Why do y'all do that to each other?"

"We mean well." Rich wrapped his arm around my shoulder. "I'm trying to help Laner through a rough patch."

"Whatever," I laughed. "Everything's fine."

"See, kid likes to suffer."

"But why? What's wrong?"

"Well," I started, "first off, she hates my work schedule. We don't really see each other on game days, except maybe having lunch once in a while."

"Why doesn't she come to the games?"

"Ooooh, well, she came to one. That wasn't particularly successful. She doesn't get the concept that I'm working there and can't just hang out for three hours."

"I tried to warn him months ago what he was getting into," Rich said. "He let his base needs call the shots, and now where is he?"

"Can we talk about something else?" I suggested, fidgeting in my seat. I didn't want to follow Emma's uplifting story with sordid details of my deteriorating love life.

"I'm sorry, Lane," Emma said. "I bet everything will work out for you."

"Don't worry about it. I just don't want to say anything bad about her. She's a good person. We just—"

"Don't belong together," Rich interrupted.

"Sometimes maybe not so much. And sometimes she's great."

Emma said her good-nights around eleven-thirty, not wanting to worry her aunt and uncle. Carson chivalrously walked her to her car, then headed for the pool table after reentering.

"That fella's love struck," I said to Rich, as I slid around the other side of the table.

"No shit."

"You think she likes him?"

"That kid don't stand a chance."

I tried to get him to elaborate, but he went all Obi-Wan Kenobi on me, talking in riddles I was too tired to wrestle with. By midnight I was ready to go.

We wandered into the adjacent room to say good-night, and found Carson on a stool, intently leaning forward with his chin on the tip of his cue stick, oblivious to the blue chalk marking his throat. Blake meticulously lined up his shot on the 7-ball. The 8 was the only other remaining on the table. Jenna's Kyle rested against the counter, talking trash. I almost didn't notice Shannon, or rather, her legs, which were all we could see, wrapped around the trunk of Kyle's friend Charlie. She was seated on a stool in the corner, pressed up against the wall by her new acquaintance. Rich and I exchanged smirks as we made our way outside. Crack Whore Girl had found a new addiction.

CHAPTER TWELVE

In honor of Mother's Day we handed out gift bags to the first 500 women through the gate Sunday afternoon. The giveaway packages were sponsored by Kerr Drugs and included a small makeup compact, a Russell Stover chocolate, some coupons, and an artificial wrist corsage. Nothing fancy, nothing you'd be all that proud of giving your own mom if you were over the age of nine, just a nice gesture to thank the mothers in the crowd. Well, try telling that to woman No. 501. I ruined her life by running out of gift bags, retail value three dollars and some odd cents. Her preteen children backed away as her volume rose, and I wished I were in a position to do the same.

"I'm truly sorry, ma'am," I said. "We only had 500 of them, and they're gone. I wish I had another to give you."

"Well, she got one," she huffed, pointing toward woman No. 500. As she spoke a fault line opened in the makeup under her left eye, revealing a wart or a mole. Or maybe a wart on top of a mole. Whatever it was, she had caked a quarter inch of foundation over it, like a handyman spackling a nail head in a wall. "I was in line before her. If it hadn't taken so long to get our tickets I would have been in earlier."

She pawed at the empty box on the table next to the entrance, searching for a gift pack I'd somehow missed, the flowers in the ribbon of her hat dancing as she jerked her head to and fro.

"I'm sorry," I repeated. "They're really all gone."

"Well, I just don't think this is fair. There should be one for every mother. It is our day, after all. I'll bet some of those women don't even have children."

Captain DesJardins approached tentatively, sizing up the situation with an amused grin, which highlighted the dimples in his cheeks.

"Is everything okay over here?" he inquired.

"Well, officer," she started up again. "My family specifically chose this game to attend because of the Mother's Day promotion, and this young man is trying to tell me that we're too late to get a gift. And I'm a mother." She puffed out her matronly figure and stomped her heel against the ground to put an exclamation point on her statement.

"You certainly are," Captain DesJardins replied. His steady, reassuring gaze and measured tone had once talked a jumper down from an overpass above I-85. She was no match for him. "I'm afraid they've run out. It's a shame you couldn't get here just a minute sooner."

"Well, as I tried to explain, we waited forever for our tickets." She glared beyond him in the direction of the ticket tower. "And it took so long to find a parking spot. It's no wonder we never come here."

"But you're here now," he said, "and it's a wunnnn-der-ful afternoon for a game."

He almost had her. She even started to smile for a second, until that puddinghead Randy Munn came barreling through the gate and clipped her with his elbow.

"Oh, for the love of St. Christopher." She staggered forward, her ironically festive bonnet sliding down over her eyes. "This is the last time—you know, I still feel like we were falsely advertised to."

"Let me call the general manager and see if he can do anything for you, okay?" the still-smiling policeman said. "In the meantime, let's move over here and let everyone else through."

She reluctantly complied, following Captain DesJardins over to the side of the barbecue stand. I wasn't sure whether to go too or tiptoe away until she dragged me back into it by muttering, "Maybe he can do something, because this fellow here was certainly no help."

A bevy of comebacks dogpiled in my brain. I was sorting through the best ones when the good captain defused me with a wink. I smiled back and held my tongue. Don appeared a moment later, even calmer than Captain DesJardins. He said nothing as she recited her complaint, letting her talk herself out.

"How about a couple of slices of pizza and some Cokes," he offered, when she had made her case. "Wouldn't that be nice?"

She nodded and followed him to the concession stand,

leaving behind a cloud of old lady perfume and a crumpled silk flower that had fallen from her hat band. After Don had seen her and her unfortunate offspring to their seats he returned to inquire how it had all started. I recounted the entire ordeal and he shot me his trademark smile.

"Sometimes you've just got to cut your losses," he shrugged. "We traded her some pizza and drinks for some peace and quiet. Everybody's happy."

That's why he was the boss. If I had been running the show I would have reached in my pocket for twelve bucks or whatever she paid for her tickets and told her to get the hell out of my stadium. With enough time at the helm, my park would have been as empty as Sumter's.

The game itself was mercifully short. Oscar Lantigua tossed seven shutout innings and the Bulls capped the homestand with a 3-1 win over the Spirits. Shortly after the park cleared out I was on the road to Raleigh to visit my own mother, who was kind enough to hold dinner for me.

My grandparents were out front on the porch swing, holding hands as they watched my dad scoop the ashes out of the bottom of his charcoal grill. Several pounds of strip steak marinated in a casserole dish on a tray table next to him. Kate sat on the steps reading a magazine, which she dropped when I approached. I hadn't seen her in nearly a month, but she looked exactly the same, down to the spaghetti-strap shirt she'd worn on my last visit.

"Hey, Kate. How you been?"

"You stink," she said, as we embraced. "You come straight from work?"

"Yeah. Thanks for noticing."

I shook hands with my dad and grandpa and kissed my grandmother before heading inside to find my mom. She was on the phone talking to her mother and smiled when she saw me. I walked over to kiss her on the cheek and I could tell she was talking about me by her expression. She listened to my grandma ramble on, then finally cut in and said, "Yeah, he just got here. They had a game today. They sure keep him busy out there." A minute later she made her excuses and ended the call.

"Forty minutes," she said as she hung the phone up. "And she didn't come up with one thing she hadn't told me at lunch yesterday."

"It's her day, too," I said. "You have to humor her."

"Please don't let me go on like that when I'm her age."

"Don't worry, Mom. We'll just tune you out."

"I'm sure you will. You're already plenty good at that."

She gave me a quick update on her mother's chronic aches and pains, none of which added up to anything more than recycled conversation, and we headed outside to join the others. I grabbed a beer from the ice bucket by the front door and sat down next to Kate on the steps.

"Thought you might be bringing your girl," Kate teased. "I've been hearing interesting things lately."

"Oh really? Like what?"

She lowered her voice. "Mom said she dressed like a hooker at the ballgame."

"I did not!" my mother protested from twenty feet away. Her hearing was practically bionic. Kate and I had to invent our own sign language as kids. "I didn't say that!"

"It's okay, Mom," I laughed. "Sometimes she kinda does."

"She's a very pretty girl, Lane. But, really …"

"It's not like she consults me about her wardrobe. Not that I usually mind it."

"Well, I shouldn't have said anything. I'm sorry. She's a nice girl. And she couldn't stop talking about you."

"She couldn't stop talking, period," my dad mumbled.

I patted him on the back and whispered, "Now you know how I feel."

"No secrets, boys," my mom scolded. "Especially about girls who aren't here to defend themselves. Where is she anyways?"

"She said she was spending the day in Pittsboro with her mom. I should see her later tonight."

After dinner my dad hauled out a jar of nickels and we played a card game called Indian my grandpa had taught us when we were little. Each player got one card that they held up to their forehead so everyone but them could see it. Judging by their opponents' cards they decided whether to toss in their nickel or drop out. High card took the pot. There are probably a dozen variations, but we always kept it simple and we always laughed a lot. And Grandpa always won. He had the best poker face. As he dumped his mountain of nickels back into Dad's Mason jar, he reminded me I owed him a round of golf, and we made a date to play Monday.

The next morning at nine o'clock sharp I met him in the parking lot of the Raleigh Country Club, where he spent so much time he had his own stool in the bar. After a short wait we hit the first tee box. Grandpa let me go first, ragging me it might be the only time I had honors all day. When I started golfing as a kid he always let me lead off. By the end of high school I had to earn the right like anyone else.

I pulled out my driver and teed up for my first swing of the year. The first hole was a long, straight par five, and I took a practice cut, coaching myself under my breath, "nice and easy, no slice." I stepped up and addressed the ball, then stood there and analyzed my stance, my balance, the angle of the club face, and anything else that popped into my head. I lifted the driver and held it at the apex of my backswing, pondering the path it was about to cut en route to the ball. Was my arm straight? Were my legs bent too much? "Don't muck it up," I thought as I ripped into my swing, connecting solidly with the Titleist. Thwack! It lifted off the ground and took a sharp right turn, high into the trees.

"Goddammit," I cursed. My grandpa never minded when I swore. I learned half the words from him in the first place.

"You're thinking too much," he kibitzed. "That swing took you half an hour. Take a mulligan and just let it rip this time."

I pulled a second ball from my pocket and teed it up. Dispensing with the practice cut, I wound up and dropped the club head right through, launching the ball 150 yards down the right side of the fairway. It bounced a couple of times, picking up more ground, coming to rest nearly 200 yards from the tee box.

"That's more like it," Grandpa said as he took my spot. "You can't think too much up here. You'll drive yourself nuttier than a three-legged squirrel."

I watched as he went through his motions by rote. He wasn't as strong as he used to be, but he had nearly flawless form. It was a rare tee shot that drifted off the fairway when he swung. He split it perfectly this time, his ball rolling to a stop about twenty yards short of mine. We climbed back into the cart and cruised after our balls.

"You see that gal of yours last night?" He jabbed an elbow into my ribs as if to jar some juicy details loose.

"Yeah. I went over there after I left."

"How's she doing?"

I shrugged. "She's okay, I guess. We had a good time."

"So? What's the story? You two've been going out quite awhile now." He halted the cart beside his ball and grabbed a five wood from his bag.

"I don't know," I replied from the cart. "No story. We're just going out."

He stopped his club in mid-backswing and stared at me. "No wedding bells? No nothing?"

"Shit, Grandpa, you sound like Trina."

He winked at me and unfroze his arms, eating up another chunk of green with his second shot.

"So she wants it and you don't?"

"I don't know. I mean, I'm still just twenty-two. I don't feel ready for that. What's the rush? And ..."

"And you're not sure she's the one?" He climbed back into the driver's seat and lightly depressed the gas pedal.

"No," I confessed. "Sometimes I'm not even sure why we're together."

"Do you love her?"

I paused until he halted the cart by my ball. "We have fun together."

"Hell, boy, I'd have fun with someone looks like that, too. I think I'd still know what to do."

I pulled a four iron out of my bag and gripped it in both hands, bending down to touch it against my toes and stretch my back out. After two practice swings I realized I was overthinking again, and I stepped back to clear my head. Brain emptied, I hacked away, lining the ball sweetly down the fairway.

"Nice shot," Grandpa said. "But back to more important matters. Do you love this girl?"

"I don't know. I guess."

"You'd know if you did. There wouldn't be no guessing involved. I ain't too old to remember how that part works, anyway."

I retook my seat, still holding my club, now stubbled with

mud and tiny grass clippings. As Grandpa jerked the cart forward, I worked the corner of my untucked shirt over the face until the iron shone again.

"What was it like when you met Grandma?"

"Things were different back then. You didn't get the keys until you paid for the car, none of this renting shit. Not that I begrudge you a good test drive or two."

"So you and Grandma never ..."

He decelerated and stared at me, his wiry eyebrows dangling down over his eyes like spider legs.

"The truth?"

"Yeah. Did you guys ever, you know?"

"Nope." He tilted his head toward me and cocked his right eye. "Not that I didn't think about it. But her daddy would'a shot me."

We laughed in unison as he halted the cart next to his ball.

"Should land this one right in the center of the green," he boasted, wrestling his nine iron loose from his bag. He swung down and popped the ball up expertly. It landed with a soft thud on the edge of the green eighty yards away. "Had the distance, little off on the aim."

My second shot had come to rest about sixty yards short of the green. I debated the pitching wedge verses the nine iron, deciding at last to go with the shorter club. It was probably a mistake. I caught the top of the ball and bladed it off to the right, cursing loudly as I chased after it. It took two more shots to reach the green, and I finished with a seven on the hole. Grandpa parred it, wresting honors just as he'd predicted.

"I didn't need to sleep with your grandma to fall in love with her," Grandpa said, as we waited to tee off on the second hole. "I felt it the day I met her down at the luncheon counter, and it's never let up since."

"I was pretty swept up when I first met Trina. I thought about her nonstop for weeks."

"Was it your heart was doin' the thinkin' there, or was it your dick?"

His bluntness sometimes caught me off guard. He seemed so wholesome when I was a kid. As I grew up I found other dimensions to him and we'd talked about all kinds of stuff most people probably hope their grandparents never think about. My middle name, Warner, was in honor of him, bonding us from the day I was born.

"What's the difference?" I laughed, embarrassed to admit the truth.

"It's a huge difference in the long run. As it seems you're learning now."

Eventually we exhausted Trina as a topic and turned the conversation in other directions. I managed to beat him on three holes, but he was so consistent he smoked me by fifteen strokes, finishing twelve over par. When we parted after a couple of drinks in the clubhouse I promised him we'd go again soon. He went back in to hang out with his buddies and I drove back to Durham.

CHAPTER THIRTEEN

On the heels of the seven games we'd wrapped up on Sunday, another week-long homestand loomed Thursday. I had next to no time to catch up on sleep, and what I had was spent over at Trina's. Wednesday night as she slumbered beside me, I stared at the ceiling thinking about what my grandpa had said. I wanted to love Trina. All the time, not just here in her bedroom. Life would have been easier that way. But I wasn't convinced she loved me as much as she loved having me around to love her. And maybe that mattered.

I rolled toward the window, careful not to rustle the bed. Without the freedom to toss and turn it was impossible to get comfortable enough to drift off. When the digital clock on her nightstand hit twelve-thirty I slipped out from under the covers and tiptoed to the living room. With the volume so low I could barely hear him, Letterman proved a suitable sedative. I awoke to an infomercial two hours later, slumped over the arm of the couch with a painful crick in my neck. In my absence Trina had claimed my side of the bed. I climbed over her and fell back to sleep.

Morning hit me like a bucket of lukewarm grits. As much fun as my job was, the week off was vital to getting recharged for the week on. The part of my brain that actually does anything useful just wouldn't engage Thursday. First I dropped my radio, cracking the plastic housing, right in front of Don. Then I lost track of innings and nearly missed the infield drag. The only thing I did with any feeling was ply myself with free alcohol after the game, and even that was abridged. Rich badgered me to drive him home when he came up from the field. I was grateful he did. We pushed our alarms back and snuck in a few minutes late Friday morning. By the time the game started my body clock was nearly back on schedule.

The team enjoyed one of its most successful homestands of the year, feasting on two of the weaker clubs in the league. At least

Salem put up a fight. The Pirates' affiliate was in town for the first four games, and played us tough, though the Bulls scored three wins in the matchup. Next a truly dreadful Peninsula club rolled in. We would have swept them but for a couple of bad calls and an error Wednesday night. The plate umpire had a brutal game. There were two plays at the plate and he got them both wrong, triggering a torrent of plastic cups and foil hotdog wrappers in the bottom of the sixth. Guess who had to help clean that up.

Don worked us all lightly the next morning, and we cut out shortly after lunch and went home. Burt, the unemployed wannabe millionaire, was snoozing on the front porch when we arrived. The three of us lounged around the rest of the afternoon, talking about the upcoming holiday weekend. I think it was Burt who first suggested a Memorial Day house party. Rich bought in and the three of us were soon batting ideas back and forth.

"We should do something cool, more than a just cookout," Rich said.

"Buddy of mine's got a deejay setup," Burt said. "Maybe I could get him over here."

"Cole's gonna be around, right?" I asked Rich.

"Yeah, they booked some studio time down here to play around with some new songs. Said it was way cheaper than D.C. He'll come."

"I know he'll come. Can we get him to play?"

Rich's eyes lit up. "You mean the whole band?"

"Why not?"

"Wait a sec, guys," Burt cut in. "You want your friend's band to play here? In our house?"

"Or on the lawn," I said. "Wherever."

"Won't that be kind of loud?"

"Possibly," Rich agreed.

"What if they did an acoustic set?" I asked. "Not as loud …"

"Yeah, yeah." Rich was more excited than I was now. He paced around the porch, measuring things off. "Drums over here, bass player could stand about here … This could totally fucking work."

"Call him, man. He's home by now, right?"

He went inside and dialed Cole's house. Fifteen minutes later he rejoined us.

"He's so in. They were looking for someplace to test their new material anyway, and they couldn't line anything up around town this weekend."

We invited nearly everyone who worked at the stadium. Emma asked if she could bring a friend of hers who was visiting from Shallotte. "Of course," I said. "Bring anyone, as long as his name isn't Blake." I didn't know too many others to invite, so we relied on Burt and our deadweight roommate, Garret, to beef up the guest list. Garret rarely did anything with the rest of us, but he was surprisingly enthused about the party.

Trina, on the other hand, was cool to the concept, until she realized I wouldn't be talked out of it. She did a lot of sighing Saturday night when Cole came over to strategize. He didn't want to go totally acoustic, but figured maybe they'd go half and half. We drank and laughed and reminisced, and since Trina wasn't the center of any of it she lost interest in a hurry. She left around nine, offering to stop over Sunday morning to help us get the house ready.

Cole broke his guitar out shortly after she split and picked a few songs for us as Rich, Burt, his girlfriend Jenny, and I clapped along. He sang the words to a couple of them, including one awesome breakup song he called "Lost It." The chorus went:

Want it. Got it. Had it. Lost it.
She put me on ice, I'm totally frosted.
When I had my chance I blew it.
She threatened to leave, but I didn't think she'd do it.

His soulful wailing sounded fantastic with just an acoustic guitar for accompaniment. I was eager to hear what it would be like with the whole band.

We finally went to bed sometime after three, with Cole camping out on the sleeper sofa down in the living room. I came downstairs around nine and found him already awake, scribbling in a notebook he kept in his guitar case.

"I had the craziest dream," he said. "It was almost like dreaming a song. I had to write it all down."

"What about?"

"You'll hear it tonight. You'll like it."

He took off a short time later, and I went upstairs to shave and shower. I'd just slathered the shaving cream on my face when Trina knocked on the porch door. I ran downstairs to greet her and rushed back up before anyone could steal the bathroom.

Fifteen minutes later, still toweling my head dry, I descended the stairs in a pair of cutoff Levi's and was greeted by an angry woman waving a scrap of paper in my face.

"Who the *fuck* is Becca?"

I threw the towel over my shoulder and examined the message as if it might reveal some hidden clue on how to defuse her. But all it said was, "Lane, Becca called AGAIN." The last word was underlined three times.

"Is this one of your honeys from the ballpark?" she asked. "I hope she shows up today because I'd love to see her."

"It's not like that."

"Oh, it's not? What's it like? Enlighten me."

"Would you calm down? You're being silly."

"Give me a reason to calm down. Why shouldn't I be upset? Who's calling you?"

"You are."

"Who else?" She tore the note from my hand. "Who's Becca and why is she calling you? Again!"

"Becca's no one."

"Goddammit, Lane." She turned to leave. "Fuck your party. I was going to help out, so I'd at least get to see you today. Don't play bullshit games with me."

"Hold on," I called, as she pushed the screen door open. "Let me explain."

"Oh, this ought to be good."

The time had come for one of Rich's private nicknames to go public.

"You're Becca."

"What?"

"Rich, well, he used to get your name confused with some girl from school. He still thinks of you as Becca for some reason."

"Am I some kind of joke to him?"

"No," I lied. "You're not. It was originally an honest mistake. He was more making a joke on himself with the reference. Ask him."

Not that she was likely to see him anytime soon, sound carrying like it did through that house. He must have barricaded his door by that point.

"You swear?"

"Of course."

She took her hand off the door and stepped timidly toward me.

"I don't ever want to be the butt of anyone's joke, you know? I don't need to put up with that."

"I know." I folded her in a hug and kissed the top of her head. "Believe me, I know."

Our guests began arriving shortly after noon. Jenny was first to show, though she was practically hired help. She did more to get the house ready than Rich did. Her presence recalled Trina to her rightful place as self-perceived belle of the ball. Jenny's urban hippie persona was a perfect counter to Trina's and they fed off each other in a peculiar way. Jenny cut up produce for a veggie tray and Trina arranged it artfully on a platter. Jenny prepared taco dip and Trina poured the chips into bowls. Satisfied she was on her good behavior, I went outside with Rich to block off a few choice spots along the curb for band parking. A battered, two-toned Buick Skylark ignored the markers we'd set up, pulling to a stop right in front of us. After a moment the passenger's door creaked open and Spanky stepped out.

"Wendell," I called out, waving to his mother, who smiled at me from the front seat.

"Shut up." He blew past me to exchange a gangsta high five with Rich. He still hadn't warmed up to me for some reason.

The early-arriving guests were mostly Burt's, and late-model Volvos and Mercedes lined the opposite curb. They were friendly and I would probably have fit in comfortably at a party with just his crowd. By two, the Bulls crew started to make inroads. Carson hiked up the street from where he'd parked. Jenna arrived with Shannon. And Emma pulled up a few minutes later, accompanied by a guy wearing a gray sweater vest, tan Bermuda shorts, black socks, and penny loafers. His gelled hair waved from a part on the left all the way across the top of his head. If they gave medals for the doubletake Rich would have earned a gold. He snapped his neck so hard when Emma's friend walked in I heard it crack from across the room.

"Whoa, nice socks, man," Rich said as he approached our new arrivals.

Emma rolled her eyes and turned away and I bit down on my lip to stifle the laugh that was trying to sneak out.

"Thank you," sweater vest replied. "They're quite comfortable."

"Excellent," Rich nodded.

"Hey, y'all," Emma said. "This is Alton. He's from down home in Shallotte."

"Alton Hobgood, the fourth," he said, extending his hand.

"Rich Farrell, the first."

I pushed Rich aside and shook Alton's hand. "Ignore him. I'm Lane. What can I get you? You guys need a drink?"

"I'd love a Sprite if you've got one," Alton lisped.

"How 'bout you Emma?"

"She'll take the same. Two Sprites, please."

Emma's lower jaw hung down, frozen in place as a maze of wrinkles carved up her forehead. Through puckered lips she silently exhaled and her face regained its smoothness as she walked toward the kitchen.

"Here you go, Alton," I said after a quick survey of the fridge. I held out a can and he took it, snapping the tab hard twice with his middle finger before cracking it open.

"For good luck," he explained, hiking up his shoulders and eyebrows, as though seeking permission to practice his dorky superstition.

Emma sighed and popped her can open, glancing longingly at my beer.

"Well, cheers then." Alton tapped the neck of my bottle with his can. He reached toward Emma as well, but she had already lifted her drink to her lips and he played it off.

As I swung the refrigerator door closed, Trina strode in rattling a glass of half-melted ice cubes. Alton scanned her up and down from her tank top to her toned legs, then took a long pull from his can as if to cool himself off.

"There you are. I've been looking all over."

"I've only been here and on the porch."

"I need more vodka."

I dumped her ice in the sink and began mixing her another lemon drop.

"Trina, this is Emma and Alton. Emma works with us at the Bulls."

"Nice to meet you both," she said without smiling. She snatched her glass and draped her arm around my neck.

"Alton's up from the coast this weekend," I said, as if Trina cared. "What do you down there?"

"Nothing, yet. I'll start up in the family business in a couple of weeks. But I just finished school. I've got to enjoy myself a little first."

"Where'd you go to school?"

"Brewton-Parker." There was a hint of a boast in his voice, as if each syllable were lifting its nose at us.

"Oh. Where's that?"

The air leaked out of his sweater vest. Emma turned her face from his and threw me a quick grin.

"It's down in Georgia, about halfway between Macon and Savannah. It's one of the top Baptist colleges in the country."

"Never heard of it before. Sounds nice, though. And congrats on being done."

"Thanks."

Trina leaned forward and pressed her lips to my ear. "This is boring," she whispered, her hot, moist breath tickling my ear lobe. Withdrawing her arm, she slipped away into the living room.

I introduced Emma and Alton to Jenny, then headed back outside to assess the crowd. The party had already splintered into segregated groups. Garret staked out the prime turf on the porch, though his clique was bumped as soon as Disingenuity pulled up and began unloading their gear. Burt locked down the living room. And the Bulls crowd gained the lawn by default.

Cole handed me a box of Disingenuity CDs and asked if I minded if he sold them.

"God no. Hell, I'll make everyone buy one."

I pulled my own copy of *Fashion Fugitives* from the shelf next to the stereo and slipped it into the CD player. We set one speaker on the windowsill to cover the people outside, and boosted the other one onto an end table next to the couch. The result was less than perfect stereophonic sound, but at the right volume it didn't really matter.

Rich and Garret fired up the grill at six and I worked the crowd taking hot dog and hamburg orders. Once the dinner mess was cleared, Cole and his bandmates began setting up. They adopted Spanky as their roadie and he rushed about running wires to the amps. After a quick sound check Alex, the lead singer, signaled to Rich they were ready.

Rich climbed the steps to the top of the porch and took the microphone, which was hardly necessary, but he opted for the dramatic whenever possible. "I'm glad you guys could all come today. We are really lucky to have Disingenuity here. They're gonna try to keep it down a little, but just in case the neighbors call the cops, Peanut and anyone else under age better not be drinking. Okay, give it up for Disingenuity!"

The crowd numbered about thirty-five people and we hooted and hollered encouragingly as the band kicked into "Chicken Soup and a Six Pack." Cole wrote it one day a few weeks before he dropped out of State when he was waylaid by a horrendous cold, and it quickly became one of their bread-and-butter numbers on tour. Though Cole wrote most of their songs, Alex handled the bulk of the singing. Cole took the mike after they'd done about six songs and switched over to his acoustic guitar. Alex broke out a harmonica and played the first few notes of what turned into "Lost It." Cole really nailed the vocals. It was even better than I'd anticipated. I felt like we were hearing a sneak preview of their breakthrough hit.

He fiddled around with his guitar strings for a minute as Spanky ran a fresh beer to the drummer. "Um, this next one is for Lane and Rich," Cole announced. "And our friend Paul. You guys haven't changed since fifth grade, and that's a good thing. A real good thing. You guys keep me grounded when I start thinking I'm some kind of rock star.

"This one's called 'Sneaking Home.' I just wrote it this morning. We only practiced it twice before heading over here, so don't hate us if it sucks."

They were surprisingly tight considering the newness of the material, but what made the song were Cole's lyrics: "I wake up some nights unsure who I am, chasing a dream that never ends. The only sure cure that I've ever found, is sneaking back home to my friends." I'd enjoyed plenty of innuendoes in his songs before, being in the tiny sliver of the crowd that was in on the joke. But this was different; it was personal, and it suddenly made me nostalgic for the days we all hung out together growing up.

After that they switched back to all electric and livened the pace up again. People started dancing on the lawn. I grabbed Trina's hand and led her to a smooth spot. She finally looked like she was having fun. Two songs later she started in on her dirty dancing routine. I never minded her grinding against me, but I preferred it without an audience. My eyes met Emma's and I shook my head to communicate it wasn't my idea. She smiled back at me as though she understood. After dancing for about twenty minutes Trina went inside to use the bathroom and I took a seat on the steps. Emma wandered over and sat next to me, her face flush from dancing with Carson Fowler. Alton surveyed us from a chair at the edge of the lawn, picking at the warts on the back of his hands.

"Nice moves," she yelled into my ear. It was hard to hold much conversation that close to the stage.

"Yeah, thanks." I shrugged to indicate again the dry humping hadn't been my choice. "At least she was having fun."

"She's pretty," Emma shouted.

"Thanks." The song ended and I didn't have to yell anymore. "You like the band better this time?"

"Oh, yeah. They sound great."

"Is your friend having a good time?"

"Alton? I doubt it."

"Why not?"

"He never does."

Cole started strumming the opening chord to "Alley Dog" and I wanted to ask Emma to dance but thought better of it. Trina returned and tugged my hand until I followed her onto to the lawn. I smiled back at Emma as Carson swooped in to take my place.

"What's up with her?" Trina shouted into my ear.

I shrugged and said nothing.

"Why's that Opie kid all over her? What happened to her boyfriend?"

"I dunno."

"She's a little plump." She popped the p's at the beginning and end of the word.

"Who cares? She's nice and Carson likes her. So what?"

"Excuse me. I didn't know you had the hots for Miss Haircut there. What's the deal with her hair, anyway?"

"You wouldn't understand." I turned away to face the street. The neighbors across the way stood on their front stoop watching the show, bobbing in time with the music.

Trina danced around to face me and mouthed, "What's that mean?"

"Never mind."

"Don't be a grump." She half-smiled at me, curling the left side of her lip up. When I didn't smile back she pushed her tongue out and shook her head a couple times.

"Very attractive," I said.

"Thanks." She smiled again. "Look, I'm sorry I made fun of your dorky friends."

"Whatever. Just forget it."

"You gotta admit it's a strange bunch. It's like you work on the island of misfits."

"They're pretty cool, actually. At least the ones who came."

"Come on. You've got Dopey Opie over there. And that little fat kid. And your chubby girlfriend there's like their queen."

"Not everyone can have your figure. She's fine the way she is."

"Listen to you," Trina said. "You growing sweet on her?"

"Are you threatened by her?"

"Ha!" she cackled. "Yeah right. Should I be?"

"Then why do you have to tear her down? You're so superior sometimes. Are you that insecure?"

Trina stopped dancing and glared at me, her mouth frozen open. "Insecure" was like the c-word to her. She wouldn't even say it about other people.

"Fuck you."

"All I meant was—"

She thrust her hand forward like a traffic cop, then turned it around and flipped me off, the red paint on her fingernail screaming as she bit down on her lip.

"Nice," I said.

"Go fuck yourself, Lane."

Trina turned away, still aiming her middle finger back at me.

She held it behind her as she marched across the lawn and up the steps. That red fingertip was the last thing I saw before the screen door slammed behind her when she disappeared into the house.

With her gone, I became the spectacle. Some gawked, others snuck more of a stealth peek, as if they were merely checking the street for passing traffic and just happened to notice me. Even the drummer prairie dogged up from behind his kit to see what was going on. There was no point in pretending Trina hadn't just castrated me and spiked my meat on the lawn. Guests who didn't know us, who only saw her using me as a stripper pole earlier, probably wondered what I had done. Even Rich, who was leaning against a flowering cherry tree near the driveway, hadn't witnessed a shitstorm of that caliber. Instead of the smirk I expected, he offered a sympathetic shrug.

"You guys okay?" he asked, after I made my way over.

"I think I just touched a nerve."

"It would certainly appear that way."

Ten minutes later, as Disingenuity was winding down their last song of the night, Trina banged through the screen door and stomped down the stairs, purse in hand. She passed through the parting crowd without so much as a glance in my direction. I started after her until Rich grabbed my arm.

"Let her go, Laner."

Her spinning tires fired a volley of pebbles at the rear bumper of my truck as she backed into the street. Shooting one final bird my way, she hit the gas and pulled away.

"Thanks for coming," Alex called into the microphone, waving his arm at the departing vehicle. "I hope everyone else isn't in such a hurry to go. Buy a CD if you liked the show."

CHAPTER FOURTEEN

By ten o'clock our last lingering co-worker was Shannon, who had hooked up with one of Burt's business school buddies. Roderick Paterson apparently found the bulimic hipster look a turn-on. Jenna panicked when it was time to go and she couldn't locate her assistant, but a search of the premises turned up Crack Whore Girl sucking face on the picnic table in the back yard. Her sarcastic tongue was so worn out from wrestling with Roderick's that she was actually pleasant as we chatted on the front porch. They were the last two guests to leave, shortly after twelve-thirty. Jenny and Burt went up an hour later, leaving me and Rich alone in the gathering dampness. I reached into the cooler and pulled the last two bottles of beer from the lukewarm bath that had once been four bags of ice.

"Guess this'll have to do it," I said, handing one to Rich.

"That was a hell of a party, man. Cole and them were great. That worked out perfect."

"Yeah. Well, except …"

"Okay, except for her. Good riddance. You put up with that shit way too long already."

"Oh, she'll be alright. She just needs a couple days to cool off."

"You really think so?"

"Why not? It's not like it's our first fight."

"Dude, I think it was your last fight. There's no way you salvage that. Why would you want to?"

I had no answer beyond a weak shrug. Nothing came to me as I twisted the cap off my beer, which held little of the seductive appeal of its predecessors.

"Hate to say it, but I think it's over," he said. "If you have even an ounce of manhood left don't call her again."

She probably wouldn't even answer if I did. I'd tried to imagine the call several times already and never got past her machine. Even if she picked up, what the hell could I say? It wasn't up to me to apologize. And she never would.

"I won't."

"You better not. She's worn your pants long enough."

"She didn't ride over me near as much as you make it out."

"Whatever. Look, if there's anything there to save, let her make the first move. If she doesn't, there's your answer."

"I know."

"I'm gonna hold you to that. Don't make me break your dialing finger."

"I won't call her. I promise."

"Good. Now what was with Emma's friend there?"

"Who knows? He was kind of a wiener."

"She grew up with him?"

"Guess so. She said their parents went to college together or something like that. Kid probably doesn't have any other friends."

My mind drifted as fatigue set in and our conversation eroded into disjointed one- or two-line exchanges before finally halting altogether. I woke up around four leaning against the porch railing, a half-finished beer pinned between my outstretched legs. I nudged Rich, who had passed out in a rickety papasan chair Burt had rescued from the curb down the street a couple weeks earlier.

"I'm headin' up, dude."

"Night," he mumbled.

When I got up at seven-thirty to use the bathroom his door was closed. I slammed four Advil and went back to bed. Another two hours of sleep was all I could muster. Unwilling to concede, I lingered in bed breathing slowly through my cotton-dry mouth, trying to trick my body into dozing off again. It hurt to open my eyes, move my head, or even think. I gave up on falling back to sleep after forty-five minutes and moved down to the porch. Misery had company in that house Monday. We all moved gingerly, practically tiptoeing about until well after noon, when the collective pain began to subside. It was a short and unproductive day off, and I was relieved when it ended.

It felt so good to wake up sober Tuesday I got up half an hour early. I read the paper and enjoyed a glass of orange juice on the front porch as I waited for Rich. We had an easy week on tap, with a three-game homestand starting Friday. This was payback for the hellish fourteen games in seventeen days that we'd survived earlier in the month. Or so I thought.

Lest we relax too much, Mother Nature opened the skies at irregular intervals. Sonny didn't mind the rain Tuesday, saying the field could stand a good watering. But by Wednesday afternoon he wasn't so appreciative when the showers rolled in. We got the call to cover the field shortly after lunch. With six of us and no wind it didn't take long.

I had just returned to the office trailer when Sonny radioed a second time.

"Guys, hate to say it, but the rain's passin' by. I can see a rainbow off in the distance."

We couldn't leave the tarp on when the sun came out or it would burn the field, so we filed back down to the diamond. Sonny, Gray, Blake, Carson, Rich, and I went through this drill half a dozen times by Friday night. As we trudged up the hill following one such exercise Friday afternoon I asked Rich why Don never joined in the fun.

He turned toward me, squinting through his left eye, mouth open wide enough I could see a strand of barbecue wedged in the gap created when he chipped his second tooth on my elbow back in junior high. "You're serious?"

"Well, I know he's GM, so maybe—"

"Dude, you never noticed anything about the way he walks?"

"Hunh? Not really."

"He's got a wooden leg, dumbass."

"Oh."

I spied on Don whenever possible that afternoon, searching for any sign of his handicap. His limp was so minor I never would have spotted it if Rich hadn't said something. There was just a slight shuffle in his right step, because his knee didn't have much bend to it. As he worked his way back toward his office after opening the gates, he paused briefly to look up beyond the tobacco warehouses across the street. A low rumble of thunder sounded in the distance. We laid the tarp down to a smattering of applause as the rain began to fall. The early-arriving fans congregated under the grandstand roof, speculating whether the storm would pass. It did, momentarily dropping the heat index, which was high for late May, and the game went off without incident. The Bulls topped

Frederick 5-2 on Del Kolb's complete-game gem. We didn't see many nine-inning efforts out of our starters, but he was so efficient he threw just 102 pitches on the night. His only mistake was a hanging slider that Keys third baseman Eddie Newsome deposited over the left-field fence in the fifth inning.

We took the precaution of covering the field after the game and hit the keg. As he departed, Sonny advised us to head home, because he wanted us back by seven to pull the tarp. That was the first downside I found to living two minutes from the park. We were convenient. My strength sapped from the frequent field maneuvers, I heeded his counsel and left after a couple of wind-down beers. Rich, however, stuck around, taunting me that I had to train my body to handle the rigors of a three-game stand. I heard him come in around two-thirty, after I'd already logged two hours of sleep.

The humidity hung so thick Saturday morning you could feel it brush past your lips when you opened your mouth. There was no breeze, no movement of any kind. My shirt clung to my skin as I sat out on Burt's ratty chair, waiting while Rich finished in the bathroom. He pushed the screen door open wearing only a pair of running shorts.

"Fuckin' A, dude." He pulled a mud-spattered t-shirt over his head. "It's too early for this shit."

"Should'a split sooner last night."

He ignored me and sat down on the top step to pull his sneakers on, having not bothered to unlace them when he kicked them off the night before. When he was dressed we climbed into my truck and headed for the DAP.

The concourse was still a mess from Friday night's game. Usually the city workers started cleaning before we arrived, but I guess they slept late on the weekends. What a concept. We shuffled down the ramp and onto the field, where Sonny and Spanky leaned up against the rail waiting.

"This it?" Rich asked.

"Yup," Sonny said. "Gray hadda take his wife to the doctor."

"What about Fowler or Blake?"

"I ain't makin' em drive in for this."

"Son of a bitch," Rich said. "Three and a half fucking guys?"

"Hey!" Spanky piped in. "Who you callin' a half a guy?"

"Cool it, you two," Sonny chided.

We'd had plenty of practice getting the cover on and off the field all week, but we'd also had at least five guys every time, which was a comfortable minimum for a dry tarp pull. Silently, we fanned out, each grabbing a portion of the edge, slowly trudging across the diamond as we folded the monstrous sheet in half. In the middle, twelve-year-old Spanky lagged behind. Considering we'd have been even worse off without him, everyone remained patient as we waited for him to catch up. Back we walked to grab the crease and pull again, folding it into quarters this time. It got heavier with each pass, but the walk got shorter so it kind of evened out. When the tarp was folded in eighths, we pushed the twenty-five foot corrugated aluminum center pipe into place and began wrapping the plastic cover around it. Rich and I, on the left side, got up a good head of steam, hoping our momentum would make the job easier, but Sonny took a slow-and-steady approach and the roll was uneven almost immediately.

"Slow down," he barked. "Y'all are messin' the durn thin' up."

We pulled back on our end as Sonny and Spanky pushed forward to straighten their half of the pipe up. See-sawing back and forth, the tarp wound up bloated and unbalanced by the time it was pushed into place against the fence.

"Good enough," Sonny growled. He was pissed we'd gotten off kilter, but without starting over there wasn't much that could be done for it now.

I sank to the ground with my back against the tarp, wishing I'd brought something to drink. Rich slumped down next to me. Neither of us spoke for two full minutes.

"I hope it fucking pours tonight," he said at last, pushing himself up. "At least it'd be worth the trouble then."

I was in and out of the main office all afternoon, radar watching. You'd think ESPN would be the network of choice in most ballparks, but the TV in Don's office almost never came off The Weather Channel. It looked like we might be in line for some fireworks. Heavy showers were sweeping up through South Carolina, putting them on track to hit us sometime after opening pitch. Each time I snuck in the office the green blobs on the screen moved a little closer.

Sonny stalked through the concourse around six, hunting for warm bodies to help pull the tarp. No experience required. But the concession stands were down to a skeleton staff already.

"Where in hell is everyone?" he demanded.

"Prom," said Carson, who leaned against the door to the ticket tower downing his traditional pre-game slice of pizza. "The high school kids are all off."

I hadn't realized it, but he was right. The only food workers were the middle-aged women who didn't miss a game for anything short of a funeral. It had to be a social thing. They only made about fifteen bucks a night.

"So no Peanut?" I asked.

"Nope. Even he got a date." Carson chomped on his pizza crust. "Mike's at a wedding. And Aaron—" He started to laugh, triggering a coughing fit. After hacking up a chunk of dough he continued. "That dork Aaron went to the prom with some girl from his church."

"Isn't he like twenty-eight?"

"Twenty-nine, actually. He said he never went to his."

"Dammit," Sonny cried, recalling us to the crisis at hand. "Lane, see if y'all can line up some volunteers."

"Where?" I didn't see anyone idly standing around looking for work.

"I dunno. Work the crowd."

He stomped away down the hill, leaving me in charge of recruiting. For some reason the first idea that popped into my head was the season-ticket holders. I headed into the stands and scanned the box seats. Give me your aged, your infirm, your suckling babes, and your whatever else it says on the Statue of Liberty. They were all represented. Anyone capable of pulling a tarp, however, was miles away. I rounded up a grand total of one guy, Eric Weeder, an intern at *Baseball America* who came to the park a couple times a week. Everyone knew it was going to pour so the bleachers were nearly empty. I gave up after twenty minutes and reported to Sonny, who was prepping the mound.

"Dadgummit!" He furiously raked the red clay, his cowboy hat bobbing with each stroke.

"We'll be all right," I said. "We've got nine, maybe ten guys."

"T'ain't enough." He spat a stream of tobacco juice into the dirt. "Y'all've only seen routine, easy tarp duty. That's nothin'. This win' tonight'll blow your ass right off the field."

By gametime the southwest sky had darkened to a deep purple, ripe cloud formations stretching up into the heavens like inverted bunches of grapes. Matt Acres was on the hill, and he was dealing. The Keys barely sniffed a pitch in the first, going down quietly, 1-2-3. The Bulls were slightly more successful. Rabbit Waterson beat out a bunt to open the frame, and reached third on a single by Martin Harcourt. But Frederick pitcher Joey Blasingame dug down and got the next three guys on a popup and two strikeouts. The sky grew darker with each passing out, casting an ominous shadow over the game. Frederick finally broke through in the top of the sixth, on back-to-back doubles by Jeremy Tyler and Hector Ulloa. The Bulls trailed 1-0 in the bottom of the inning, with left fielder Luther Hudson at the plate when the rain started falling, popping like cap gun blasts against the dirt on the warning track. The drops were sporadic at first, but huge and hard to ignore.

"Come on, come on," Sonny muttered, as Hudson stepped out of the box to wipe his bat under his arm pit. "Call the durn game."

The base umpire split his time between watching the sky and tracking the action on the field. You could tell he wanted to get the game in, but it became increasingly evident it wasn't going to happen. Blasingame enticed Hudson to ground out and had worked the count to 2-and-2 on shortstop Dain Gregson, when he slipped throwing the next pitch. I figured the plate ump would call time then for sure and usher everyone into the dugouts, but he just ignored it. Frederick's manager rode him from the top step of the visitor's dugout, yelling, "Come on, someone's going to get hurt!" Gordy McNulty gave it to him in stereo from our side of the field.

When Gregson swung through the next pitch he darted off the field looking almost glad he hadn't gotten on base. By the time Roger Gale stepped up to bat you could barely see him. The first pitch from Blasingame sailed ten feet over everyone, into the screen, finally prompting the umpire to call time. As the Keys cleared off the field, we rushed on pell-mell. Gray and Rich hustled a small cover to the pitcher's mound, while Spanky and Batboy Eddie battled to get the plate protected. The rest of us began tugging on the big tarp, pulling it back far enough from the fence to drop in behind it. There were only four of us at first, and Weeder had no idea what he was doing, making him almost more of a hindrance. A couple of latecomers straggled into place as we lowered our shoulders and planted our muddy sneakers against the base of the wall.

"Hey, y'all," a female voice called from my right. "What do I do?"

It was Emma. God love her for picking the worst possible night for tarp initiation.

"Just do what I do," I yelled above the roar of the storm, as she lined up next to me, leaning into the roll.

The tarp came unrolled kind of wrinkled and crooked, on account of the shitty job we'd done that morning, and you had to watch your step or you could easily trip where it was bunched up. Once the pipe was clear we spaced out, waiting for Rich and the others to get in place. I grabbed a fistful of slippery polyethylene and on Sonny's command we surged forward. Emma kept up with me pretty well on the first trip. The only casualty was Blake, who lost his footing near first base. We sprinted back across the slick cover for the second pass. The wind picked up and swirled through the bowl of the stadium, drowning out Sonny's voice though he stood less than twenty yards away.

I lowered my head and dug my fingernails into the tarp as I waited for the line to move. Progress was slow and by the time we got the second section unfolded the infield was so swampy you could have piloted an airboat across it. On the dash back for the last pull, Emma slipped and fell. When I heard her scream I turned, but my feet kept going, the soles of my shoes so caked with infield clay I might as well have been on roller skates. My legs went up, my head went down, and I landed hard on the walkie-talkie in my back pocket. My first thought was I'd broken my right ass cheek. My second was I couldn't breathe. The rain streaking through the stadium lights mesmerized me as I lay there fighting to catch my wind. I was so wet already it didn't matter that it was pelting me in the face, falling into my open mouth. It actually felt refreshing. Had Spanky and Emma not begun tugging on my hands I'd have been content to lay there a moment longer. The three of us were the last to reach our places in line for the final run.

"Keep it low!" Sonny yelled. The wind had let up momentarily and I could hear him again. "Don' let the wind get under it!"

I held the tarp barely off the ground, just behind my knees, and motioned for Emma to do the same. Sonny dropped his arm like a flag at a stock car race and we all bolted forward, making good progress for the first thirty feet. I turned my face away from the driving rain and trained my eyes on the grass, which moved under me at a slower and slower pace until we stopped altogether. Down the line Batboy Eddie had fallen. The tarp soared overhead, filled like the sail on a clipper ship.

"Stop! Stop!" Rich bellowed. But half the crew didn't hear him until Eddie had been buried.

I left my spot in line to run down and help control the other end. Blake crawled under the tarp and pulled a dazed Eddie out. Of course, he always looked dazed.

"Coño motherfucker," Rich roared. "Stay on your damn feet."

Eddie howled as Rich swore at him while trying to corral the flyaway tarp. Once the air got under it like that your best hope was prayer. We overloaded to that half to regain control, and my original side, now manned only by Sonny, Spanky, and Emma, lofted up. It was getting to be a lost cause and we were barely to the pitcher's mound. Laughter carried up from the Bulls bench, where a handful of players hooted and hollered in the relative shelter of the dugout. Rich unleashed a torrent of obscenities, shaming three of them into helping out. It wasn't enough. We got the tarp as far as the third base cutout, but it was so heavy with rainwater we couldn't pull it over the line. Without the players we'd never have even gotten that far. Rich was all for giving it another shot until a flash of lightning lit up the sky overhead, followed almost immediately by a tremendous clap of thunder.

"Everybody off!" Sonny waved his hands toward the side of the field. We scampered across the diamond, ducking into the tunnel, muddy and defeated. Eddie passed around towels borrowed from the Bulls clubhouse, and the guys peeled off their sopping shirts, wringing them out and hanging them over whatever was handy.

"What about me, y'all?" Emma asked. "I need a new shirt."

I summoned Spanky, whose bangs were so matted against his face he could barely see.

"Spank, I got a job for you. Run up to the souvenir stand and get Emma a dry shirt."

He clicked his heels together and gave me a salute, then took off into the rain. I knew he'd do it. He'd had a crush on Emma since the day she started.

"He's so cute," she cooed.

"The feeling's mutual. If he were old enough to drive he'd be cruising by your house every night."

"Ohhhh. Don't tease him."

"He likes it."

"You guys are so mean to him," Emma whined.

"He loves the attention. He wants to be razzed. He mopes if you ignore him."

Spanky returned a moment later, holding a rolled up Bulls t-shirt, which he handed over with a smile.

"He'll help you change, too, if you want," I said.

Emma blushed, and Spanky kept smiling, like a fourth-grader in love with his teacher. He would have.

"Shut up, Lane," Emma said. "Where am I gonna change?"

I nodded toward the storage shed. She was in and out of there in fifteen seconds, probably afraid if she took too long someone would pull the door open on her.

The damp radio in my pocket hissed and popped and I heard Don's static-laced voice. "The umpires have suspended the game. I need some bodies up here before I make the announcement."

"This is Lane. I'm on my way."

"Is Carson down there? The ticket office could get hit. He needs to be there. How about Emma?"

"We're coming."

I pulled my soaked shirt on and stepped back into the rain, which showed no sign of letting up. Outside of a couple of kids splashing around in the downpour, the crowd was packed into the grandstand or under the awnings in the concourse. When we were in place, Don radioed Nick, who made the announcement.

"Folks, we're not going to be able to complete tonight's ballgame. The Bulls will pick up tonight's game where it left off in the bottom of the sixth, starting at one o'clock tomorrow. That will be followed by a full nine-inning game against these same Frederick Keys. Drive safe and thanks for coming."

If I had a dollar for every fan who listened closely to his entire message, I might have been able to buy lunch. We were barraged with questions from fans, some irate they hadn't seen a full game, as if we had any control over the weather. I'd never been so relieved to see the park empty out.

Sunday morning was another early affair, but this time pulling the tarp off the diamond was only an appetizer. The third-base line, which had never been covered, was underwater. The rest of the infield dirt was so soft and muddy my feet sank in up to my socks. I had to lift my knees high on every step just to keep my shoes from getting sucked under. Even the pitcher's mound and home-plate area begged for attention, because the umpire had waited so long to halt the game. We had six hours to get the field playable, and it was an all-hands-on-duty chore.

There were eight of us out there, marinating in our own sweat as the morning sun turned the waterlogged diamond into a sauna. Normally lazy Blake was the only one with any energy, running around the infield barking orders when Sonny went up to the office to take a call from his wife. In an effort to avoid him I grabbed a squeegee and helped Peanut push water away from the infield. Next we leveled the deep spots in the outfield so the excess would evaporate more quickly. The others dumped bag after bag of dusty Diamond Dry on the field, raking furiously, tamping down earth until the clay firmed up again. In between a few showy tamps, hyperactive Blake was offering tips to everyone. I thought Rich was going to swing a rake at him.

When Emma arrived from church shortly after ten she hauled down a tray of ice-cold Cheerwine that disappeared in a matter of seconds.

"This looks good, y'all," she said. "I thought it would be worse."

"You should have seen it three hours ago," Spanky said. "It was a mess. We've been out here—"

"Spanky," Emma cried as Rich yanked the twelve-year-old's shorts to the ground from behind. Spanky's pint-sized unit had sprung to attention in his Fruit of the Looms, betraying his affection for the intern. Emma covered her eyes and turned away as he scrambled to pull up his shorts.

"Asshole," Spanky screamed, turning to find Rich rolling on the damp ground, his arms wrapped tight over his belly as he laughed. The junior field hand flung himself at his mentor, flailing away blindly as the rest of us cheered like prisoners watching a fight in the yard. Within moments Rich pinned him and made him cry for mercy.

"Oh, let him up," Emma pleaded. "Y'all are *so* cruel to him."

Rich pulled him to his feet and insincerely apologized and we all got back to work.

Neither manager complained when Sonny informed them batting practice was canceled due to field conditions. Half the time they didn't take it for a day game anyway. By one o'clock the only substandard area remaining was the third-base line, which had been dramatically improved. There's only so much drying agent you can mix into that surface. It passed the umpires' inspection and the Keys were waved onto the field for the continuation of Saturday night's game.

The Bulls trailed 1-0 as Roger Gale stepped into the box, with a one ball, no strike count, and only a few hundred spectators in the stands. The original scheduled time for Sunday's game was two o'clock, so only fans that knew about the makeup game were there to see Roger slam the first pitch he saw off the center-field wall for a leadoff double. He advanced to third on a passed ball and scored the tying run a minute later when William Durante grounded a single past the second baseman. And that was it. Neither team scored again through the end of regulation. On the plus side, the game moved along quickly. But we were facing a doubleheader and extra innings were the last thing anyone wanted on this steamy ninety-degree day. Mercifully, Dain Gregson ended the affair with a solo homer to lead off the bottom of the tenth, kicking off a thirty-minute intermission.

Outs in the second game came as precious as runs had in the first. The two teams combined to push across nine runs in the first inning, and the floodgates never closed. After storming to a 12-6 lead, Frederick held on for a 14-11 victory in a contest that featured two grand slams, four hit batters, and nine stolen bases, including a swipe of home. But the most impressive statistic of the homestand was the nine tarp pulls, dating back to Wednesday. It wasn't a record, at least not according to Johnny Layne, who boasted his Gastonia crew had pulled the tarp thirteen times in a four-game series back in July of 1972. Of course, he was known to stretch the truth beyond recognition from time to time, so we might have been within our rights to brag a little.

CHAPTER FIFTEEN

Fourteen times. This one probably was a record. In the three hours before lunch Thursday, Carson dropped no less than fourteen references that tomorrow was his birthday. There might have been more, but I didn't start keeping track until the hints were so deep you couldn't help but trip over them. Rich and I flashed a count to each other every time he looked away, and we made a game out of who could change the topic first whenever Carson would mention the impending holiday.

Rich finally bit as we were filing out of the park to head for lunch. "So, what's this one, twenty-two?"

"Twenty-three." Carson's freckled cheeks were stretched almost to his ears. I hadn't seen a kid that excited about a birthday since second grade.

"You want us to take you out to the strip clubs after the game?" Rich asked.

Still grinning like Howdy Doody, Carson glanced from Rich to me, unsure what to say.

"There's a nice one out toward Burlington," Rich added. "Or we could stick closer around here."

"Well, I never—" Carson started.

"Oh, good night," Emma interrupted. "Y'all are joking, ain't ya?"

"I dunno." Rich pried open the passenger's side door on his Civic. He stood back a moment to let a blast of hot air escape. "Carson sounds kind of interested."

Emma folded her arms across her chest and shook her cropped head. "What is it with boys and them clubs? Most of them girls got diseases, you know."

"No they don't," I laughed.

"They certainly do! They did a show about 'em on *60 Minutes*."

"Don't touch the girls, Carson," Rich said. "She's probably

right."

Carson's smile vanished and he turned away. I was guessing he didn't want Emma to chalk him up as just another pervert that hung around stuffing dollars into strange girls' panties. Emma opened her mouth as if to speak but closed it a moment later. She backed away from Rich's car, shaking her head and not looking any of us in the face.

"We were just kidding," I said. "They wouldn't let Carson in anyway. He still looks like he's only fifteen."

"Do not," he insisted.

He did, though. That smile was half of it. With a straight up expression he could have passed for a high school senior. But his brush cut and wide eyes reminded me of Homer Price from these chapter books I used to read in grade school.

The temperature in the car had dropped enough for Rich to lean in and unlock the back door. We climbed in, no one saying anything until Rich walked around and opened his side.

"Where do you really want to go tomorrow?" I asked.

Carson, riding shotgun, turned around and flashed his goofy smile at us again. "Well, I've been calling for Chapel Hill all season. Maybe …"

"Sure," I said. "We can probably swing that. If Emma's okay with it, I mean."

She glared at me, then turned to face the window. I could see her in the rearview mirror and she was smiling, biting down on her lip like she didn't want the rest of us to know she wasn't really mad.

Despite Rich's threat to saddle Carson with an inflatable girlfriend Friday night, we let him off easy with a paper crown from Burger King, which he sported all throughout the game. He was still wearing it when we found him later at He's Not Here, where meat market meets lawn party in Chapel Hill. It's a veritable village square of college kids trying to hook up. They set a bar up out near the entrance where they pour draft beers so big you almost need to hold them with two hands. Emma got a free soda, on account of being our driver, and she was pleased with that. The interns made about half of what we did.

We worked our way through the crowd and located King Carson, who had established a beachhead on an empty bench. I hopped up and scanned the sea of faces to see if we knew anyone else.

"Jenna and Shannon are here," Carson said. "They were in line ahead of me."

"They just ditched you?" Rich asked.

Carson shrugged. "Jenna was meeting her boyfriend."

"Who's Shannon meeting?" I asked.

"The night is young," Rich said. "She's got plenty of time."

We manned the bench for a while, watching the crowd. With school out there was a good mix of revelers, including several game-day staffers from the Bulls. We saw Sue and Stacy from the right-field beer stand and they chatted with us for about five minutes before retreating again into the pulsing mass of bodies. I watched them until the crowd swallowed them. When I turned my attention back to our bunch my sidekick was missing.

"Where's Richard?"

"He went that way." Emma pointed over by the stairs.

"Bathroom?"

"He didn't say. Just took off all of a sudden."

"Interesting."

"Uh-huh," Carson mumbled, just to stay in the conversation. He was still smarting from his belated and clumsy denunciation of nudie bars, which hadn't won him any points with Emma. That was a topic best left dead. Now he was facing a dilemma. He wanted to look cool in the event any young ladies cast a glance in his direction, which didn't seem likely with him wearing that stupid crown. At the same time he didn't want to risk alienating Emma any further. When a girl from his apartment complex waved at him from across the way, he apologized and slipped away through the crowd.

"I don't know what to do with that boy," Emma confided when he was gone.

"What do you mean?" I had a hunch, but I didn't want to let on that his infatuation was so obvious it had become an inside joke at the ballpark.

"He's sweet. He really is." She turned her head to watch him talking to his friend about forty feet away. "But I get the feeling he wants something from me, you know?"

"Yeah."

"What am I supposed to do?"

"I dunno. He's a nice guy. But if you're not interested …"

"It's not necessarily that. I just, I don't think it's a good idea to date anyone you work with."

I lifted my nearly empty cup and touched it to her Sprite. "Amen to that."

"You worked with Trina, didn't you?"

"Uh-huh. We met at the bank. It was too much after a while. I had to transfer."

"Imagine if you still worked there."

"If I still worked there, I wouldn't work there anymore."

"What?"

"I'd quit."

"Oh, I get it now. But back to me. Do you think I should say something?"

"Naw." I knew how Carson was. The shame was he seemed about her speed in a lot of ways. "Things could get weird if you did. Maybe more awkward than now. Just don't encourage him and he'll figure it out in time."

Emma leaned up against me, resting her weight on my arm, and smiled. "I need you around to think for me sometimes. I just don't know how to handle these things. I'm not a heartbreaker. Look at me."

"Don't sell yourself short."

"Oh, come on. Your girlfriend was like a magazine cover. I'm just a dumpy, frumpy girl from Shallotte, who won't let anyone touch her good parts."

"Spanky loves you."

She giggled. "Now he's gonna be a heartbreaker."

"Chubby kid in the bowl cut?" I asked between sips. "We're talking about the same Spanky, right?"

"Give him a couple of years."

I felt a knuckle in my back and turned around to find Rich had resurfaced, a full beer in his hand.

"Dude, why didn't you tell me you were going for a refill?"

"I wasn't. I had to talk to someone."

"Becca here?" I couldn't recall the names of any of his other girlfriends, it had been so long since he dated.

"Close."

"Who?"

"Rae Ann."

"The ex-virgin?" I winced as the words left my lips, but when I looked over at Emma she smiled on like before. She hadn't heard me over the crowd.

"She's taken a dramatic turn since then," Rich said.

"Look what you started."

"I wasn't sure she'd talk to me, but she was really cool about everything."

"How cool?"

He extended his forearm. There was a phone number written in black ink just above his wrist. He shrugged casually as if it were no big deal.

"Look, Emma and I need refills," I said. "You coming, or you holding down our spot?"

"Lead the way."

We met up with Jenna on our return trip, and surprise, surprise, she had lost track of her assistant. "That girl gets around," she said, catching me off guard. Shannon put on a front that they were some dynamic duo, but Jenna chewed our ears for a little while on that score. "She's gone through four guys in, what, a month?"

"Slept with, you mean?" Rich asked.

Jenna nodded and Emma blushed.

"Damn, she's giving it out like government cheese," Rich said.

As the crowd thinned out we found her on a bench by the wall with No. 5. When Jenna headed over Shannon waved her off, indicating she had lined up her ride home.

"She's gonna catch something," Jenna said.

"What's wrong with her, y'all?" Emma asked. "That's a little extreme, ain't it?"

"She's a skank," Jenna mumbled.

"They should do a *60 Minutes* on her," Rich said.

"What? It's not funny," Jenna pleaded as we filed out past the bouncer. "I have to work with her. I have to be her friend. You guys have it easy."

CHAPTER SIXTEEN

A heavy hanging sky belly laughed thunder all morning Sunday, threatening showers, which held off until shortly after the game started. We were interrupted twice by rainfall, and the crowd thinned out long before the game ended. Jenna's left-field picnic cancelled, leaving us with a smorgasbord on our hands when we closed the gates. Hamburgers, fried chicken, rolls, baked apples, sweet corn, and cole slaw, all there for the picking.

Sonny detained his grounds crew to repair some of the field damage and they were the last to partake. The bedraggled bunch ascended the ramp after the rest of us had dug in, Peanut toting a mammoth black bat over his shoulder like Mighty Casey's wimpy cousin. He limbered up and took a few cuts after loading his plate.

"Hey, slugger," I called. "Think fast." I fired a dinner roll across the concourse at him. His swing looked like a flamingo lifting a sledge hammer at the county fair. He barely made contact.

"Gimme another one," he called, his mouth full of chicken. "I wasn't ready."

Rich underhanded his bread to me and I went through my windup, throwing another strike. Peanut swung hard and lined it back over my head off the wall.

"That's better, man. Nice stroke. Where'd you get that bat?"

"Luther. He cracked it in the third inning." Peanut walked over and handed me the lumber. A fresh piece of white tape covered a hairline crack ten inches up from the handle.

"Let me take a couple cuts."

He scurried over to the banquet table and gathered the remaining rolls, which were peppered around the lobby of the stadium moments later. Grinning mischievously, Peanut grabbed something from the end of the table and hid it behind his back. "Hit this." An apple spun out of his hand and I pounded it with a mighty *THWACK!*, showering the concourse with apple sauce.

"Boys, boys," Jenna cried. "You're making a mess."

"City'll clean it up tomorrow," Rich said. "Don't worry about it."

I handed the bat over to my housemate, who sent several rounds of fruit fireworks rocketing through the concourse. Jenna and Shannon rated each hit for style from under the cover of the concession-stand awning. It took a roof shot to earn a ten, though their grading got tougher after the first dozen ears of corn were deposited up out of our sight.

"Can I hit?" Emma begged. "Just once."

She stood in front of the fence wearing an intense look of concentration as Rich lobbed a pitch into her wheelhouse. Emma spun through her swing, laughing as the fallout showered down upon the rest of us.

"It looks like snow, y'all," she panted. "Let me hit one more time."

Within fifteen minutes we'd emptied the aluminum trays of apples and steamed corn. I found a corn cob that had merely been fouled off earlier still virtually intact and underhanded it to Peanut.

"One more," I called. "This one's going *over* the roof."

He sent the corn plateward and I unloaded. Through the maize explosion I watched aghast as the cob sped toward the wall, where Blake and Mike were huddled, talking and trying to ignore us. It slapped Blake solidly in the back of the shoulder, transferring the buttery coating to his shirt. He turned slowly, his head angled slightly forward, big dumb eyes staring at me, like a bull contemplating a charge.

"What the hell?"

"Sorry, man," I laughed. "My bad. I was trying to clear the roof. Sorry about that."

"You're gonna be sorry."

"Easy, man," Mike said. "It was an accident."

Blake bent down and retrieved the corn cob from where it had dropped at his feet. "I'd like to take this thing and shove it up your ass—sideways."

"Dude, I didn't mean anything." I stepped toward him, trying to stifle the smile that was undermining my show of remorse. "We were just having fun. Sorry."

"Yeah, I can have fun, too."

Blake reared back and unleashed a wicked throw, freezing

me in my tracks. The corn cob approached in slow motion, twirling end over end, the few remaining buttery kernels glistening in the light. A pathetic gasp escaped my lips as the cob slammed into my windpipe, knocking me off stride.

"Oh my gosh," Emma shrieked. "Lane, are you okay?"

Clutching my throat, I gulped for air, nodding violently as Blake guffawed thirty feet away.

"Serves you right, dickhead."

"That was uncool, man." Mike withdrew a couple of steps. "Really."

"Kick his ass, Lane," Peanut exhorted from a safe distance over by the nacho stand.

Blake laughed more boisterously, beckoning with his hands as he rolled his neck from side to side. "Bring it on, stickboy. It's go time."

I rushed him, wary of the meathooks spinning in small circles before his chest. With a dart to the left and a duck to the right I eluded his first swing and notched a glancing blow off his left bicep. His arm was as soft as it was big, and my fist would leave enough of a bruise to prove I'd connected. He telegraphed his next punch, which I easily evaded. Hopping forward and back, always keeping on the balls of my feet, I skimmed him a couple more times, never doing any damage, but never absorbing any, either.

As I danced out of his reach he straightened and dropped his arms. My eyes followed his gaze, landing on the scowling face of our general manager.

"Go home," Don ordered. "All of you. Now."

Don's stern voice and angry expression haunted my dreams, robbing me of all but two hours of broken sleep. Contrite and exhausted, I slipped into the ballpark Monday morning feeling too emasculated to look any of my co-workers in the eye. I hid at my desk reading the same lines in the morning faxes over and over, comprehending nothing. Rich finally relieved my agony when he entered the office at nine-thirty and said, "Don wants to see you."

I trudged across the stadium concourse through the splattered mess of fruits and vegetables now drying in the morning sun. The sickly sweet smell of overripe apple lingered in my nostrils as I pulled the door to the main office open. Blake stood in the outer room staring out the window like a child kept in from recess. He looked at me with scared eyes, and for the first time since we'd met I felt a sliver of kinship with him.

Don kept us waiting for two minutes as he leafed through a stack of papers on his desk. Whether he was reading them or merely torturing us, I couldn't guess. It felt like torture, though. At last he looked up and summoned us into his office. We stood side by side a couple of feet apart, shoulders drooped, heads hung low, awaiting our sentence. After a moment Don cleared his throat and began.

"That's a new one by me. A food fight and a fist fight in the same night."

I opened my mouth to explain, apologize—grovel—but the words died in the back of my throat, arrested by the hardened expression of the hanging judge on the other side of the desk.

"If you guys can't get along, I can find two guys who can. I don't have time to babysit. That's not how things run around here."

"Sorry, sir," Blake mumbled.

"Yes," I added. "I'm sorry."

"I want that mess cleaned up. This morning—before it dries. And don't forget the roof."

"I, um," Blake's voice faltered. "I didn't hit any of the food last night."

Don's icy glare left me and landed full force on my mulleted adversary. "I don't care. Clean it up or go home."

"Yes, sir," we responded in unison.

Don dropped his eyes back to his desk and we turned to withdraw.

"Lane," he called. "Stay put."

Blake smirked at me and headed for the door. When he was gone Don spoke again.

"I expected more out of you. I thought we'd gotten lucky to find you at the last minute this spring. Until last night I was impressed with your work. You were really forcing your way into the plan."

What blood remained in my face drained straight away. I could feel it falling from the top of my head into my cheeks and down to my neck. Between that and the window unit pumping cold air into my ear I felt woozy enough that I leaned back against the wall for support.

"I'm sorry. It won't happen again."

"You need to be smarter all the way around. Why would you mix with a kid like that?"

"How do you mean?"

"He's twice your size. He would have killed you. You've got to learn to walk away."

He gave me a grim, paternal smile, like my dad used to after reaming me out for cutting class in high school, and dismissed me with a nod toward the door. I emerged to find the sun still shining, the birds still singing, and Blake looming sullenly with a pair of Hefty bags in his hand.

"What'd he say?"

"Nothing much. Just reminded me how lucky I was to work here."

"Yeah. I feel real lucky today."

Blake handed me a plastic bag and started rubbing the mouth of his with his thumbs to coax it open.

"I'm sorry, man." I extended my hand. "Truce?"

"Sure." He clasped my hand with his sweaty palm. "Truce. Let's get this shit cleaned up."

We wandered the concourse picking up corn cobs and stale rolls and soon realized the bulk of the food waste was not going to be easily cleaned by hand. Every square foot of wall and floor was caked with dried corn, apple, and cole slaw. I couldn't recall anyone hitting the slaw, but there it was, hardening in the sun. Blake ran for a hose and a bristle brush and we set to work spraying everything down, forcing the waste down the storm drain as a troop of seagulls heckled us from above. Rich and Gray filed out on their way to lunch and offered half-hearted encouragement, and I longed to join them. Weak from hunger, I brushed down the final wall, my head throbbing from a night of no rest.

"Thank God we're done with that," Blake said as he turned the hose off. "I'm beat."

"We still got the roof."

"Fuck."

I mounted the ladder first, poking my head above the roof to find the gulls feasting on corn kernels and apple pulp, pecking for tidbits among the gravel.

"We might catch a break up here. Maybe we can just grab the big chunks."

The birds screeched as we joined them, taking to the air and dropping down again a short distance away, where they found more lunch. Stooped low, we scoured the roof for corn cobs and other remnants that were too big for the gulls to take, plucking them with our sticky fingers and dropping them into our bags.

"Lane," Blake called. "Check it out."

He chucked a tattered flip-flop sandal across the roof. It skipped twice and stopped at my feet.

"Can't blame that one on us." I stashed it in my bag.

"Find anything else good?"

"No." I scanned the horizon, seeing nothing but tar-coated stones. Off in the distance toward left field a speck of white caught my attention. "Wait. There's something down there."

I dropped my bag and set off to investigate. Blake followed. The speck grew into a baseball as we approached.

"Foul ball."

"Let's see it."

I flipped him the ball with a high, arching trajectory and it landed softly in his fleshy mitt. As we walked back to the ladder we tossed the ball back and forth, each testing the other with throws slightly out of reach. Blake lobbed a high fly over my head and I jogged after it a couple of steps, catching it Willie Mays-style with my back to him. I reciprocated with a pop fly of my own, which he let bounce in front of him before corralling. I winced when it hit the roof.

"We're right over Don's office," I said. "Bad idea."

"Right. Here, let's go."

With a behind-the-back motion he sent the ball my direction, again slightly over my head. I tracked it like an outfielder, skipping back a step and tapping an imaginary glove. The impact stung the palm of my hand, which I shook briefly after stuffing the ball into my back pocket.

"You doing anything for lunch?" I asked, as I felt for the ladder with my foot.

"Naw."

"Wanna grab a sub?"

"Sure," he shrugged. "I'm starving."

* * *

"You went to lunch with him?" Rich asked, as I sprawled out on the front porch nursing a beer later that afternoon.

"Is that so hard to believe?"

"Yeah, it is. Yesterday you hated each other."

"Blake's not so bad."

"You're just saying that because you guys got busted. What'd you talk about anyway?"

"High school, mostly. He played two years for Cary."

"When we played?"

"Yeah. He played left field and pitched sometimes in relief."

"I don't remember him."

"Only guy he remembered on our team was Cole, yelling shit from the dugout."

"'Be the ball, Richard!' That always killed me."

I sat up and mimicked Cole working the crowd from the bench. My head hurt when I laughed, but it felt good and the tightness in my gut began to loosen.

"You ever piss Don off?"

"No. Not that I know of."

"Don't. I never want to see that face again. That look that said I disappointed him, that was the worst part. And how he said I was forcing my way into the picture. Now, who knows?"

"There's no openings anyway."

"Someone's bound to leave. What about you?"

"Fuck you. Just drink your beer, you damn vulture."

CHAPTER SEVENTEEN

The road to the big leagues is riddled with detours, as Nelson Ray learned when the second half of the season opened. The organization did some roster shuffling, dealing the reliever right out of the pack just twenty-four hours after it appeared he'd survived. With three pitchers on the disabled list the club couldn't afford to cut him the day the half ended. But Andy Mills responded to treatment for his tendinitis and threw a strong bullpen session before Thursday's second-half opener at Peninsula, and Nelson ran out of time. Don called me back into his office Friday morning and asked if I'd go pick the reliever up at the airport as he made his way back from Virginia.

I pulled my truck into short-term parking and entered the airport on the baggage-claim level, checking the monitor for USAir Flight 1753 from Norfolk. After a short wait at security I reached his gate, just as a stream of passengers filed in from the skyway. A hundred people paraded by, but no Nelson and I wondered if Don had given me the correct flight information. The gate attendant smiled and asked if I was waiting for my grandmother. No, I replied, just Nelson. She was nice enough to check the computer to confirm he was on the flight, but before she could pull the log our man emerged, pushing an elderly woman in a wheelchair.

I hailed him and he introduced me to Rita Barnhart, who greeted me warmly as he guided her slowly into the concourse. They continued their conversation all the way to the baggage claim. I tossed in a few "uh-huhs" and "ohs" to try to fit in, but they seemed to almost forget I was there. Their chat was finally interrupted when a middle-aged man in a rumpled, forest-green suit shot through the revolving door, tripped over a suit case, and faceplanted on the tile floor.

"Oh, there's my Peter," Mrs. Barnhart sighed. "Born two weeks late and he's never caught up."

"Mom," he huffed, picking himself up off the floor. "Sorry. I had a meeting and then the traffic and … uh, who are these guys?"

She introduced us to her son and said good-bye to Nelson, who stooped down to give her a hug. "Good luck with your baseball, dear," she said. "I'll be rootin' for ya."

Peter chased after her suitcase, his untucked shirttail flapping from beneath his coat as he waged a valiant battle to pull the bag from the conveyer belt. Sweating and swearing, he wrestled it to the floor. Perspiration matting his hair against his head, he hefted his mother's luggage up and laid it across her lap. As he wheeled her toward the exit, she turned in her seat and waved to Nelson until they disappeared through the revolving door.

"Nice woman." Nelson pulled his own bag off the belt. "We talked the whole way. Her husband was in the same unit in France as my grandpa. Small world, hunh?"

I didn't know what to say. I'd expected to find a justifiably mopey ballplayer, lamenting his poor luck and lack of opportunity. Instead I found a boy scout. He looked for all the world as though he'd just signed his first contract. It was almost unnerving.

He tossed his duffel into the bed of my pickup and beat out a cheerful tune on the roof as he waited for me to reach across and unlock his door. I drove him to his apartment in North Durham and he talked the entire ride. Not just small talk, either. It was like we were old friends from college or something. I wanted to feel bad for him getting cut, but I couldn't. He was happier than I was. When I dropped him off I asked him what he was going to do now.

"I'll make a couple of calls, who knows?" he said. "If nothing opens up, I'll go back to school in the fall. I need twenty-five more credits to finish up my teaching certificate."

I shook his hand with a tinge of disappointment that the reliever who couldn't shoot straight was riding out of town.

Two hours later he pulled into the parking lot at the DAP, all smiles. I wondered for a moment if the team had changed its mind; perhaps someone else had gotten hurt. But he wasn't there for a second shot. He wanted a final tour of the park so he could say good-bye. He stopped every employee and thanked them for whatever help they had given him over the past couple of months, leaving an astounded crew in his wake.

His class act was the buzz of the park, overshadowing the rest of the roster moves. Center fielder Rabbit Waterson, who never got things going at the top of the lineup, was dropped down to Macon to clear room for the Braves' first-round draft pick, Cleotis Anthony. A five-tool stud from UCLA, he signed with Atlanta the day after the draft for a $500,000 bonus, a good portion of which he'd already invested in jewelry. Clyde Knowles was moving down a rung as well, mainly to work on converting to catcher. Matt Acres was the sole Bull promoted, climbing one notch to Double-A Greenville. He was being replaced in the rotation by left-hander J.T. Gaines, who had spent the first half of the season in extended spring training rehabbing his elbow following ligament-replacement surgery.

Two of Paul's teammates were also joining the club. Reliever Goose Grascyk, a flame-thrower who had closed out games for Macon, joined the bullpen as a setup man. And third-year pro Dominic Verotto would take the at-bats at third base that used to belong to Clyde. Despite Paul's current hot stretch, he had no chance to make the jump. The system was backed up with quality second basemen. Juan Escarola at Greenville was the most highly regarded of the bunch, but he was being held off by Al Metzger at Triple-A Richmond. And Paul was basically replicating what Martin Harcourt was doing for the Bulls.

Goose Grascyk could not have provided a starker contrast to the man he replaced. Nelson was tall and lean; Goose, short and stocky. Nelson couldn't crack 90 mph with a gale-force wind at his back; Goose flirted with triple digits on a regular basis. Nelson was beloved by his teammates; Goose, well, did I mention he flirted with triple digits on a regular basis? That was about the only nice thing his colleagues could say. He was an effective reliever. He had a big-league arm. But he was a bush-league human being as we all learned the day the Bulls returned for their first home series of the second half.

Goose and the other new guys had to scramble to get settled into their living quarters when the team returned from Hampton, where it swept Peninsula. Not a big deal for most of them, but his apartment was objectionable. I overheard him bitching to Sonny that it stunk, it had no view, and the neighborhood was so dumpy he knew his car would get broken into. Sonny sent him to Don, and the buck stopped right there, which did nothing to shrink the size of the chip on Goose's shoulder. You'd guess he was a spoiled bonus baby the way he glared and scowled his way through the park. Wrong. He was a twenty-sixth-round pick with a lot to prove, which in his case was immensely worse.

The only guy who was glad to have him around was Matt Hamer. Reporters love good quotes, and Goose was liable to unfurl some doozies. Take Monday night, for example. Durham's newest reliever got the call to open the eighth inning against the heart of the lineup that had sparked Kinston to the best first-half record in the league. Strikeout. Grounder. Strikeout. Side retired. On came Warren Yauch for the ninth inning to close out the win. Only he blew the 4-3 lead and the Indians won the game.

Not only did Goose tell the Durham beat writer he felt strong enough to go two innings and the Bulls would have won if Gordy had left him out there, he also claimed he would have struck out the side in the eighth if the mound had been in better shape. Now mind you no Bulls pitcher had complained about the condition of the mound all season. Sonny poured so much love into that heap of dirt his wife ought to have been jealous. It was immaculate. But it wasn't good enough for Goose.

Tuesday morning's *Herald-Sun* was a hot item around the yard. Those quotes were the subject of numerous conversations, and they did not sit well with the grounds crew.

"Who does this guy think he is?" Peanut queried loudly and repeatedly until we told him to shut up. "Why doesn't he just go straight to Atlanta if he's so great?"

It didn't take much to stir Peanut up. He loved to talk, and he was extra blusterous this week, having gone full-time now that he'd finished high school. I noticed he toned his act down when the players began arriving. He even fumbled out a "Hey, Goose!" as the muscle-bound fireballer cruised in, earning a disdainful stare for his efforts.

"Jock sniffer," Spanky taunted him, initiating their daily wrestling match. Peanut had six years on him, but Spanky nearly matched him in weight and had picked up some useful moves fighting to stay out of the trash can all year. Rich broke them up after a couple of minutes and they prepared the field for BP as I wandered back to the office.

Due to an earlier rainout, our team photo giveaway had been pushed back to tonight. I hauled two cartons of pictures over from the tower and Gray and I stationed ourselves on either side of the entrance, racing to see who could distribute his supply first. He won, burning through his pile about a minute before I did, though it should be noted I had to chase him back to his side of the traffic flow on several occasions.

I unloaded the last of my stack on a high school kid, who slipped it into the first garbage can he passed. At least he didn't drop it on the ground like dozens of others before him. Within spitting distance of where we stood fans had chucked at least twenty team pictures, footprints across the front or back, depending upon how they had fallen. I stooped to pick a handful up and felt a tap on my shoulder.

"What, I don't get one?" a vaguely familiar voice asked.

It was Andy Quinn, my old boss at the Durham bank branch. He was trailed by a smartly dressed woman with short, sandy brown hair.

"Here." I handed him the trampled souvenirs. "Take your pick."

He brushed the photos aside and grabbed my hand instead, shaking with a firm, almost bone-crunching, grip, the links on his watch band jangling as we shook. "How the hell have you been, man? It's good to see you again."

"Likewise. I figured you might show up here sooner or later."

"Lane, this is my wife, Irene."

"It's very nice to meet you," I said.

"Same to you." Her perfectly manicured, coral and white nails tickled my palm when she reached to shake my hand, much more delicately than Andy had. "I remember hearing your name come up several times last summer."

"She only heard the good stuff," Andy whispered with a wink.

"It was all good back then," I laughed. "Seems like so long ago."

He clapped his arm around my neck and I winced as his watch connected solidly with my shoulder blade.

"Holy cow, you got a license for that?"

"Sorry, man. Still getting used to it. Check this thing out."

He lifted his wrist for closer examination and I found myself staring at a gorgeous platinum Rolex, with diamond chips where the numbers should be and intriguing dials that I was sure must have charted the tides or barometric pressure or something fantastic.

"Oh, man," I said. "That's some timepiece. They must have given you a hell of a raise."

He leaned forward and whispered into my ear, "It's fake," as though he were more proud of that than he would have been to own a genuine Rolex.

"Looks flashy."

"That's just it. Only a jeweler could tell. My brother-in-law got it up in New York for a hundred bucks. He knows a guy, who knows a guy … they're not selling this model on the street corner, put it like that."

Andy's wife gazed impatiently around the concourse, as if she'd heard this one before, and I dropped further inquiry into the origin and acquisition of his counterfeit chronometer.

"Where are you guys sitting?"

He extracted his ticket stub from the breast pocket of his t-shirt, which unlike his watch looked inexpensive, but wasn't. It was the kind of shirt you saw in GQ magazine for $105 and wondered why anyone wouldn't just buy the seven-dollar version at Penneys.

"General admission. Doesn't matter where we sit, right? We usually wind up in the bleachers down past third base."

"Well," I said in my best mock-mafioso voice, "I know a guy, who knows a guy, who could get you better seats."

"Now that's what I'm talking about," Andy exclaimed. "Lead the way."

We had a couple of season tickets next to the home dugout that had been cancelled at the last minute that we used for special guests. I guided them down into the box-seating area and found our seats open.

"Outstanding," Andy said. "Now this is more like it."

"No problem." I shook his hand again and was about to leave when he grabbed my shoulder.

"Hey, I almost forgot. I'm sorry things didn't work out with you and Trina."

I knelt down beside their box to get out of the way of the spectators behind them. "Well, we had a nice run." I was burning to know what version of events he'd heard, but didn't feel comfortable asking.

"She's quite a gal," he said, disregarding an abrupt look from his wife.

"That she is. I'm sure she'll land on her feet."

Andy raised his eyebrows tellingly and glanced away.

"Or maybe she already did?" I asked.

"Maybe I shouldn't be talking about this stuff. I don't want to get caught in the middle."

"That's cool. Just tell me one thing. Is she okay?"

"She looks fairly content," he said. "But it's early yet. She's only been seeing him a few weeks."

"That sure didn't take long."

Andy offered an apologetic shrug as I left. Wasn't his fault. I would have eventually asked her out even without his prodding.

Back in the concourse, Gray and I kicked off a half-hearted game of body-part bingo. To win you had to spot various, often disturbing, body parts before your opponent. A gut hanging out under a t-shirt, a plumber's crack, a side boob. I surged ahead on half an ass cheek, courtesy of a woman whose shorts were riding high in the back. But the game soon petered out because there wasn't enough of a crowd to sustain it.

By the fourth inning the night was starting to drag. I leaned against the front gate talking with Harvey, who hadn't torn a ticket in nearly thirty minutes. He was retelling me a story about his beloved Brooklyn Dodgers when the walkie-talkie in my back pocket crackled to life. It had been as quiet as the crowd tonight. I figured Don was buzzing to let us know some of the game-day staff, like Harvey, could start packing up.

"Anyone down near left field?" Don called. "We've got a fan in here who says there's a fight about to break out down there."

I ripped the radio out of my pocket and pushed the talk button.

"This is Lane. I'm in the concourse. I'm on it."

"Thanks. Let me know what you find."

I hoofed it down the hill to the third-base bleachers, not sure what to expect. Our average disturbance involved an over-lubricated fan or two, and usually came later in the game, right after beer sales were cut off. As I rounded the corner, Faith flagged me down from the auxiliary souvenir stand.

"Oh, Lane," she called. "I think there's some kinda argument going on down there." She pointed toward the bleachers. "I think it might be Joe."

"Vendor Joe?" I couldn't think of any other Joe, but no one ever called him just plain Joe, except to his face.

"That's right. He's been getting heckled something fierce."

I hustled down to the fence by the bullpen, where the Kinston relievers were all staring up into the stands. Their line of vision led directly to the disturbance above. Scaling the bleachers two at a time, I arrived just as Vendor Joe was lifting his wire basket of peanuts, popcorn, and licorice ropes over his head to free himself up for the main event. Three rows up, a portly oaf in a faded Dale Earnhardt t-shirt towered above him, waving his arms and barking to the nearby crowd, as if they were all co-conspirators in his haranguing of the mentally overmatched salesman. "Programs! Programs! Lucky number scorecards!" he mocked. His corpulent wife shoveled nachos into her mouth like Cookie Monster, as their two chunky kids, stained with a cheese and mustard medley, laughed and rooted on their old man.

His throat and cheeks swelling, Joe growled like a treed cougar, cleared his throat with a phlegmy cough, and spat into his palm. "You—and your entire family—are just a cheap cut of meat!" He rubbed his hands together, slicking them up with his own saliva, then balled his fists so tightly his knuckles whitened. Again he growled and coughed, only this loogie he held in reserve, perhaps to be launched during combat. Then came the dancing, shifting his weight from one foot to the other with awkward hops, like a dyspeptic boxer trying to stave off crapping his trunks.

"This is Lane," I called into my radio. "We need Captain DesJardins, pronto."

"I'm right behind you."

Sensing the situation might not hold until he arrived, I leapt in front of our resident huckster to try to break things up before any punches were tossed. Joe freaked. All he saw was someone flying in from the corner of his eye. I think he had some kind of 'Nam flashback. He screamed and lowered his head into my back, hurtling me into the side railing as his antagonist went ballistic on him.

"Crazy vendor on the loose!" He flapped his arms and turned to work the crowd of drunks egging him on. "I'm the psycho vendor guy! Watch out!"

Joe let out some kind of kamikaze war whoop and lunged forward, grabbing the guy by the ankles. He parted his lips and sank his teeth into a doughy calf. At least that's what it looked like from where I had collapsed, ass over teakettle, against the rail.

"Yeeeooooww! The vendor bit me!"

As the rowdy rained blows down upon Joe's back, I struggled to my feet and surged up the bleachers. Captain DesJardins arrived, trailed by Carson, Gray, and two other police officers. Between the six of us we pulled him off Joe, who was curled up in the fetal position, spitting out chunks of flesh.

"He bit me," the obnoxious fan cried. "The vendor bit me." He twisted and fought as one officer wrenched his hands behind his back and cuffed him. A fresh gash in the back of his right leg oozed blood down over his dingy tube sock.

"Show's over, show's over," Captain DesJardins declared. The crowd, many of whom had boisterously supported the inebriated bully, now cheered as he was led away, followed by his trailer-trash family, who filed out so nonchalantly I half suspected it wasn't their first such exit.

"You all right, Joe?" Gray asked, stooping to put an arm around the peddler, who mumbled belated and unintelligible threats under his breath. Gray supported Joe to his feet, and I helped collect the snacks that had spilled out of his basket during the fracas. We descended the bleachers to the opening notes of the William Tell Overture. Lined up in my place for the mid-game drag was young Spanky, beaming like a lighthouse as he toed the first-base line. When his turn to hit the dirt came he stepped onto the infield and kept pace with Rich, staying an even ten feet back all the way around the diamond.

I cut through the stands and arrived at the field entrance on the first-base line just as the crew was exiting the diamond. Rich and Peanut high-fived Spanky, whose round face was parted by a toothy smile.

"I thought for sure you'd trip over second base," Peanut chided.

"I saw it the whole way," Spanky said, as he rolled his chain-link mat up. "I just wanted to make sure I got close enough."

"Hey, it's Wally Pipp," Rich said when he spotted me. "Spanky stole your job, dude. He's better at it than you, too."

They all laughed, Spanky the loudest. Finally he was part of the gang, and not just the tag-along kid brother. I darted at him, lifting him off the ground as if I were going to toss him in the trash barrel. After he squealed for a few seconds I let him down.

"How's the fight?" Rich asked, pushing the last of the drag mats into place in the storage bay under the grandstand.

"Pretty good, actually. Vendor Joe bit some drunk who was hassling him." I re-enacted the melee, and the guys ate it up.

We learned Wednesday morning that the brawl wasn't the only bullet on the crime blotter that night. Don announced several players had reported money or other items missing from their lockers after the game. In total someone had made off with $550, a gold chain, and a silver cigarette lighter. The victims included Francisco Acevedo, Cleotis Anthony, Miguel Orlando, and Goose Grascyk.

"I don't want to jump to any conclusions," Don said. "But we have a problem on our hands. If you see anything suspicious, please report it directly to me."

Under normal circumstances I could have milked my Vendor Joe tale for the rest of the homestand. But the only one who wanted to talk about that anymore was Joe. Whispers and gestures carried the new top story to all corners of the ballpark. For the rest of the week we acted out a game of Clue, convicting in absentia anyone who wasn't within hearing distance. "I suspect Blake Mungo, in the clubhouse, with the sticky fingers."

The only person I knew for sure didn't do it was me.

CHAPTER EIGHTEEN

Grandpa left two messages for me Sunday morning, an hour apart. The first time I was down in right field checking out a hole Cleotis Anthony drilled through the fence in BP. He literally hit a baseball through a plywood sign. Granted the wood was old and somewhat soft, but it was an impressive feat nonetheless. The second time Gramps called we were at lunch. I'm sure there would have been a third if I hadn't phoned him as soon as we got back. His crisis turned out to be a stump that had to come out of the yard so he could extend the herb garden bed. The tree in question had been cut down ten years before I was born, but for some reason he didn't decide the trunk needed to come out until he was well past his physical prime, and then all of a sudden it was an emergency.

I found him in the backyard Monday morning, sitting in a lawn chair under a shade tree, cradling a glass of sweet tea in his hand. He was leaned back in his seat, his straw hat tilted down over his eyes, and I thought he was napping when I first got out of the truck. As I approached he slid his hat back and stiffly pushed himself up.

"Hey, there he is," he called. "Thanks for coming."

"Sure thing, Grandpa. I've got nothing better to do on my day off, right?"

"That's the spirit."

We shook hands and I followed him to the garden gate, which he carefully nudged open with his foot.

"Bees," he explained. "Careful what you touch up front here. They love the salvia."

Lining the white picket fence, fragrant stalks of purple flowers teemed with honey bees and yellow jackets. I hugged the other side of the path as I passed. Their low buzzing was soon drowned out by the racing call of the cicadas in the woods behind my grandparents' lot. We cut through the garden to the back gate, where Grandpa stopped and leaned against the fence. On the other side rested a pair of shovels and a pickaxe.

"You know if you'd have done this before you put the garden in you could have yanked it out with a truck."

"Would'a, could'a, should'a, didn't. This garden wasn't half this size when I started it. I never thought I'd need the room."

The stump measured two feet across and was soft in the middle when I poked at it with my shovel. We started out on opposite sides, digging a ring around it, hoping to get enough leverage to pop it loose. I planted my shovel in the dirt and jumped on it, riding it down into the ground. Grandpa's scoops were shorter and quicker.

"So, any word from that girl of yours?"

"Who? Trina?"

"That's her. Your mom said it was all over."

I stabbed at a root with my shovel a few times until it gave way, then slid it under and leapt aboard.

"Yup," I said at last. "I haven't heard from her but once since Memorial Day. She called our house around two in the morning a couple weeks ago. I think she was drunk."

"What'd she say?"

"I couldn't really make it out. There was a lot of noise, music and laughing. She was probably at a club. I thought I heard her sister telling her to hang up."

"She was such a sweet gal."

I arrested my shovel and stared at him for a second, then shook my head and laughed. "I'll give you hot, Grandpa. But not sweet."

"You say to-may-to, I say to-mah-to."

"Weren't you the one telling me not to think with my dick?" I wiped the sweat out of my eyes with the bottom of my t-shirt, which was already damp with perspiration. A moment later I lifted it over my head and hung it on the fence. "Damn, it's hot out here. You got any more of that tea?"

"Grandma'll bring some out shortly."

"You look like you could use a drink worse than me."

Grandpa belched deeply into his fist, straining his face in the effort. "It's this goddam heartburn." He pulled a handkerchief from his back pocket and mopped his forehead. "Burns like hell."

"How often do you get that?"

"Couple of times this week. Usually goes away with Tums."

"Want me to go fetch some for you?"

"I got 'em right here." He smiled and patted his front pocket. "They go better with tea, though. You mind running in and helping your grandma with that? She might have fallen asleep in there for all I know."

I cut through the garden and jogged across the yard, reaching the back entrance just as my grandmother was negotiating the screen door balancing a pitcher and two glasses. I gave her a sweaty hug and relieved her of her load. Grandpa emerged from the flowers and resumed his seat on the lawn. I sat down Indian style next to him.

"You think you can handle that stump on your own?" Grandpa asked when we finished our break.

"Why? You running out of gas already?"

"I think I tweaked my back earlier."

"That's awfully convenient," I kidded.

"It's hell getting old, Lane. Ten years ago I could have done this without you."

"You're not old, Grandpa."

"My back is."

He leaned against the gate and supervised as I completed the moat and took the pickaxe to the roots. He summoned enough strength to help me rock the stump loose, but I needed a rope and a two-by-four from the garage to pull it out of the hole. I dragged it to the tree line at the back of the yard and rolled it into the underbrush. When I finished, Grandpa was sitting on his lawn chair holding a pair of twenty-dollar bills against his knee.

"Here," he said. "You did all the work."

I waved it away and sat down on the grass. "I'm not taking your money, Grandpa."

"You earned it. That was a lot of work."

"Forget it."

"Take the money."

"No way. You got any beer in the fridge? I'll call it even with a beer."

"We do. Should be in the door."

I washed up and visited with my grandma for a few minutes, then returned outside with a couple of bottles of beer in tow to find

Grandpa stuffing tomatoes into a plastic grocery bag.

"At least take these. They're gonna go to waste. We can't eat them all."

"What am I gonna do with a dozen tomatoes, Grandpa?"

"Take 'em to the ballpark and share 'em with your friends."

He likewise loaded me down with a pint of blackberries and a bunch of scrawny carrots before I left. I turned my desk into a farmer's market Tuesday and found good homes for most of the produce. The berries were gone by the time Rich and I left for lunch.

We returned to find Emma stewing at her little computer table, muttering to herself. She didn't even look up when we walked in. Curious, I snuck up behind her and peeked over her shoulder at the screen. It was blank.

"Writer's block?" I inquired.

"What?"

"Why the long face?"

She spun her chair around and tried to look cheerful. "It's nothing."

"Are you sure? I've never seen that frown before. Something happen when we were gone?"

"It's no big deal."

"So something *did* happen?"

Emma popped up out of her seat and paced across the floor, spinning back toward me as she reached the wall. "Alton called. He's coming back to Durham on Thursday."

"And that's a bad thing?"

"I have to entertain him, just like last time, only this week I have to work. What am I gonna do with him, y'all?"

"Wait, why is he coming?"

"I don't know. He's got nothing better to do. I swear his daddy doesn't want him around the office so he plants ideas in his head to get him out of the way."

Emma sank into her chair and hung her head over the back so she was staring up at the ceiling. Her breast heaved, then fell as a weighty sigh rolled into a moan.

"He's a pain in the ass, y'all."

"Oh my God," I laughed. "You said the ass word."

Her body quivered and a giggle worked its way through her

clenched teeth.

"He told my dad that I took him to a party with drinking and fornication."

"Fornication? Who even talks like that?"

"That's not my point."

"Wait. Who was fornicating at our party?"

"Probably no one."

"Maybe Shannon was."

"Okay, maybe her, but can we get back on topic?"

"I thought he was a friend of yours. What's wrong with him?"

"He is. I've known him since I was born. We were best friends in high school. But he's just never grown up since then. He tells the same jokes he told when we were fourteen. He says the same things. I've heard them all a thousand times."

"So tell him you're busy and can't visit with him this week."

"It's not that simple."

"'Cause of your parents, you mean?"

"Well, that too."

"Is there anything I can do to help out? Maybe take him off your hands for a while?"

Emma shrugged and mulled the suggestion over. "I don't know. Maybe you could show him around the park. Take him down on the field or something."

Alton arrived at ten-thirty Thursday morning as we were blowing up red, white, and blue balloons for our Fourth of July celebration. He was more sensibly dressed this time, with short white socks protruding from his running shoes and a starchy polo shirt in place of his sweater vest. His hair still rolled in a spasmodic wave away from its part, as if Babe the Blue Ox had licked him across the top of the head.

I ran interference for Emma all morning, butting into their conversations and steering the talk back on course when he hijacked it with classic anecdotes from junior high. After lunch I offered him a tour of the park, which he reluctantly accepted after asking Emma three times if she minded.

"Is she okay?" he asked as he followed me down to the field, his hands stuffed deep into the front pockets of his shorts. "She seems a little off today."

"Emma? She's probably a little tired from working so much, that's all. She's a very hard worker."

We halted short of the gate to let Rich and Blake silently pass with a protective screen for the pitcher's mound. Rich still couldn't stand him and made no pretense otherwise.

"I just worry about her up here," Alton said.

"Why? She's fine. She's got her aunt and uncle here for her."

"There are a lot of bad influences in a city. She's not used to that."

"Wilmington's a city, ain't it? I think she's had a chance to see everything there."

"I don't doubt it. That's why I tried to get her to come to Brewton-Parker with me. It's a better environment."

"Maybe she just wanted to be closer to her family."

"That's what she said. But …" Alton trailed off. I crouched down to tighten the hose faucet, which was dripping onto the warning track.

"But?" I prompted him.

"She's changed. She's not the same as she used to be."

"We all change, Alton. It's part of growing up. I don't know how she used to be, but she's the nicest person I've met all summer."

He stopped and surveyed the field, and I took advantage of the opportunity to play back his lines in my head so I could relay them to Emma after he'd left.

"Can we go in the dugout?" he asked at last. "I've always wanted to sit in one."

"Sure. Whatever you want. I can show you the bull later if you're interested."

When I dropped him back in the office an hour later Emma mouthed a "thank you" to me and introduced her friend to Johnny Layne, who was already stuffing programs with the day's game note inserts. He coaxed Alton into assisting and I left to help Jenna and Shannon hang patriotic bunting along the front of the stadium.

Emma dragged Alton down to the press box when the gates opened at six and camped out there for the rest of the night. I stopped in just long enough to hear Nick Henry grilling Alton on life in a small town, then cruised down to the field to give Rich the afternoon recap. He and the rest of the crew were waiting by the dugout for batting practice to end so they could prep the field. Dom Verotto, the new Bulls third baseman, passed by on his way off the field and slapped hands with Spanky before descending into the dugout and grabbing his bat and helmet. Our pint-sized co-worker gushed as his new hero loosened up with a weighted bat in the on-deck circle.

"Don't get all star struck, Spank," I said.

"Fuck you."

"You only like him because he's never thrown you in the trash can."

"Not yet," Rich added.

We watched Dom take half a dozen hacks from the left side, then turn around and take six more as a righty. He bent down and touched his bat against the ground and rose when a fan called him from the railing. Bat on his shoulder, Dom strode over and shook hands with a snappy dresser whose tiny curls were gelled tightly into place atop his head. A flashy, quarter-inch-thick gold chain hung down over his silk t-shirt.

"Who is that guy?" I asked.

"Who?" Rich replied.

"The guy Dom's talking to. He looks familiar for some reason."

"Dunno. Never seen him."

I closed my eyes and thought for a moment, paging through the catalog of images stored in my head.

"I got it. I think Trina knows him. We ran into him at Red Lobster one night."

"Small world," Rich said. "Why don't you go ask him how she's doing?"

"Because I don't care."

"There may be some hope for you yet."

I spied on Dom's friend a couple of times throughout the night. He sat in the fourth row behind the screen with another man, possibly his buddy from Red Lobster, but I couldn't tell for sure. They were gone by the fifth inning. Most of the capacity crowd stuck around to the bitter end of a ten-inning loss to watch the fireworks display that began fifteen minutes after the game. The park didn't clear out until eleven-thirty.

As we sipped our beer and congratulated ourselves on a successful night, Don emerged and broke the news that our clubhouse thief had struck again.

“That’s impossible,” Rich said. “The only guys in or out of there all night were players.”

“It’s possible,” Don said. “That loudmouth Grascyk got hit again. And two others. They lost over two hundred and fifty dollars between them.”

“Do they have any leads? Any suspects?”

“Everyone and no one,” Don said. “It could be anybody.”

CHAPTER NINETEEN

Spanky rocketed to the top of many suspect lists when he arrived at the park Sunday styling in a brand new pair of Air Jordans, toting a fresh Sony Discman CD player. That was a lot of flash for a junior high kid on the free-lunch program at school. I didn't figure Spanky for our thief, though I casually mentioned to Rich that his timing looked suspicious at best. He conceded that, but shredded the case against his junior assistant. Sunday was Spanky's thirteenth birthday; the gifts were from his godmother in Charlotte.

The strain of the ordeal weighed on the staff as the five-day homestand wrapped up. The entire crew was playing detective, spying around corners on each other and lingering outside doorways to overhear scraps of conversation. The players were even more on edge. I crossed wires with Goose Grascyk on Monday afternoon as I was coming out of the clubhouse after dropping some papers on Gordy's desk.

"You got business in here, dude?" Goose demanded.

"Yeah, I work here."

He stared at me cross-eyed, twitching like he had Tourette's. "No shit. I work here, too, man." He took a step toward me. "And we've had a few problems in here lately, which is why I get a little suspicious."

"So I've heard."

"I got my eye on all you guys. If I catch someone, they're gonna be sorry." He pounded his right fist into the palm of his left hand, then turned and continued on to his locker. I slipped out to the tunnel to finish wetting myself.

To sooth the nerves, I proposed a fun outing to Fayetteville to see Macon play on Friday night and several of my co-workers jumped on the idea. Even Don made the trip. We organized three car pools for the hour-and-a-half drive down. Don carted his wife and two sons in his car. Carson took Blake and Peanut and lobbied hard for Emma, but she slipped in Rich's Civic with us. Which meant we got her puppy-love admirer Spanky as well.

It hadn't taken me long to convert Emma into a Paul Giordano fan. After a few days she became almost as eager to check the morning faxes as I was. I introduced her and the rest of our group to Paul along the railing as the Braves took batting practice. Fayetteville was the most convenient stop on the schedule for Raleigh folk, and he had quite the cheering section on hand, including his parents and his girlfriend Nicole. His college coach also made the short drive up from Pembroke. We erupted when Paul rifled a hard single to center in the first inning, though it turned out to be the highlight of the evening as he finished 1-for-4 and the Braves fell to the Generals, 6-1.

I tried to talk Rich into returning Saturday night, but he was acting all mysterious, making hush-hush plans on the phone with someone, so I drove down on my own late in the afternoon. Paul took a little break and climbed into the stands with me, where we caught up as Fayetteville took BP. He'd rebounded from a demoralizing late-May slide, lifting his average back up over .290, and was feeling good about the way he'd been playing in the second half. He asked me about things with the Bulls and I told him all about our recent crime wave.

"No kidding? Same thing happened in Macon early in the year."

"Seriously?"

"Yeah. Maybe three or four times. Guys lost a bunch of money, some jewelry, a CD player."

"You lose anything?"

"Nah. I don't carry that kind of dough around. Mostly it's the Latin guys and the hotdogs."

"Why the Latin guys?"

"Most of them ain't got bank accounts. They keep all their money on them. Crazy, really."

"Whatever happened? Did they catch whoever was doing it?"

"Yeah. Well, I ain't convinced myself. Goose Grascyk, he got hit a couple of times, and he was sure it was one of the clubhouse kids. People got in an uproar and the kid got fired, and it all stopped. But I don't know. I used to talk to that kid a lot. I still can't quite believe ..."

He stopped talking when he realized I was traveling down another road of thought.

"Goose, huh?" I said. "He's been threatening us all ever since this started."

"I sure don't miss him," Paul laughed. "Though it was nice having an hombre like that on the staff."

"He's off his rocker, man."

"Yeah. He always seemed amped up, sprinting out of the bullpen like a maniac. I think he's on something."

"Speed, you mean?" I asked.

"Uh-huh. They tried to crack down on that stuff in spring training, but guys still use it."

"You ever try it?"

"Once, at Pembroke the week before finals. Struck out three times and couldn't sleep all night. That cured me pretty quick."

I waited up for Rich that night, reading a battered paperback copy of *Summer of '49* in the dim light on the front porch. Every ten minutes or so I'd drift off, then rally, read a few more paragraphs and repeat the cycle. He finally arrived home around one. It took surprisingly little effort on my part to worm the details of his date out of him. He'd taken Rae Ann out to dinner, then for a drive up to Falls Lake.

I told him about my conversation with Paul and he perked up, slapping the side of his head to signify a cognitive reaction had occurred.

"Of course. Goose. It all makes sense."

"What does?"

"What you just said about Goose stealing everything."

"I said what?"

"Didn't you just say that Paul thought Goose did it?"

"Um, no, not exactly." I dog-eared the page in my book and tossed it onto the papasan chair. "But that might explain a few things. Like why this never happened until he joined the team."

"We just need to catch him in the act now."

"If it's him, you mean."

"It's gotta be him."

"So he's stealing from himself?"

"That's a front. Oldest trick in the book."

"How are we going to prove it?"

Rich rubbed his temples as if he could somehow massage the answer out of his brain. After a minute he shook his head and let out an exasperated sigh.

"I don't know," he admitted. "Let's think about it for a couple of days. We'll come up with something."

I was eager to talk to Paul again, but Rich begged out of Sunday night's game, reluctantly confessing he had a follow-up engagement with Rae Ann. I hectored him in retribution for all the Becca comments he had made, but my heart wasn't in it. I liked Rae Ann and had always thought Rich had screwed her over the first time they dated. Maybe he recognized it as well. He'd grown up a lot since then.

Not wanting to drive down alone again, I called my sister Sunday morning. Kate had been my baseball buddy one spring when we were at State together. She mainly went to scout for boys, an effort I sabotaged more than once by caressing her hand or rubbing her back when I caught her making goo-goo eyes at some prospective suitor. That might have been why she stopped going with me. She was mildly tempted by the Fayetteville trip but already had plans with her girlfriends.

Another name rumbled around in my head. Emma. I debated inviting her, fearing I'd make her uncomfortable at work. It was bad enough she had to tiptoe around Carson. I didn't need to creep her out, too. I thumbed through the phone book, looking for any Wrights that lived on Hope Valley Road, which was as precise as I knew her address. There were two listings: Abel C. Wright and Warren and Bethany Wright. I started with Abel and hit the mark, catching her just as they returned from church.

"It's not a date or anything," I explained, trying to put her at ease. "I just wondered if you wanted to go to the game tonight. Not a big deal if you can't go, I'll just—"

"I'll go. You shouldn't have to go by yourself."

"Don't feel obligated. I've gone to lots of games by myself. I went last night."

"No, I had fun there on Friday."

I pulled into Abel Wright's driveway a couple minutes shy of four. The curtains in the front window rustled and a moment later a young girl in a pink Sunday-school frock pulled the door open. She stood on the porch staring at my truck with large, round eyes.

"Are you Lane?" she asked, as I climbed the steps.

"Yes, I am. Who might you be?"

"I'm Hannah." She glanced bashfully down at her white patent-leather shoes. "I'm six."

"Can you tell Emma that I'm here, Hannah?"

She scampered inside the house, and I followed as far as the threshold. Emma's aunt rushed out of the kitchen, wiping her hands on her apron.

"Welcome, welcome," she said. "Emma will be down any moment."

Hannah stormed back into the room, giggling, and circled around her mother's legs, peering out at me from behind a billowing skirt. Footsteps thumped down the stairs from the second floor. Emma appeared a moment later, wearing navy shorts and a matching sailor blouse with an oversized white bow at the collar, toting a worn baseball mitt. She corralled her kid cousin and kissed her good-bye, hugged her aunt, and turned toward me, her face flushed.

"Ready?" I asked.

"Yep. Sorry to keep you."

"We have plenty of time," I said, backing out the yet open door.

She waved good-bye and followed me down the porch steps. I opened the passenger-side door of my pickup for her and she climbed in. When I pulled my door open a faint hint of lilac perfume wafted across the cab. Emma set the baseball glove on the dash and wrestled her seatbelt into place.

"You planning on getting a game of catch in?" I asked to break the thin layer of ice that had settled over the truck.

"The glove, you mean?" She slid it off the dash and slipped it onto her left hand. "I almost got hit by a foul ball Friday. Y'all were so wrapped up you didn't seem to notice. My uncle gave me this for self-protection."

"Uncle Abel?" I chuckled, as I swung the truck around so I was pointing toward the road.

"We call him Abe, actually. Where'd you get Abel?"

"Phone book."

"Ahh. No one calls him that, 'cept my grandma. I figured you didn't get it from me."

The now familiar drive flew by as we chatted about Bulls stuff, both co-workers and players. Before it seemed possible we'd gone that far, we pulled into the Riddle Stadium parking lot. We found Paul leaning against the rail, talking to his parents. I reintroduced Emma and we all chatted for a few minutes. When Mr. and Mrs. Giordano retired to their seats I turned the talk to Goose.

"You know, I thought about it last night after the game, and I kinda wondered the same thing," Paul said.

Emma wasn't fully up to speed, but she guessed along enough to know where we were heading. "I wouldn't put anything past him, y'all," she said. "He's a bad apple."

"How do we catch him?" I asked.

Paul shrugged. "That ain't my field a' expertise. But if you need a hand on the inside, look up J.T. Gaines."

"Yeah?"

"J.T. frickin' *hates* Goose. If you want someone to keep an eye on him, he might help. Just tell him I told you to ask. We roomed together in spring training."

Watching the game with Emma reminded me of attending games in college with Kate. Emma knew more about baseball, though. I didn't have to explain stuff like what a balk was or why the batter could run to first on a dropped third strike while she pretended to care and flirted with some guy in the next row. We sat behind Paul's parents with Nicole, who latched onto Emma so quickly that by the third inning they were running to the restroom together. Paul rewarded his fan club with his fourth homer of the season in the third and an infield single in the seventh.

It was nearly midnight by the time I pulled back into her uncle's driveway. Nestled in the web of his mitt was a South Atlantic League baseball I'd gloved for Emma as it caromed back at us from the last row in our section.

"Thanks for going," I said.

"Are you kidding? I had a blast. That Nicole's a lot of fun, too. I'd go again tomorrow, but Hannah's got a dance recital and I promised her I wouldn't miss it."

I stared dumbly across the cab, the synapses and neurons in

my brain fraying apart as I wondered if this still didn't count as a date. I wanted to ask if her co-worker policy applied to me or just Carson, but I didn't dare risk the awkwardness.

"See you tomorrow," she said, breaking the pregnant silence as she lifted the door latch.

"Yeah, good night. I'll see you at work."

CHAPTER TWENTY

Blake glommed onto us Monday as we were hauling some unused equipment from the tunnel across the street to the fire tower and wound up inviting himself to lunch. I hadn't exactly grown to like the guy, but I could tolerate him most days, which was more than Rich could say. Then again, I didn't work on the field with him, so I never felt like he was weaseling out of tasks that would fall on me. He offered to drive and we piled into his low-rider truck and headed to the food court up at the mall. As soon as we were inside Rich peeled off, leaving me and Blake in line at the barbecue place. My lunch rang in at just over five dollars, which was unfortunate because my pocket held only four.

"Hey, can you spot me a couple bucks?"

Blake dug in his back pocket and pulled out a wallet so thick with notes it hung open like a panting mouth. He freed two bills and handed them to me.

"Thanks, man. I'll pay you back tomorrow."

"Don't worry about it."

"You rob a bank or something?"

Blake jutted his rounded chin out and glared down his nose at me. "I didn't steal it."

"Easy. I was just kidding. It's a nice wad. Sorry."

"I just don't want anyone suspecting me, with everything going on, you know. I ain't involved in that."

"That's cool. I didn't think you were."

He shrugged and picked a fry off his tray as he waited for his change. "I had a pretty good weekend, just put it like that."

"You *won* all that?"

"Most of it."

"How?"

"You want in on the action?"

"No, man. Sorry. Forget I asked."

I spotted Rich sitting at a table in the middle of the crowd and made my way toward him. Blake followed. "I could get you in, if you want," he said in a hushed voice. "Boxing, cars, baseball, whatever."

"Nah. I don't think that's for me."

"You sure? I'm calling in a couple after lunch. I could easily place one for you."

"That's all right. I don't have the dough for that anyway."

"Suit yourself, dude. I pulled in two hundred bones over the weekend."

"Wow."

"Hey, listen," he whispered as we approached the table. "Don't mention it to Rich, will ya? He, you know."

"Yeah," I nodded. "Don't worry."

Rich moped throughout lunch, barely saying ten words the whole time. Blake ignored him right back, leaving me to track two disjointed, and frankly pointless, conversations. When we returned to the stadium Rich followed me into the office and dropped down in Sonny's chair.

"What the hell did you let him come to lunch for?"

"What? What could I say? Fuck off? Stay away from us?"

"I needed to talk to you."

"About what?"

"Let's walk."

I followed him out into the parking lot. Every twenty feet he twisted his head and peeked over his shoulder like he was being trailed in a spy movie. We walked the chain-link fence until we reached the gate and cut back in down by right field.

"Where are we going?" I asked.

He looked at me crossly and kept walking behind the outfield wall. "I don't trust anyone around here anymore," he whispered. "No one but you and Sonny."

"Glad I'm still on the list."

"Keep talking to Blake and you won't be."

My earlier promise taunted me, daring me to break it. I knew Rich would enjoy it, especially if it were followed up by news of big losses the next weekend. But I kept my tongue in check and followed him to the magnolia tree behind center field. He leaned against the trunk and took one last look around.

"I've got an idea."

He pulled a well-worn, eel-skin wallet from his pocket and tossed it to me. I flipped it open and rifled through. The slots in the front held a Winn-Dixie shopper's club card and a bus pass, but the rest of it was empty.

"What's this?"

"Bait."

"For what?"

"A Goose. We're gonna load that up with a little dough and hide it in the clubhouse."

"Whose wallet is it?"

"I snagged it from the lost and found. Someone must have cleaned it out and turned it in."

I folded the wallet up and handed it back. "How much money are you putting in there?"

"None." He pushed my hand away. "You're putting in forty bucks."

"Why me?"

"I came up with the idea. You come up with the money."

"I'm broke."

"Go to the ATM. And one more thing."

"What?" I hated when Rich was in charge. He became clever Tom Sawyer and I morphed into bumpkin Huck Finn.

"You're off the drag team."

"What? Why?"

"I need you to watch the clubhouse while we're out on the field."

"What about Sonny? He could do it."

"I don't want to bring him into this yet. Just let Spanky take your place. When we drag, you're on watch."

I ran to the bank and made a withdrawal, then recorded the serial numbers of two twenty-dollar bills and stuffed them into the wallet. We stashed it in the side pocket of a duffel bag that was hanging in the stall vacated by Nelson Ray a few weeks earlier. I was just going to set it on the top shelf, but Rich said that looked too obvious.

Each morning we checked our Goose trap and found it untouched. No one had ever been so disappointed to learn their wallet hadn't been stolen. We couldn't take it personally; our thief abstained throughout the three-game stand against Frederick.

Operation Gander, as we came to call it, was hardly the only thing on Rich's mind. He had been bugging me to catch a game in Burlington since the Indians' season started in mid-June. We headed over Saturday night to take in their Appalachian League showdown with Bristol. This was a matchup of clubs heading in opposite directions. The home team was off to a great start, while the visiting Tigers already had a half nelson wrapped around last place in their division.

The baseball was secondary for my friend, however. It was time to renew his acquaintance with the Indians staff and ingratiate himself in case an opening arose after the season. Matty Benbo, the general manager, was in his fourth year in Burlington, and by Rich's calculations it would be his last before moving on to a bigger market. Matty had apprenticed as the assistant GM directly out of nearby Elon College, climbing to the top spot after learning on the job for two years. His right-hand man, fresh-faced Turner Wyand, was poised for a similar jump this offseason. Rich was angling to fall in line behind Turner.

The first thing he needed to learn was the route to the park. Though I'd seen Paul play there twice last year when Pulaski came through, I'd gotten lost both times. I still wasn't sure which exit to take off of I-85. We debated the point for several miles until I settled the argument by swerving onto the offramp. Things looked vaguely familiar, even more so the second time we hit the traffic circle in picturesque downtown Graham. "Go straight!" "No, I think we want to turn right." "Hit the next light and take a left." "Where the fuck are we?" If you traced our route it would look something like Billy's travels in the Sunday Family Circus.

Burlington Athletic Stadium was more than adequate for Rookie ball, but no one will ever get lost in its ambience. The physical structure could be picked up and plopped down in any small town in America and serve as a suitable home for minor league baseball. That, in fact, was how it came to Burlington from Danville, Virginia, in the late 1950s, as Matty informed us on our quickie tour of the facilities. The one thing they had over Durham was plenty of parking in a large grassy lot next to the stadium. It was nearly full by game time, due in no small part to the second annual "NASCAR Night at the BAS" promotion. Baseball may have been a passion for many folks in the Carolinas, but NASCAR was a close second behind God in their hearts. Matty tapped into this fervor by securing three stock cars for display in the park. Unlike ours, Burlington's concourse was big enough to drive through, and the vehicles were parked, hoods up and doors open, ready for inspection. I passed by several times on my way to the concession stand and restroom, seeing the same pit-crew dreamers out there each time. They were so lost in carburetors and gear shifts they never came in to watch the game.

Matty and Turner had precious little help running their show. Their game-day staff was primarily high school kids, with a handful of retirees sprinkled in as a stabilizing element. But like the game on the field, the action in the park moved a couple of ticks slower than things in Durham, and it all averaged out just fine.

On a packed night like Saturday, the BAS got a-rockin' with a deafening cacophony of children stomping on the aluminum bleachers. We sat a row behind a couple of Bristol pitchers who were charting pitches for their teammates, the bush league ritual to force off-duty starters to pay attention to the game. A long, slender kid with pimples on his neck and nose was reading the numbers from a radar gun and shouting them to his more-seasoned companion, who recorded them on a clipboard along with the pitch type and location. We talked to them briefly, and they confessed awe at the volume of the crowd.

"This is about four days' worth of attendance back in Bristol," the older pitcher said. "Most nights it's so quiet you can hear people talking from down on the field."

"These people here are crazy loud," the kid added.

They really were. Every cheer, every groan, every footstep echoed off those metal bleachers making it tough sometimes to concentrate on what was happening on the field. By game's end I had a splitting headache. Rich seemed almost glad. It gave him an excuse to track Turner down again to bum some aspirin off him.

I found the trail home with surprisingly little difficulty. Rich jabbered the entire ride back about how he would love to move over to Burlington after the season ended. "It's the next logical step," he said, about a dozen times. I asked what happened if Matty didn't leave and there was no opening. He said he'd bet his left testicle Matty was leaving. No one that promising stays five years in the Appy League.

We fell silent shortly before reaching Durham, Rich dreaming about the next rung on his ladder while I wondered how that might help me move up with the Bulls. If he migrated west, I'd probably have a job throughout the winter, assuming I didn't get myself fired before then. If he didn't, they might cut me loose until springtime to clear my huge salary off the payroll for a few months. As much as I would hate to see him go, I was rooting for him.

CHAPTER TWENTY-ONE

Rich's next schmoozing opportunity lay just around the corner. This was a big one. Don had authorized almost all of the full-timers to travel up to Frederick for the Carolina League all-star game on Wednesday.

Because that teetotaling party-pooper Aaron wasn't going, I got stuck collecting an assortment of Bulls souvenirs for the all-star charity auction. Monday morning I raided the Ballpark Corner shop of t-shirts, caps, pennants, and a couple of coveted jerseys. Faith killed my buzz a little with her puppy-dog eyes when she mentioned how Don had given her some false hope earlier in the year that she might be invited. Even when Aaron passed she was left off the roster. That ought to have told her right there where she fit in the organization. I sympathized with her for a few minutes, then slipped through the curtain into the back room to gather the merchandise on my list.

Owing to *Bull Durham*, we sold nearly as many No. 8 jerseys as all the others combined. Everyone fancied themselves a Kevin Costner. No one ever stopped in looking for Robert Wuhl's number. The quietly competitive Don suggested grabbing an 8 for the auction, giving us a leg up on the rest of the league in fundraising. I hoisted myself up to stand on the second shelf and sifted through the uniform tops, pulling out a winner after a couple of minutes of searching. Leaping the four feet down to the floor, I lost my balance and crashed into a stack of seat cushions. They scattered in several directions, revealing two neatly folded blankets and a body pillow. Intrigued, I examined the bedding and detected a faint hint of White Linen perfume.

I reconstructed the wall of cushions and carted the goodies down to the trailer, where I joined the knot of slackers lounging around outside. There was little work being done as everyone chatted about the upcoming trip to Maryland. Those who had been to past all-star events regaled the rest of us with stories of home-run contests, celebrity banquets, and after-parties. Emma sat quietly on the stoop, soaking up the late-morning sun as the rest of us discussed room arrangements and carpools.

"You don't seem very enthused," I said, after drifting over next to her.

She looked up at me, shielding her eyes from the sun with her hand, and replied, "I'm not going."

"Why not? It should be a lot of fun."

"Don only got ten tickets. No room for the interns."

"What? Shannon's going, isn't she? I heard her talking about it this morning."

She lifted her eyebrows and mouthed the words, "I know."

I nodded my head toward the field and slipped away from the others. Emma followed a moment later.

"What gives?" I asked when we were alone down in the bowl of the stadium. "How come Government Cheese gets a ticket and you don't?"

"Well, she didn't exactly get a ticket," Emma explained. "But I'm sure they'll sneak her into the dinner. She's going to bunk with Jenna."

"Can't you share a room with someone?"

"There's only one room for girls."

"So, you'd have to share with them?"

She started to open her mouth, but just sucked in a deep breath and nodded. The corners of her eyes sagged down toward the edges of her mouth, which was drawn into a forced smile. We walked on in silence.

"No can do, hunh?" I asked at last.

She shrugged, and I thought for a moment she might cry, but she exhaled and the threat passed.

"It's not that I can't get along with her ... but, I, ya know, I don't want to feel like I'm intruding all the time."

"Jenna'd probably be glad to have you along. And you could always hang out with us during the day."

"It's okay. I'm going to go home to see my parents."

"Well, if you change your mind, we'll make room for you in our car."

"Thanks, but I'm leaving this afternoon for Shallotte."

Emma boosted herself up on top of the first-base dugout. I

jumped up next to her. We sat there for a couple of minutes, neither of us saying anything. I didn't want to talk about the trip anymore because I didn't want her to feel like I was rubbing it in her face. So I watched her kick her short legs out and bang the heels of her sneakers against the side of the dugout. Kick. Bang. Kick. Bang. I leaned my shoulder into hers to throw her off stride, but she kept kicking and banging her heels. The harder I leaned the faster she kicked until she finally stopped kicking and started pushing back.

"Knock it off," she giggled.

"Knock what off?"

"Stop shoving me with your bony shoulder."

"Bony? That's muscle."

"Yeah, right," she laughed, still pushing back until she stopped suddenly. "Don," she murmured.

Our GM stood at the top of the walkway nearest his office, waving his arm to catch our attention. "Lane!" he yelled. "Phone call!"

Don didn't normally answer the phone, but with everyone else in goof-off mode he was the only one inside when it rang. I jogged up after him and pulled a chair up to the desk outside his office. After grabbing a pen, I punched the flashing button on the phone. "Lane Hamilton."

"Lane, it's Mom."

"Hey, Mom. What's up?"

"I have some bad news. Your grandpa's in the hospital. Your father is—"

"What happened?"

"We got a call from Dr. Tooker about an hour ago. Your grandfather had a heart attack."

Dr. Tooker was a retired physician who had delivered me and my sister when we were born. He golfed with my grandpa a couple of times a month at the country club.

"Is he okay?"

She let out the sob she'd been holding back since I answered the phone. When she spoke again her voice was thick with grief. "I don't know. Your father said he'd call from the hospital, but he hasn't yet."

"What happened?"

"He was golfing with Dr. Tooker, and ... he just collapsed."

"I'm coming home, okay. I want to see him."

"You better hurry."

But I didn't. I couldn't. I didn't even hang the phone up until thirty seconds after she did. For two more lost minutes I stared at the desktop, autistically clicking the button on the pen until Don walked out and arrested my thumb. Through fogged eyes, I looked from him to the Bic and back. "Sorry," I said, when I realized what had drawn him from his office.

"Everything okay?" he inquired, knowing, of course, that it wasn't.

I shook my head. A drip trickled down the inside of my nostril and I wiped the back of my hand across my nose. "My grandpa had a heart attack."

"I'm sorry."

"I just saw him last week. I can't believe this."

"You should go."

I thumbed a tear away and another rolled into its place. I looked up at stoic Don and wondered how he would react to news like that. Would he cry if it were his grandfather? Did he ever cry? He was as calm as a cigar-store Indian most of the time, food fights aside. I simultaneously envied and hated his self-control. He smiled a smile no one else I know could have pulled off in the wake of such a call, and I pushed the chair back and got up. Out in the concourse Emma had resumed her spot on the stoop, watching half-heartedly as the rest of the crew swapped stories. I approached slowly, hoping to attract Rich's attention without breaking up the party. Sonny halted his tale midsentence when he noticed me, and the rest of the group turned, one by one.

"Y'allright, man?" Sonny asked.

I squinted in a vain effort to squeeze the tears back into my eyes. "My grandpa had a heart attack."

"He gonna be okay?" Sonny asked.

"I don't know. I hope so. He's pretty tough."

Emma circuited the crowd, surveying me with her soft eyes as she approached, her recent doldrums dismissed. She slipped her arms inside mine, buttressing me with her embrace as that audacious shock of blonde hair tickled my chin. I pulled her tight, entwining my hands together behind her back as the others huddled around offering words of encouragement.

"You still going?" Carson squeaked, when the murmur died back down.

"I don't know. Depends."

But I knew. If Grandpa pulled through I wouldn't leave. And if he didn't … if he didn't … I couldn't get past that part. What if he didn't? I clung to Emma and tried not to think about him dying. After a minute I excused myself and entered the trailer to rinse my face in the bathroom before making the drive to Raleigh. When I returned, Emma handed me a scrap of paper torn from last week's media notes. Her parents' phone number was neatly penciled in the margin.

"Call me if you need anything," she whispered.

I nodded, then waved good-bye to the others with as much heart as I could muster and trudged to the parking lot. The house was empty when I arrived and I found a note on the table in my mom's handwriting. She and Kate had gone to meet my dad at Wake Medical Center. I drove to the hospital and found them pacing the hall outside the emergency room. My dad and grandmother were praying together on a bench against the wall.

Kate saw me first. She shook her head solemnly, her nostrils pinched in and shoulders trembling as she approached. I began to cry as we hugged. Mom cut in and our tears mingled as the three of us pressed together in the middle of the thoroughfare, oblivious to the pageant of carts, wheelchairs, and foot traffic streaming past in both directions. We broke our huddle when a resident in scrubs emerged from the double doors nearest us. He spoke in a low tone to my grandmother, and she listened intently as he explained what had happened. I couldn't hear him, but in her face I read there was still hope.

They wheeled him down the hall a couple minutes later, and we followed as far as the elevator. He was moving up two floors to a recovery room. Kate and I took the stairs and were there when they rolled him out of the elevator. His face looked anguished when they pushed him past us, like he'd fallen asleep in the middle of an argument.

We had to wait fifteen minutes as they hooked him up in his room. Then they told us to keep to three visitors at a time. My parents and grandma went in first. As soon as the nurse turned the corner Kate and I slipped in after them.

Grandma held his hand and mumbled out a prayer. When she finished she bent down and kissed him on the forehead. "Hang in there, you old jackass," she said as she stood up. That's when I knew he'd be okay. He had to be. Grandma wasn't crying anymore. We all took turns talking to him. I had some crazy idea I could make him laugh in his sleep. He smiled once, when I told him I'd go track down Trina for him. At least it looked like it to me. No one else saw it. Maybe it was just the way his lip was curled up.

As the afternoon dragged on we spoke less and less. Trying to communicate with Grandpa had long since lost its entertainment value. I did a lot of staring out the window and pacing up and down the hall. At first I thought if I walked away for a little while I'd come back to find some improvement. Maybe Grandpa would even be sitting up in his bed eating a bowl of Jell-O or ice cream. After awhile I was walking just to kill time. I'd come back and find everyone where they were when I left, the monitors by Grandpa's bed still whirring and beeping at the same intervals. The lack of change wasn't all bad. After all, his heartbeat had stabilized, albeit with a bit of assistance. But it sure was boring.

My mom had had enough by eight o'clock. Kate and I went with her, leaving my dad and grandma to stand sentry. I made two calls when I got home. The first went to Rich, who had already made plans to ride up to Frederick with Sonny. The second went to Emma. She must have been hovering near the phone. I never even heard it ring on my side.

"Harlan Wright residence," she answered.

"Emma?"

"Yes, this is Emma."

"Hey, it's me. Lane."

"I know. How's your grandfather?"

"You always answer the phone like that?"

"Like what?"

"Arlan Wright residence."

"It's Harlan, with an H. And yes. My father is a town alderman. He gets a lot of calls."

"Oh. No one ever calls my dad, unless they're trying to sell him something."

"How's your grandfather doing?"

"Still fighting. He's unconscious, but his heartbeat is steady."

"That's good news."

"Yeah. Could be the machines, though. He's hooked up to about a dozen different things."

"Sounds like they're doing their job. What's his prognosis? Did they say?"

"Not exactly. I didn't get the impression they really knew. Or maybe they didn't want to tell us."

"I bet you he'll pull through it if he's made it this far."

"I hope so. But it would be nice to see some improvement. I was at the hospital for more than seven hours and nothing changed. It's emotionally draining just sitting there all day watching my grandma stare at his bed."

"Which hospital is he at?"

"Wake. My dad and grandma are still there with him."

"Just keep thinking positive thoughts. They say it's always darkest before …"

"Before what?"

I heard a muffled discussion filtered through a hand over the phone. What I could make out sounded like, "Yes … okay … I will … no … it's just a friend from Durham … okay." She never actually raised her voice, but it was clear she was irritated.

"Lane? Sorry about that," she said, when she returned to our call.

"That's okay. Was that your dad?"

"No, my mother."

"What'd she want?"

"It's not important."

"What were you saying before?"

She laughed. "I don't remember."

"You said, it's always darkest before something."

"Oh, the dawn. It's an old saying."

"What's it mean?"

"Well, when things are at their worst … Lane, hold on one second."

I heard the skin of her palm rubbing against the mouthpiece as she covered the phone again. This time I couldn't pick out any of the conversation.

"Lane," she said after about thirty seconds. "I'm sorry about that. I need to go."

"Everything okay?"

"It's fine," she sighed. "I'll see you Thursday at work, okay. Hang in there. Your granddad's going to be okay."

"Thanks."

I slept in my old room that night for the first time in more than four months. Exhausted as I was, I wasn't the least bit sleepy. So I stretched out under the top sheet, just thinking about Grandpa. I remembered the day he taught me to bait a hook when I was five, and how he would always let me stay up late watching shows my parents wouldn't when he babysat. I had nightmares for a week after we watched *Jaws* one night when my parents were at a wedding. Eventually Kate, who fell asleep on the couch before the first shark attack, ratted us out. I recalled the scolding he gave me after I bragged to him about copying my report on Switzerland out of the encyclopedia in fifth grade. My teacher had given me an A, but Grandpa convinced me to turn my plagiarizing ass in. He was also the one who taught me how to read the break on a curve ball in high school. He was my only grandpa, my mom's father having passed away when I was just a baby, and he had more than made up the difference.

I returned to his room Tuesday morning to find my dad and grandma still there. Grandma figured she wasn't going to sleep anyway, so she might as well stay. My dad wouldn't let her do it alone. They were quiet, but in slightly better spirits than when we'd left the night before. No news was good news. Grandpa was still drawing breath, and because Dr. Tooker had started CPR almost immediately after he fell, his doctor was optimistic he wouldn't suffer any serious brain damage if he came out of it soon. But he couldn't, or wouldn't, guess when that might be.

By the time I went home that night I knew all the shortcuts to the cafeteria and newsstand and which stairways came out where, relative to the much slower elevators. I did a lot of walking, because just sitting there was making me more coño than Batboy Eddie.

Grandma was slumped in a chair asleep when I arrived Wednesday morning. It didn't take much to convince my dad to take her home for a while. He needed a nap and a shower himself.

He was smelling pretty gamy after his two-day vigil. I promised I'd call if there were any update, though we all recognized, at least to ourselves, that we might be facing a long wait.

Alone at last, I felt less self-conscious talking to Grandpa. I read him the baseball stories out of the morning paper and shared a couple of things I found in *The Sporting News*. I moved from one side of his bed to the other, but never saw any difference in him. He sure didn't follow my voice or blink his eyes or do any of the things I'd read about patients in a coma doing. But his monitors kept beeping and his IV kept dripping and he was still on the right side of the turf line.

I gave up on talking him back to life and reclined in the chair my grandma had spent the night in. The pillow smelled of her fabric softener, which was strangely comforting, and before long I dozed off. Sometime later I was shaken awake by a hand on my shoulder. Emma's round, hazel eyes were looking down into mine when I cracked my lids open.

"Hey." I thumbed the saliva out of the corner of my mouth. "What are you doing here?"

"I thought I'd stop in to see how you were doing. And I put together a little bouquet for your grandfather."

A small blue vase containing daisies, a couple of orange lilies, and some yellow wildflowers sat on the table by his bed.

"He'll like those. He's got daisies like that in his garden."

"How's he doing?"

"Holding steady, I guess. I haven't seen any change since Monday afternoon."

"At least he's not getting any worse."

"True," I said. "Still, it gets a little boring sitting here watching him do nothing all day. Thanks for coming. I wasn't expecting to see anyone from work."

"Have you heard from them?"

"Yeah, Rich called last night. They had some kind of luau party. They're supposed to all be golfing today in a best-ball tournament. Then the game's tonight, at seven, I think."

"Sounds like fun."

"Yeah," I shrugged. "If I knew Grandpa was going to sleep all week, maybe I'd have gone up."

"You had no way to know. Besides, what if something had

happened?"

"I know. I'd never forgive myself."

Emma nodded. "You made the right call."

"How was your trip? I thought you weren't coming back until tomorrow."

"Well," she started, then paused. "It was a little stressful. Two nights was plenty enough."

"What happened?"

"Oh, I had a big argument with my dad." Emma put her hand to her face and covered her eyes for a moment before forcing a half a smile. "It's a long story. I don't want to bore you with it now. But next time I go home I need to have a long talk with him about—"

"BURP!"

We both turned toward the bed, where the author of the belch was surveying us through heavy eyelids.

"Grandpa!"

He nodded, then moved his lips, touching them against each other unsurely as if he were feeling them for the first time.

"Press the call button on the side of his bed," I ordered as I pushed myself up out of my chair. "He's awake!"

Emma raced around the hospital bed and jammed her thumb down on the red button. Grandpa eyed her as he weakly moved his hand up to his face. He fingered the oxygen tube running into his nose, then looked back in my direction.

"What the hell happened to me?" he rasped.

"You had a heart attack, old man," I laughed. "You scared the piss out of us. We thought you were a goner."

"Not yet," he whispered. "The big guy said it warn't my turn."

CHAPTER TWENTY-TWO

We had surpassed the 200,000 mark in attendance at the end of the last homestand, but Don had his sights set on 300,000—and topping Frederick. In order to reach that goal we'd need to average almost 4,800 fans a night over the final twenty games. It was doable if the weather cooperated. At our Friday staff meeting he challenged us to each think up one suggestion for boosting attendance, which we'd report back next week.

I thought that was the end of his agenda, but he sucker-punched us with a list of detailed cleanup tasks. Rich and Blake were forced to cooperate in straightening up the tunnel, which had gotten sloppy as the season wore on. Carson, Jenna, and Shannon had litter duty outside the park. And I got stuck with the rat-bat tower, along with Emma, Peanut, and Spanky. The shipment of team logo baseballs for our upcoming ball-night giveaway had arrived late Thursday afternoon, when Don was the only one around to unlock the storage unit. He'd been dismayed by the conditions. He handed us a collection of supplies, including a snow shovel and a box of contractor-strength garbage bags, and told us to clean "down to the slab floor."

We raided the tunnel for lighting sources and hiked across the street. When the door creaked open, I stretched up on my tiptoes, feeling for the spike nail in the cinder-block wall above with the handle of my lantern. The back of my hand brushed a thick beard of cobwebs, setting every hair from my fingers up to my neck at attention.

"Ugh." I yanked my arm down and snapped my wrist hard to shake away the clammy tickle.

"What?" Emma gasped behind me.

"It's nothing. Just a spider web."

She took a tentative step across the threshold, leaving one foot planted firmly in the brilliant sun outside as her eyes acclimated to the dim light indoors. Only a short shock of blonde hair peeked out from the green bandana she'd secured over her head. Peanut squeezed between her and the door frame, playing his powerful flashlight off the far wall. Its beam disrupted a napping bat, sending him wobbling across the ceiling and up the stairwell.

Emma's shrieks drowned out the squeals of the fleeing tower dweller. Ever-sympathetic Peanut laughed so hard he coughed up a pink wad of bubble gum. There was no five-second rule in the tower.

"I can't do this, y'all," Emma moaned. She clamped her arms around my midsection, cinching them so tight I could feel each of her fingers individually gripping my stomach. "Please don't make me spend the day in here."

I led her back out into the sunshine, where she waited as the rest of us conducted a thorough pest patrol. Aside from a dead rat, which Spanky bagged with the casual expertise of an Orkin man, our search turned up nothing. We broke the room down into quarters, clearing each in turn, scraping the mounds of bat guano from the damp concrete floor and assessing the merchandise. The cardboard on many of the boxes had decomposed to the point our fingers punched through when we tried to pick them up. Several resisted our efforts to slide them across the floor, having been cemented in place by time. We deemed much of the merchandise worthless and noted the wasted inventory on a pad Don had given us. With frequent fresh-air breaks, we made it through the first floor with no physical sickness to report.

After lunch it was on to the second story, which was more of the same, only stuccoed with a layer of pigeon shit. We brought it up to standard shortly before three. Spanky headed up another flight to scout the third floor.

"No way, amigo," Peanut said. "I got places to go and people to see. It's gonna take me an hour to shower this funk off already."

"Hot date tonight?" I asked.

"Hell, yeah. Dinner and a movie, and prob'ly a lot more."

"Yeah, right," Spanky said, descending the stairs, having been overruled on advancing to the next level. "Does this chick have a mustache like the last one?"

"Shut up, punk." Peanut thrust the festering shovel toward Spanky, who ducked behind Emma. "She's a sophisticated college girl. Very attractive."

"Are we done in here, y'all?" Emma was looking to escape both the lingering stench of rodent urine and the battle between our teenage co-workers. "I'm heading outside."

I flung a trash bag over my shoulder and followed her downstairs. "Where'd you meet this girl?" I asked, when Peanut came down.

"Party last weekend at a friend's. Lots of hotties."

"If things go really well and you reach a point where you don't know what to do, maybe Spanky can coach you through it."

"Har-de-har-har."

"I'm just saying Spanky's been around the block a few times. Right, Spank?"

Spanky grinned broadly and folded his arms across his chest, like a young man with proud secrets to guard.

"No, y'all, that's horrible," Emma said. "You have not, Spanky? Have you?"

The youth blushed and looked away, then shook his head, acknowledging she was correct.

"Don't go and do that stuff yet, Spanky," she pleaded. "Save yourself for the right girl."

"Yeah, Spank," I said. "Save yourself like Peanut has."

"Shut up, man," Peanut protested from inside, where he was collecting the lanterns. "Why would you assume that?"

His hands were visibly twitching as he handed the lights down. Guys never like to talk about their virginity, especially when there are women nearby.

"You can tell," I assured him.

"Well, you're wrong. Very much wrong."

His discomfort was nothing compared to Emma's. Attempting to ignore our conversation, she struggled to lift a bag of bat waste into the bed of my truck, which I'd parked outside the tower after lunch. I locked the door and hustled down to help her. We loaded the bags two deep and hauled them to the dumpster in the stadium parking lot, completing one of the most distasteful chores of the summer.

"So, what about you?" I asked Emma, as we walked back to the office.

Furrowing her spider-web-encrusted brow, she wagged her forefinger at me. "Don't be crude, Lane. I told everyone before I was saving myself."

"Not that," I laughed. "I meant, what are you doing tonight?"

"Oh." She cracked an embarrassed smile, and shrugged her shoulders slightly. "No plans."

"Ballgame? Burlington and Greensboro are both home. Your choice."

She chose Greensboro. I picked her up at six and we drove Interstate 40 west. We parked across the street from War Memorial Stadium and breezed in through the pass gate. After watching the first three innings from behind the plate, we moved down to the cheap seats in left field for a different vantage. Greensboro's park was one of the oldest in the minor leagues, even older than Durham's, and wide open with tons of foul ground. Down the line where we sat it felt like the game was a mile away. Or maybe that was just in my head. As we walked back to the car, I slipped my hand around Emma's. I might as well have been in eighth grade for the thrill that gave me, but after Trina it felt good to walk in baby steps.

Don looked like he was going to cry when we met Monday morning to go over our brilliant stretch-run ideas. A second Chicken night (good luck planning that one). An old-timers game (see previous comment). Emma got a little warmer with Church Bulletin Night, though with only two more Sunday games slated, it was a little late to get the ball rolling on that classic. My apprehension grew with every pained sigh that escaped Don's lips.

"Um." I felt every eye in the room on my face as I cleared my throat. "I know we kind of do stuff with Duke already, but I was thinking of a College Night thing when school starts back up."

"That's been so done," Blake sneered from the far end of the table. He was still smarting from Don's out-of-hand rejection of his mud-wrestling match. "Be original."

"It's better than yours," I countered.

"Give it a rest, guys." Don tightened the tortured grip on his thinning hair. "Continue, Lane."

"Well, I was figuring maybe we could get a band out front before the game. Someone popular with the college radio stations." I traded glances with Rich, who nodded, probably wishing he'd thought of the idea. His Circus Night suggestion had earned a stinging "some of you guys didn't put much thought into this" from Don.

"And maybe all the between-inning games could be battles between representatives of the local schools," I said. Seeing Don stroking his chin as if he didn't hate the idea, I started improvising. "We could even challenge the schools with some kind of prize for who turns out the biggest crowd..."

"I like it," Don said. "Flesh it out a little and get back to me."

I ran for the phone the moment he adjourned the meeting, desperate to track down Cole. The best I could do was leave a message with his dad, who was lounging by the pool in the back yard, talking on a portable phone that sounded like it had been dropped in. "Don't forget," I pleaded. "Don't worry, Lane," he assured me. If I had a nickel for every message Cole missed when we were growing up I could have hired the guy a secretary.

When I hung the phone up I found Emma standing in the doorway of our office, leafing through a stack of paper.

"You seen the fax from the Braves today?" she asked.

"The media notes?"

"Yeah. It wasn't in my box. Or yours."

"I didn't get it. You need it for the game notes?"

She tabbed through her faxes once again, licking her finger as she flipped the pages.

"Nah," she finally said. "I've got enough else here."

"How'd Paul do last night?"

Emma pulled the Macon fax from the middle of her pile and scanned it quickly. "Went two-for-four. Pair of singles and a stolen base. He's on a roll."

"Sure is." I slid the top drawer of my desk open and pulled out a weathered sheet of notebook paper. "By my calculations he's hitting .310 since the beginning of June."

Emma snatched a pen off the corner of the desk and scribbled a note on the top of her fax. "Thanks. I'll use that."

Engrossed in her notes, she nearly collided with Ashandra on her way out. The office manager snorted loudly and glared after her as she walked away. When Emma had disappeared Ashandra turned back to me. "Your flags are here."

To celebrate Boy Scout Night we had ordered 500 mini U.S. flags for the kids to hold as they paraded onto the field for the national anthem. I spent the bulk of the afternoon tearing boxes open and neatly stacking the flags on a foldup table in the main concourse. Shortly after the gates opened I was swarmed by boys in blue and brown uniforms, clutching and grabbing and knocking flags to the ground. The support sticks, topped with a sharp point, quickly became weapons. Sword duels broke out on my left and right. When the red-faced scout leaders and pleading den moms restored order, I marshaled the troops down to the field, where we found Martin Harcourt and Dom Verotto waiting.

Ignoring the occasional side skirmish, Martin welcomed the boys and shared how he had been involved with scouting for eleven years, rising to the rank of Eagle Scout in high school. Dom hadn't made it quite as far, though his father was still a troop leader back home in New Jersey. After their opening remarks they fielded some baseball questions from the kids and Dom let a few of them swing his bat as he offered pointers on their stances. With Jenna's help I ushered the kids off the diamond at five after seven to prepare for their grand entrance. As we marched past the dugout I spotted Dom's friend with the shiny shirt leaning casually against the railing, working his teeth with a gold toothpick and chatting with a couple of the Bulls.

A color guard comprising four older scouts carrying full-sized flags led the parade back onto the field. The younger boys weaved in and out of line brandishing broken mini flags as their troop leaders barked threats through clenched teeth. Undisciplined as they were up close, from the grandstand it was sheer choreographic genius. The stadium hummed with the sound of proud parents snapping keepsake photos.

Once the kids cleared off the field they were no longer my headache. I swung by the press box to catch my breath and slam a slice of pizza. I'd just leaned back in my seat when my radio crackled to life.

"Hey, Laner," Rich buzzed. "You there?"

"Yeah."

"Switch to channel eight."

We carried out side conversations on an alternative frequency so as not to raise Don's ire. Channel 7 was for official business only.

"What's up?"

"You sitting down?"

"I am actually. Why?"

"We got a Becca sighting to report."

"No shit?"

I walked to the door of the press box as Emma and the beat reporters observed.

"Where's she sitting?" I asked after a quick scan of the crowd turned up nothing.

"About the third, fourth row back, just behind the screen."

I peered out the door again. This time I spotted Trina sitting a couple sections down from the dugout. Her teased-out hair splayed over her bare shoulders and her elbow rested atop the muscular forearm of Dom's mysterious buddy.

"I got her," I said. "You notice who she was with?"

"Thought you'd like that."

"What's going on?" asked Emma, who had joined me at the door.

"Oh, nothing. Trina's here. We're just trying to figure out who's the guy she's with."

I tore my eyes off my ex and found Emma staring into the crowd, not necessarily focusing on Trina so much as avoiding looking at me.

"Why does it matter?" she asked.

"Doesn't really. But I bet she was seeing him before we broke up."

I moved away from the opening and plunked down in the seat next to Matt Hamer, who hopped up and took my spot at the door.

"Who are we talking about here?" the Durham beat writer inquired. "Point her out."

"That bimbo in the fourth row, about four sections down from here." Emma pointed her finger straight at Trina.

"Bimbo?" I laughed.

"Well, isn't she?"

"Yeah, kind of. I just didn't think you used words like that."

"Words like what? Bimbo's not a bad word."

"But you're so … *nice.*"

"I know that guy," Matt cut in. "Used to play quarterback at Chapel Hill High."

"What's his name?"

"Landon Dowager. You know the Dowager family?"

I shook my head.

"Loaded. His old man's got money falling out his ass. I think the grandpa or great-grandpa hit it rich after the Depression when the stocks bounced back. Landon's dad's a lawyer or CPA or something like that."

"What's Landon do?" Emma asked.

"Nothing. He's a playboy. Dropped out of college when he never got off the bench. He had a football ride to Wake Forest. They tried to convert him to a slot receiver, but he didn't have the hands."

"Must be nice."

"Yup," Matt said. "He's got money. That's probably why she likes him."

"He can have her. I'll consider myself lucky if I can make it through the night without running into her."

My good fortune ran out in the top of the seventh. I was hiking up from the tunnel, where I'd hid out for a bit after serving my watch, when Trina popped out of the women's room. I tried to pretend I didn't see her, but she grabbed me by the elbow and foiled my plan. It wasn't realistic anyway. My head naturally jerked in her direction when I saw that much bare skin. By the time I realized who it was I'd already been nabbed.

"Hey," I said. "Look who's here."

"Hi, Lane." She smiled and spread her arms. I stepped forth into the obligatory phony hug and quickly separated.

"What a surprise. You enjoying the game?"

"Sure are. We've got great seats."

"We?"

"We." Her smile wasn't nearly as malicious as I'd pictured it in my head. "Me and Landon."

"Oh, great. I hope you guys are having a wonderful time."

"You wanna meet him? You might like him. He's a big baseball fan. He knows a lot of the players."

"I would. But I was on my way up to the ticket office. They're running low on tickets—or something." I winced, but she didn't know enough to realize I was freelancing and it passed unchallenged. "Maybe another time."

When we parted at the top of the stairs I lingered, admiring her ass as she worked her way down toward the field in her three-inch heels. I made no effort to hide it, so I shouldn't have been shocked to have gotten caught. Still, my heart nearly burst through my ribs when a meaty paw clamped down on my shoulder.

"I can't believe you let her get away," Johnny Layne gummed. "That's a damn fine piece right there, boy."

"I didn't let her get away. I escaped."

Johnny cocked an eyebrow at me and grabbed my chin. "You ain't goin' queer on me, are you, son?"

"What is it with you old guys? You and my grandpa both. Man, he had a thing for her."

I broke free of Johnny's grasp when we reached the concourse and made my way across the street up to the Ballpark Corner store, where I laid low until the game ended. When the stadium had cleared I rendezvoused with Rich at the keg and listened to his f-bomb-enriched description of the moment he discovered Trina was in the house. He was playing the crowd when a dour-faced Don interrupted and informed us there had been another report of players losing money from their lockers during the game.

"This is getting out of hand," Rich said.

"It's past out of hand," Don replied. "Arnie is threatening to kill our affiliation if this doesn't end."

"What are you going to do?"

"For starters, we'll station an officer outside the tunnel."

"I tell you no one came through there tonight," Rich insisted. "One of us was down there the entire time. When I went onto the field, Lane took my watch."

"I don't know what to say," Don said. "It happened. I wish to God it hadn't, but it did."

CHAPTER TWENTY-THREE

Rich shushed me twice on the short drive home. Before I even cut the engine, he sprinted up the steps and through the front door, leaving me shaking my head in the driveway. By the time I entered the house he'd ripped his swimsuit calendar off the kitchen wall and was stooped over the table with a black marker in his hand. He flipped June to July and back again, marking X's on the days where locker-room incidents had occurred. At last he capped his pen and threw it on the table in disgust.

"What?" I asked, when I finally dared to break the silence.

"I was hoping there'd be more of a pattern here. These are just three kind of random days."

I grabbed the corner of the calendar and pulled it toward me. After analyzing his notes for a moment I asked, "What would a pattern have done for you?"

"Duh. We would have known when Goose would strike again."

"Are you still sure it's Goose? He's been robbed too, remember."

Rich popped the door of the fridge open and pulled out a dubious pitcher of tea, raising it to the light to check the bottom for sediment.

"Want some?"

"If that's the best we've got."

"It's all we got."

He lifted two glasses out of the dish drainer and emptied the pitcher.

"Goose is the only one to get hit all three times," he resumed. "Isn't that a little convenient?"

"So you said before."

"I still think it's a setup to throw everyone off."

"How do we prove it?"

"We need some shinier Goose bait. Our wallet was a dud.

Goose knew that was an empty locker so he never bothered to look there."

"Can I have my forty bucks back?"

"If it's still there tomorrow it's all yours. But be thinking of a replacement."

"What good's that gonna do if all we got is a dead locker?"

Rich took a long pull on his tea, swishing it around in his mouth for a moment before spitting it into the sink. "This shit is awful."

No argument from me. It was tart and smelled more like turpentine than I preferred my tea to smell. I followed suit and dumped my glass.

"We need a guy on the inside," Rich said. "I was thinking of asking Dom Verotto or maybe Roger Gale."

"Better yet, when I saw Paul in Fayetteville he said he thought J.T. Gaines would help us if we asked him."

"I don't really know him that well."

"Paul roomed with him in training camp. He said J.T. couldn't stand Goose."

"He could be our guy then. We need something to plant, though."

"I've got one idea. I'll see what I can do tomorrow."

"We've got time. Nothing's gonna happen the rest of the week."

"How do you know?"

"Goose might be a mouth-breathing jackass, but he's not stupid. He'll wait for the furor to die back down a little."

Securing our new Goose bait was my top priority Tuesday morning. Nervous about making any Operation Gander calls from our office, I hastened across the street to the Ballpark Corner store promptly at eleven to relieve Faith for her lunch break. When I got there I found the door bolted and a little note taped to the glass: "Back in 20 minutes." After pacing in front of the entrance for a moment I gave up and headed back down to the park. Just as I reached the main gate, Peanut turned the corner in front of the shop. I waited for him as he skipped across the street.

"Where you been, man?"

"Why?" he asked. "Someone looking for me?"

"No. I was looking for Faith, though, and the store was locked."

"It's open." He pointed up to the blue and orange building. "I just walked past."

Something didn't calculate. I had too much on my mind to crack Peanut, however, so I let him slide. The door was indeed unlocked. Faith glanced up from her paperback romance novel and smiled when I entered, just as she did every morning. Had I not spied the note on the counter by her elbow I might have convinced myself I'd imagined it all. I studied her through the window as she backed her car out of the driveway, then took a seat at her desk and made my call.

Rich and I began watching for J.T. shortly after two, wanting to catch him before he entered the clubhouse. When he arrived we enticed him into joining us for a short tour of the right-field picnic area. He proved amenable to our plan, and I handed over the faux Rolex that my old boss Andy had so kindly loaned to the cause. J.T. agreed to advertise it for a day, then stash it in his locker Wednesday night.

Every night the rest of the homestand he checked in with us on his way out. "Watch is still there," he'd say. He seemed almost disappointed, but Rich wasn't surprised. While many were quick to credit the increased security outside the clubhouse, Rich felt sure it was only a matter of timing.

In one sense I was glad of the mystery. It captured the imagination of our co-workers, allowing me a little room to pester Emma without popping onto the radar. If anyone was gossiping about our lunch dates it didn't reach me. Though Monday was an off-day we kept our lunch streak going. I talked her into a picnic at West Point on the Eno with surprisingly little effort. Her co-worker dating policy wasn't as stringent as originally advertised.

The park encompasses a two-mile stretch of the Eno River up in North Durham. We used to take class trips every spring back in grammar school. One year we did a play about the woods in the amphitheatre there. I was a tree. My only line was, "I provide oxygen so you can breathe." Somehow I flubbed it. I guess that's why I was a tree and not a beaver like Rich, who had seventeen lines and got his picture in the newspaper.

I recreated our school tour as best I remembered it, leading Emma through the West Point Mill, which dated back to the Revolutionary War. We poked around some of the other buildings for a while, then spread our meal out on a picnic table next to the river. After lunch we loitered on the bridge over the sluice, watching the waterwheel slowly creak its way around. Emma spotted a great blue heron on the other side of the river, and we crossed the bridge and softly treaded through the underbrush to get a closer look. He took no notice of us, staring intently into the slow-moving water, scouting for his own midday meal. We'd been perched on the bank for a few silent minutes when he rewarded our patience by piercing the mirror-like surface and ripping a small fish from the stream. He downed his lunch with a gulp and took to the air a moment later, lifting off gracefully, the tips of his wings grazing the water as they flapped.

We toured the trails on the north side of the river for an hour, then traversed the bridge and entered the woods on the south side. When we'd had enough of the forest, we trekked along the river's edge, stopping occasionally to watch yellowbelly turtles basking on a downed tree, lined up end to end like cars in a traffic jam, each driver craning his neck as if to see over the shell ahead. A low, slow point, littered with large, friendly rocks served as our path to a small mass of land in the river. We explored this island as if we'd discovered it, though it was clearly visible from the picnic table where we'd eaten our lunch. The blistering August sun drew the perspiration from my pores as we rested on a smooth, round boulder. I peeled my shoes and socks off and dangled my feet in the cooling stream. Emma followed suit, and we sat on our rock, lost to the rest of the world.

"I could stay here awhile," she said, breaking a long silence. "It's so soothing and beautiful."

"I'm in no hurry." I lifted my feet from the numbing water, triggering a series of soft plups as the nearby turtles slid off their log into the river. When my ankles had thawed enough to regain some color I dropped them back in.

"Everything's a hurry sometimes," she said. "The summer's gone by so fast. Two weeks from now I'll be back in school."

"Shhhh." I put my finger over her lips. Withdrawing it, I leaned down, eyes closed, and found her mouth with mine. She anticipated the move, parting her soft lips slightly and tilting her head. I'd never waited so long to kiss someone, and I didn't want it to end. I held it as long as was comfortable. When we parted, her unblinking eyes searched my face, seeking reassurance I wasn't toying with her. She must have found it, because she leaned back in for a second go-round. We spent the better part of the next hour growing familiar on our rock of solitude.

A couple of children splashing in the river nearby broke the mood. After they invaded our island we crossed the stone trail back to the bank. Emma had plans to meet her aunt and uncle for dinner, so we meandered back through the park, stopping frequently to reenact the first kiss. In the car she regained her decorum, slapping my hand away when it landed on her knee.

"I'm driving, y'all. Be careful."

We laughed easily all the way home, savoring the waning moments of a precious afternoon. When she dropped me off I waved good-bye from the porch steps and slumped against the pillar, where I lounged until Rich pushed the screen door open. He sat down next to me.

"How'd it go?"

I recounted my afternoon, minus the good parts, and he chucked me on the arm.

"This one just might work, Laner. She's the anti-Trina. I like her. Don't fuck it up."

I made my rounds Tuesday morning, swinging by Emma's desk on some false pretense, drinking in the lilac vapors as she twirled the hair above her ear. A summer of growth had begun to tame her mane, which was long enough now to lie flat most of the time. Whispering in a poor attempt to conceal our alliance, we made plans for dinner.

The next two nights were a blur of Mexican restaurants, a trip to the planetarium, a stroll across the UNC campus, two rounds of miniature golf, and ice cream on Ninth Street near Duke. We tripped up the sidewalk sucking on our cones as Wednesday evening wound down, window shopping for obsolete home remedies at McDonald's Drug Store and scouting out potential lunch spots.

"I got my schedule today," Emma said, when we dropped to a bench to finish our rapidly melting dessert. "It's gonna be a tough semester."

"I'm so glad I'm done with all that." I dabbed a napkin at the sticky chocolate congealing on my wrist. "My last year felt like it took forever."

She crunched the tip of her waffle cone and licked her fingertips clean. "I love school, ya know. I just don't want it to start."

"Yeah." I balled my crusty napkin up and batted it with my hand until she snatched it out of the air. Two minutes elapsed before I put voice to the thought running through both of our brains. "We have to take advantage of the time we have left together."

She nodded. I leaned over to kiss her, but she didn't lift her face, instead turning away to hide her rising tears.

"Are we doing the right thing, Lane?"

"Going out, you mean? Sure feels right to me. Or did you mean—"

"No," she paused and wiped her eye with her napkin. "That's what I meant, going out. I'm having fun. I really am. I just wonder about the future."

Emma rallied Thursday morning, greeting me with a stack of faxes and a sleepy smile. We lassoed Rich into joining us for lunch and made a festive party of three. As they chatted across the table I couldn't help but note the contrast from my time with Trina, and I wondered if Landon's friends were missing him at lunch these days.

Back at work, Emma and I collaborated on planning a booster club trip to Lynchburg the following weekend. When Don asked for volunteers I nearly sprained my elbow throwing my hand up. Emma didn't have so much at stake, but she poured herself into it all the same, drawing up flyers on the computer and authoring the announcement for Nick to read over the PA throughout the homestand.

We teamed up again when the gates opened Monday night, manning a table in the concourse where fans could sign up for Saturday's trip. There was room on the bus for sixty, including us. Randy Munn reserved a space for himself and his mother. The Ryans broke out their checkbook and held two seats. By the time the game started we had filled over half the bus. My only problem was I didn't know what to do with the money. Don had told me to hold it until all the signups were done because he didn't want it getting mixed in with the game-night bank. I wound up stashing a wad of cash and checks under a notebook in my desk drawer before I left for the night. Rich berated me all the way home for not locking it in the office safe, which I didn't even know existed. "With everything that's going on lately, that's a free shot for anyone who stumbles onto it," he lectured.

I memorized the cracks in my ceiling that night. Every time I closed my eyes Don appeared asking for the bus trip money. Sometimes I'd recognize him right off, other times he'd start out as someone else, lurking in the hazy corners of my dream before revealing himself. He fired me at least a dozen times before the sun came up.

There were only two cars in the stadium lot when I arrived Tuesday morning, a new course record from our house to the park under my belt. I jogged through the entrance and took the stairs to the office trailer in one leap, ripping the door open so forcefully a muffled pop echoed off the walls as they adjusted to the sudden change in air pressure. Across the room Blake stood frozen, like a raccoon caught in the unwelcome glare of a motion-activated floodlight.

"Hey, man," he said, his eyes as round as twin moons. "You're here early."

"Yeah, I had to take care of something. What you up to?"

"Nothin'. Just hadda send in a perscription for some sinus meds."

He shifted his body as I approached, keeping himself directly between me and the fax machine. I brushed past him into our office. After offering up a quick and muddled prayer, I slid the bottom drawer of my desk open. Everything was as I'd left it, the signup sheet and money nestled safe in their hiding spot.

The trailer door opened and closed. I strained to hear whether someone had entered or Blake had left. All was silent. I shoved the money into my front pocket and shuffled down the hall to check the fax machine. A long roll of paper cascaded over the edge of the table down to the floor where it looped and doubled back over itself. I scrolled up until I found the Macon report. Paul had gone

3-for-4 with a double and a homer, and there was a note about his thirty-one game errorless streak coming to an end in the eighth inning.

The machine made a series of three short beeps and began humming loudly as another page was printed. The words "ERROR REPORT" across the top caught my eye.

"Send failed," it read, followed by a time stamp. In miniature below there was a copy of a hand-scrawled message:

"LD – hears this wks order:

#1 – 5 doz.

#2 – 10

Also, put $40 on Terry Norris Sat., and $25 on Rusty on Sun. Thats all I feel good abt this week. Still can't get myself to put anything on preseason football.

See you tonite, B"

Sinus meds, my ass. Blake was faxing in his bets. Or trying, anyway.

I showed it to Rich when he came in and he went all Sherlock Holmes on me. Only unlike Sherlock Holmes, he had no answers.

"How do you bet five dozen on something?" I asked.

"Maybe that's code for sixty bucks. You know, five times twelve."

"Why didn't he use code on the rest of it?"

"Cause he's a dipshit."

"Maybe, but who's LD?"

Rich thought for a minute, then shrugged. "We had this kid working part time last year, Dick Hamrick. We all called him Little Dick. Maybe—"

"And did he like being called Little Dick?"

"Not particularly, no."

"So maybe LD ain't what someone would call him, if they were faxing him."

"Maybe not," he admitted.

After about twenty minutes of that we stashed the error report in the bottom drawer of the desk and got on with our work day.

Emma beautified our booster club table, decorating it with balloons and streamers to give it more eye appeal as fans poured through the gates. We did garner more attention, but most of it came from people wondering what we were giving away. I wasn't an accomplished enough salesman to talk a freebie seeker into parting with $50 for a bus trip, and they inevitably drifted on without signing up. They had a harder time turning Emma down and would at least engage her in conversation for a while before making their excuses and heading off to their seats.

"This is tough, y'all," she said, after all but closing the deal with a young couple. "We're never gonna fill that bus."

"We're all right. We've sold enough spots to cover our expenses. The rest is gravy."

"Well, in that case," she laughed, leaning back in her seat and resting her feet on the corner of the table, "I'm done with the hard sell approach."

"You can't quit on me."

"I hit my quota yesterday."

She reached over to tickle my ear. I squirmed out of the way and responded with a pinch of her side. "St-o-p-p-p," she giggled. "No fair. You have longer arms." Emma dove back at me and I caught her wrist, causing her to lose her balance and slide off her chair. She collapsed in a fit of laughter on the concrete. As I pulled her up she abruptly turned serious and sat primly in her seat.

"Hello, Alton," she said.

I turned and found her childhood friend staring agape, his cowlick saluting us from atop his head. He made no effort to speak and I wondered how long he'd been standing there.

"Hey, Alton." I stood and extended my hand. "I didn't know you were coming."

He ignored me and glared through Emma, his dark eyes hardened like coals. "So it's true."

Emma clenched her jaw and tried to return his black look, but it plumb wasn't in her nature. Her eyes softened momentarily. She glanced up at me, then back at him. "So what's true?"

"What's going on?" I asked.

"I think you know better than I do," Alton replied.

He spun away and fought like a salmon through the stream of incoming fans. We watched him push his way toward the gate, weaving around the turnstile past a confused Harvey. The ticket taker yelled after him for a moment, then shrugged emphatically and resumed ushering folks into the park.

"What is going on?" I asked Emma when Alton was out of sight.

"Apparently I'm being stalked. I don't know how else to explain it."

"But why?"

"Lord knows, Lane," she sighed. "I don't understand him."

She excused herself and slipped off into the trailer, leaving me to piece together the mystery of Alton Hobgood, IV. I was at a distinct disadvantage, knowing only what they themselves had told me of their history, and I made no headway. My thoughts were reclaimed by work when Nick's first booster club announcement brought me a couple of customers. An inning later I packed the table up and migrated down to the tunnel to seek Rich's counsel.

He wasn't any help, though he had plenty to say about Alton, a.k.a. Freak, Nutbag, Windbag, Douchebag, and Gomer. "That kid weirded me out from the start," he said several times as we monitored traffic in and out of the clubhouse. There wasn't much. Only Dom Verotto and Andy Mills passed through the tunnel.

Rich grabbed his drag mat and made ready to hit the field when the William Tell Overture sounded. I leaned against the fence watching the crew rush onto the diamond. My stomach somersaulted when I spotted Goose Grascyk marching in from the bullpen.

The great flaw in our plan was we had no way of knowing what was going on inside the locker room. So what if someone took our watch. How could we prove it? We'd discussed stashing Spanky in the laundry cart to spy throughout the game, but decided we couldn't trust him to keep his mouth shut. With Tom Sawyer busy across the diamond Huck Finn improvised. Tiptoeing through the shadows of the tunnel I slipped in the clubhouse door behind the burly right-hander. As Goose marched toward the john I flattened myself against the wall, stealing forward slowly and silently to the corner. Venturing out just far enough to peer around the edge I came face to face with an irate gorilla in a Bulls uniform.

"I thought I warned you, man." He pounced forward, grabbing me by the front of my shirt. "What the fuck are you doing in here?"

His breath reeked of sunflower seeds; beneath his curled lip his gums were packed solid with gray husks. He twisted my collar so tight the skin on my neck was caught in with it. I clamped my fingers around his wrist and pushed, every muscle in my stomach tightening as I fought to free myself. But his one arm was stronger than both mine together. Goose slammed me back into the wall, my head ricocheting off the cinder block with a hollow "tock," like a coconut bouncing off a sidewalk.

"You're either in here to steal more shit from my locker or to watch me take a piss. Either way I'm disturbed by your presence."

Slumped against the base of the wall, I fumbled in my back pocket for my walkie-talkie, never tearing my gaze from a right foot that was poised to strike forward into my ribs.

"It's not like that, Goose."

"How is it then? You're a thief or a faggot. Or maybe both."

He leaned down and grabbed my left ear, pinching it tight in his fingers as he lifted me from the floor. Reason and talk were going to lead nowhere. I took a swing with my left hand, skipping a harmless blow off his thigh that only managed to piss him off further. He kneed me hard in the gut and I collapsed again. By rolling onto my side I was able to lift the radio to my mouth.

"Help," I rasped. "Clubhouse. Hel—"

Goose punted the radio from my hand. My best hope was to somehow get to my feet and scramble. I knew I was quicker than he was. If I could just put something in between us I could buy some time. As he lifted his leg for another kick I spun around and jabbed my right foot into his groin. He staggered back a step and I rolled away, pushing unsteadily to my feet.

Goose recovered quickly and was only a step behind as I reached the laundry cart. Not having quite enough room to get behind it, I circled the wheeled basket, spurred on by the hot breath on my neck. He stopped suddenly as his pea brain hatched a plan. Grabbing the side of the cart he rammed it straight at me, pinning me between it and the wall. The handle dug into my midsection, knocking the wind and fight out of me. Goose grinned as he pulled the cart back and slammed it forward again. I tried fending it off with my outstretched hands, but he was just too strong. The last thing I saw before my head connected with the wall again was Rich, Sonny, and Officer Pickett, one of the park's Durham PD regulars, burst into the clubhouse.

I felt like I'd been out for an hour when I opened my eyes, but it had actually been less than a minute. Sonny and Officer Pickett had moved Goose a safe distance away and were holding him back as Rich knelt over me. A moment later Don stumped in, followed by Captain DesJardins. Goose pointed to me and bellowed, "There's your thief!"

"Say what?" Rich snapped. "Goose is the one who's been stealing from his teammates. Just like he did in Macon."

Goose did a double take. "How'd you know about Macon?" he demanded. "I lost almost five hundred bucks there in April."

"Shut it," Captain DesJardins yelled at both of them. He ordered Goose back to the bench by his locker and turned to us.

"Why are you boys in here?" he sighed.

"I followed Goose in," I said, massaging the lump on the back of my head. "Wanted to catch him … in the act."

Rich drifted over to the far wall in front of J.T. Gaines' locker. "A-ha!" he cried. "It's gone!"

"What's gone?" the captain asked.

"The Rolex. It's missing. J.T. said he left it on the top shelf of his locker."

Goose pawed in his bag, yanking out a wallet. "I'm missing a hundred bucks," he cried. He slammed his billfold into his locker and surged forth, catching Sonny and Officer Pickett by surprise. They clung to him as he steamed across the room, like tacklers riding a running back who refuses to go down.

"Stop acting like an ass," Don shouted, halting the beast in his tracks. I'd almost forgotten Don was there, he'd been such a non-factor to that point. "You've got two choices, Goose. Either go back to the bullpen for the rest of the game, or go to the police station while we sort this mess out."

The hulking reliever returned to the field under the watch of Officer Pickett. Captain DesJardins summoned two more officers to contain the clubhouse until after the game. Rich and I came clean on our sting operation, telling Don and the police captain all we knew about the thefts in Macon and why we suspected Goose. I thought Don was going to bite through his bottom lip before we could finish. After a deep sigh and a shake of his head he actually chuckled for a moment, then told us that while he admired our creativity, if we ever did anything like that again he'd fire us on the spot. We went about our business the best we could for the remainder of the game, knowing that someone would be unmasked when it was over.

Don waylaid Gordy after the conclusion of the Bulls' 6-3 loss. They whispered at the entrance to the clubhouse as two Durham police officers stood by like stone idols guarding an ancient tomb. A murmur rose among the players huddled in the tunnel waiting to enter their locker room. I should have been up in the main concourse, but I was too curious to see how this would play out. Finally Gordy gave the players the okay to enter.

Forty-five long minutes later, the door opened and Don emerged.

"Well," Sonny greeted him. "What happened?"

"We got our man," Don said with a grim smile.

"Goose?" I suggested, as we crowded around our leader.

"No." Don shook his head. "He didn't do it. It was Dominic Verotto."

"Dom Verotto?" I exclaimed. "Are you sure?"

"The money, the watch, and a gold bracelet were found in the bottom of his bag."

"Are you sure he wasn't set up?" Rich asked.

"It was him. He confessed it in Gordy's office. He's apologizing to his teammates now."

"But why?" I asked. "He just threw his career away."

"He had some issues. He's got a gambling problem, for one. High-stakes poker. Boxing. NASCAR. He got in a hole and had to cover his losses."

Rich emitted a long, low whistle and Don excused himself. The players began filing out in twos and threes, whispering among themselves. J.T. Gaines paused as he passed by.

"You were close, bro," he said. "Macon guy. Wrong Macon guy, but you were onto something."

"Yeah," Rich said. "Still kinda wish it had been Goose."

J.T. laughed and slapped him on the shoulder, then continued on his way. I heard the clubhouse door bang open and turned to see Goose emerge. Not wishing for an encore, I retreated a couple of steps to the mouth of the tunnel.

"Hey," he called. "Hold on a second."

Rich stepped between us as the pitcher approached. Nine times out of ten when a raging maniac appeared I had his back. Tonight my self-preservation instinct kicked in and I took another step toward the exit, figuring Rich deserved a shot or two for having been so convinced it was Goose in the first place.

"Hey, man," Goose said, staring through Rich at me. "I, uh, I'm sorry for what happened in the locker."

He extended his arm, offering a conciliatory handshake. I wondered if it were some trick to get me within punching range, but I took a chance and grabbed it.

"I, well, I snapped. I've lost a thousand bucks from my locker this year, and, well, man, I just didn't think it could be one of my teammates, so I suspected you guys."

"Fair enough," I shrugged. "We suspected you."

Goose chuckled, releasing my hand and offering his to Rich, who took it briefly.

"No hard feelings?" Goose said.

"Nah." I waved my right hand through the air. "No hard feelings."

He was still an arrogant bastard, but at least he wasn't trying to kill me anymore.

CHAPTER TWENTY-FOUR

Up until Tuesday night no one had a bad thing to say about Dom Verotto. The stories in the morning papers played up his long Boy Scout career and featured quotes that started, "He seemed like such a nice guy …" Stunning though it was, the news was a tremendous relief to everyone in the ballpark, most especially Don, who sprang for donuts and greeted us as we arrived to work Wednesday morning.

"I thought I told you to leave the heavyweights alone," he kidded as I dug a maple twist out of the box. "Even Dom wouldn't have taken you at a thousand to one."

I was too preoccupied with Alton's visit to completely enjoy myself. The strain grew as the morning elapsed with no sign of Emma. She finally rolled into work around ten-thirty, looking like she hadn't slept all night. She weaved through a small crowd in the concourse, not making eye contact with anyone, and disappeared into the trailer. I followed her in a few minutes later.

"I don't know," she mumbled when I asked her what was going on. "I don't really feel like talking about it now. I need to get the game notes done."

"Maybe we can talk at lunchtime," I suggested.

Emma massaged the bags under her eyes with her fingers and shifted in her chair so she was facing the computer. "I'm not sure about lunch. Let me get back to you."

I withdrew and left her a wide berth the rest of the morning, checking back into the trailer again at noon to learn she'd already slipped out.

"I don't know what's going on with that one," Ashandra said. "She got a phone call about half an hour ago, didn't hardly say two words, then hung up and walked right out the door."

By the time she returned I'd given up looking for her. She sought me out as I was painting over some graffiti on the third-base souvenir stand.

"Hey," she said. "Sorry about lunch."

"It's all right. I went with Rich."

She cracked her lips into a smile as if it hurt and I noticed she'd applied makeup to her swollen eyes.

"I'll go with you tomorrow."

"The last lunch." My stomach knotted and I wished I hadn't said that.

She didn't respond. The scratching of the bristles as I dabbed the paintbrush over the gang hieroglyphics on the door took the place of our conversation. The fresh coat contrasted sharply against the existing blue, which had faded over two years in the sun, and I realized I'd have to repaint the whole thing.

"I'll go get the table ready," Emma said, after watching me paint for a couple of minutes.

An hour later, all signs of vandalism finally eradicated, I hauled my supplies down to the laundry room and dropped the brush in the utility sink. The stream from the faucet was so forceful blue paint spattered up the sides of the tub and onto the wall. Drops hit my hands and arms, even reaching as high as my neck. I was too distracted wondering what had gone wrong with Emma to bother wiping them off. Had anything I'd done pushed her so far over the side? Had I rushed her? By the time I'd been seeing Trina this long I'd already stressed through a home pregnancy test. Had I moved any slower this time around I'd never have even gotten as far as asking Emma out. I reached down to flip the brush and froze when I detected the clicking of cleats on the concrete floor behind me.

"Hey," J.T. Gaines whispered. "I got something for you."

"Yeah?"

"Last night, after Verotto got hauled off a bunch of us went down to Chapel Hill. That rich kid was at He's Not Here buying guys drinks like he always does."

"Landon?"

"Yeah, that's his name. Always walking around with that hot brunette."

"That's my ex-girlfriend."

"No kidding?"

"Don't act so surprised."

"Sorry. Anyway, after a couple of rounds he starts popping

off about how Dom owed him a bunch of money. Eight hundred bucks, a thousand bucks, whatever. The amount got higher the more he talked."

"Owed him money for what?"

"Gambling debts, I guess. Dom was probably looting the clubhouse to pay that fucker off. It's funny, I thought that guy was just a greenie peddler, but Dom never touched those things."

"Greenie peddler?"

"Yeah, that kid was always sucking up to everyone. Everybody's pal. Just his way of doing business. Fucker gave me his pitch a couple months ago that he could get me whatever I needed. Speed, steroids, whatever. I wanted to knock his teeth in."

"Why didn't you?"

"Gotta protect your teammates. Word gets out, it's pretty obvious who his customers are."

"Who are they?"

"I can't go there, man," J.T. laughed. "But it ain't the whole team or nothing. Just a few dipshits. Your boy Goose might be one of them."

"Now what?"

J.T. patted me on the shoulder and smiled. "That's your department, bro. I'm just passing along some information."

I finally had one over Rich, and I parsed it out slowly to him. When I started explaining the gambling connection he tried to tell me he'd figured it out on his own earlier in the day. He didn't see the amphetamines coming, though. And because he wasn't the one with the scoop he seemed inclined to dismiss it at first, like I was just making it all up. Tom Sawyer could be such a smug bastard. After brainstorming for a few minutes on a second sting operation, we decided to hand this one off to the professionals. I headed to Don's office and told him what we'd learned. He sat there unblinkingly taking it all in. "I'll handle it," he said. And that was that.

Emma begged off of working the booster club table and sought sanctuary in the press box. Only two fans signed up, so I hardly needed her help. In her current mood her company wasn't much use, either. When she reported to the DAP in a despondent funk again Thursday morning, I shadowed her, moving in when she was at last alone.

"We still on for lunch?" I asked.

"Um," she hawed, searching for an excuse, anything to spare my feelings.

"We oughta talk a little. Please?"

She assented, and we snuck out shortly before one and headed to a sub shop on Main Street, small-talking our way through the drive. After ordering our sandwiches we sat down on the picnic table out front, away from the rest of the diners who valued the air conditioning indoors over the beating sun and oppressive humidity.

"I'm sorry, Lane," she started, before I could. "I think I may have made a mistake."

"How do you mean? I thought we were having fun."

"We were. I was. I should still be. I'm just so confused now about what I should be doing, and what happens after next week. I don't think I ought to get you involved."

I stared at my plate, fingering the silver bag of potato chips as my appetite dried up.

"It'll all work out," I said. "If we want it to."

She nibbled at the edge of her sub, her eyes darting everywhere but at my face.

"It's not that simple," she replied at last.

"How do you mean, because of Alton?"

She inhaled a deep breath, gurgling mucus in the back of her throat, and her eyes welled up.

"I'm so sorry, Lane."

"I still don't get it. Why? What changed?"

"My dad called yesterday morning," she sobbed. "He wanted to congratulate me on my engagement."

"What?"

"Alton asked him for my hand."

Emma laid her sandwich down and rested her head on her forearm as her body convulsed. I moved around to her side of the table and rubbed her back as she wept.

"What did you say? I mean when your dad told you."

"Nothing. I just asked him to keep it a secret until I came home."

"You're not really marrying the guy are you?"

She dabbed her eyes with her napkin and shook her head. "Of course not. I hate him."

"I still don't understand. How'd it all get this far?"

"My dad loves Alton. He dated Alton's mom in college. They've been really close ever since. He's dreamed of this day ever since I was in diapers."

"What about you?"

"I went along with it for a long time, when I was young. I don't know why. I guess I wanted to please my dad. When I was fourteen I told Alton I loved him. He made me promise we'd get married someday. I was just a kid."

"And he still is."

"I told you, he's never grown up."

I pulled Emma toward me and squeezed her tight. She rested her head on my shoulder for a minute before breaking free.

"I'm sorry, Lane. I should have told you before."

"How could you know?"

"The signs have been there. The threats. He brings that stupid promise up every couple of months. I tried dating in college but could never find a good match. I wanted to bring someone home to my father while Alton was off at school so I could show him how happy I'd be. But I couldn't."

"And now Alton works for your dad?"

"No, for his dad. But the companies are pretty closely tied. It's almost the same. Why do you think I came to Durham for the summer? I had to get away from him. From them."

She picked up her sandwich and pecked at the edge a little, munching in silence as I watched the cars pass by on Main Street. I pulled my plate across the table and started working on my lunch.

"What now?" I asked.

"I'm going back to school next week. And I need to talk with my dad. That's all I know."

"What about us?"

Emma turned her face toward mine and her eyes apologized as her mouth couldn't. The tears leaked out and down both sides of her nose. She let them stream forth without trying to wipe them away.

"Maybe someday," she said. "I need to be alone now. I have

to finish growing up so this won't ever happen again."

I pondered what to say next but couldn't come up with anything. Appetite shot, I tossed my half-eaten sandwich back on my plate.

"I hope you can forgive me," she whispered.

"Of course," I said. "I don't understand it, but I'm not mad at you."

"Thanks."

"At least tell me you're still in for the booster club trip."

"Sure. I mean, if you still want me to go."

"Absolutely. Please come. It won't be the same without you."

CHAPTER TWENTY-FIVE

I dropped Emma back in the trailer office and walked down to the field, where Rich and Sonny were retooling the warning track behind home plate. It had slowly lost mass over the past month and Roger Gale had stumbled chasing a popup the night before due to uneven footing.

"You seen Peanut?" Rich asked.

"Nope."

"That durn kid ain't never where he oughta be." Sonny leaned his rake against the wall and wiped the sweat from his brow. "If he warn't leavin' for school this week, I'd kick 'im solid in the ass."

"When's last time you saw him?" I asked.

"Half hour ago," Rich said. "About the time we started doing some real work."

"If I see him, I'll send him your way."

I had a hunch where he could be found. Exiting the stadium down by left field, I snuck up the street, tiptoeing the final twenty yards to the Ballpark Corner shop. The front door didn't budge when I tugged on the handle. My curiosity piqued, I backed into the driveway, out of view, and waited.

Ten minutes later the snap of the bolt sliding out of the lock arrested my attention. Peanut poked his head out the door, glanced left and right, then skulked down the hill to the park. I crept out of my spot and sidled up next to him.

"Ahhhh!" he screamed when I slapped my hand down on his shoulder. "What? Oh, it's you, Lane."

"Where you been, man? Sonny's looking for you."

"Oh, right. I know. I'm on my way now."

"What's the rush?" I guided him away from the entrance, past the ticket tower and down the street.

"Where we goin'?"

"Walking. Talking." I shot him a sly look out of the corner of my eye. "You helping Faith?"

"How do you mean?"

"I went up to the store. Door was locked. Ten minutes later, you came out."

He stopped and turned to face me, his forehead raining perspiration, his left eye suddenly afflicted by a tic. "It ain't what you think, man. I hadda take a shit. I went up there to use the can."

"Ohhh," I said. "So, out of courtesy, Faith locks the door when you take a dump up there? I'll keep that in mind next time I have to go."

"Yeah, whatever."

I leaned close as if to tell him a secret. After a couple of theatrical sniffs, I pulled back and grinned at him.

"White Linen?"

"Say what?"

"Your perfume there. Is it White Linen? Very popular these days. I believe Faith wears it as well."

A flustered Peanut turned toward the front entrance of the park, then back toward me and my grin. "Look, I don't know what you're getting at, but …"

"Relax, dude," I laughed. "I won't tell anyone."

"Won't tell anyone what?"

"I saw the pillow and the blankets up there in the back room." I paused for effect as his face whitened. "So you're poking Faith. I was wrong. You're not a virgin." I slapped him on the back. "Congratulations."

"It's not what you think, man."

"So you're not banging Faith in the storage room?"

"Well." He flashed a shifty smirk. "There's more to it."

"Holy crap, is Spanky up there, too?"

"No, man. Not like that."

I smiled and waited for him to elaborate. He kicked the sidewalk with his right foot a few times, then took a deep breath.

"She was giving me, you know, lessons."

"Wow!" I had most of the pieces in place, but didn't see that one falling in. "How'd you do?"

"Not bad. I'm getting better."

I nodded my head toward the storage tower and started walking. He followed.

"You can't go up there anymore, dude."

"What? We've got one more session."

"Peanut, man, do you know what would happen if someone caught you? I mean, someone besides me?"

He shook his head and bit down on his lip.

"You'd both get fired. I know you're leaving for school, but you want to work here next summer, right? And think about Faith. That's her full-time job, man."

He nodded as though the message had sunk in, but said nothing.

"Look. No one else can know about this," I said. "You can never tell anyone. I promise I won't. But if anyone finds out, Don'll fire her. No question."

I threw my arm around his shoulders again and steered him back toward the front gate.

"She was really helping me, you know," he said.

"Well, I'm sure you were helping her, too. But now you've got a warning track to repair."

Rich told me later that Sonny worked Peanut over pretty good for his delinquency. Tough love from a cuddly country bear didn't weigh too heavily on an eighteen-year-old kid days away from college, but he worked as hard as his scrawny ass was capable, probably dreaming the entire time about one more go across the way.

He was hardly the only distracted student in our midst. Emma was off in another world, and some of the game-day hands were screwing off more than usual. But it was Crack Whore Girl who injected the most drama into the night. On my traditional sixth-inning trip to the left-field picnic area I encountered a furious Jenna, standing with her hands on her hips and straining her eyes across the field.

"You seen Shannon?" she asked.

"No. Haven't been down there yet. Why?"

"She ain't answering her radio. We've got forty-five people over there and I need to know what's going on. She's been worthless this week."

"This *week?*"

"Okay, season. But this week more than usual."

"You want me to watch your picnic so you can look for her?"

Jenna glanced at the urchins tearing around the canopy, and shook her head. "No. I can't. I've got to fetch them ice cream in a couple minutes or they'll pull the tent down."

"I'll walk around to right field. If I see her I'll give you a call."

"Thanks, Lane."

Unlike Jenna's raucous affair, the picnic guests in the right-field area were all adults, who weren't unleashing their furious energy on the facilities. Which was just as well, because their hostess had abdicated her watch. I strolled through the bleachers searching for her, to no avail. As I swung back toward the picnic area I came upon a middle-aged woman pounding on the women's room door as a six-year-old girl danced in place, her hands clutching the crotch of her pants.

"Excuse me," I said. "Is everything okay?"

"No," she bellowed. "Someone's locked the door in there. My daughter's gonna wet herself."

"Locked? It's never supposed to be … oh, never mind. There's another one just up the hill. Can she make it?"

I led the way toward the main concourse and pleaded on the girl's behalf with the women ahead of her in the line that extended out the door as her mother fumed about the conditions down below. Emergency averted, I returned to the right-field restroom, rapping loudly on the door. No answer.

"Sonny?" I called into my walkie-talkie. It echoed back at me a hair later. *"Sonny?"*

"What-*what?*" he responded.

"You got a key for this bathroom down near the right-field beer stand-*beer stand?*"

"Wha'ch'all need the key for-*key for?*"

"The women's bathroom-*bathroom,*" I paused. The echo wasn't coming from my radio. It was coming through the door. "It's locked-*it's locked.*"

"Hold on-*hold on.* I'll send Spanky-*Spanky.*"

I cut my radio off, and put my ear to the bathroom door. Static crackled faintly on the other side. Spanky rushed up with a ring of keys, holding a brass-colored one apart from the rest. I waved him on and he slipped it in the lock.

"Hold on a minute," a voice cried from the other side of the door.

"Shannon?" I asked. No reply. I nudged Spanky, who turned the key to the left. As the lock creaked out of place, our missing intern jerked the door back.

"What's going on in there?" I asked.

"Nothing," she retorted, patting herself down briskly. She brushed past me and headed back to her station.

I pushed the door open and stepped inside. Everything looked as it should.

"Whatever, man," I muttered. "I am so not gonna miss her, Spank."

He took the key ring and trotted off toward the tunnel as I leaned against the wall, puzzled. Two teenage girls who had been lingering a short distance away approached. I waved them on. "It's open now. Go for it."

I pulled out my radio to call Jenna, then decided it would be best to keep this off the air. Three steps from the bathroom I was frozen by a scream, echoing through the cinderblock structure. I turned to see one of the girls fly out the door.

"Hey," I called. "Everything okay?"

She halted, her eyes bugging out of her head as she gasped for air. Pointing back to the bathroom she stammered, "There's … there's a guy … inside."

"This is Lane," I called into the walkie-talkie. "I need Durham PD down by the right-field beer stand. We have a bathroom incident."

Within thirty seconds the game was an afterthought. Every fan in the right-field bleachers was turned toward the restroom, as three police officers swarmed in. Captain DesJardins pushed the door open and waved his men inside. Brimming with curiosity, I crept in after them. The second girl cowered by the sink, as a man's voice spoke calmly from the far stall. "Look, I'm not gonna hurt you. It's all a mistake."

The voice stopped when the clickety-clack of the officers' shoes against the tile floor announced more company had arrived. Officer Pickett commanded him to come out. When the door swung open a stocky fellow with a port-wine birthmark on his right cheek stepped forward holding his hands in front of him.

"Charlie?" I asked.

He waved meekly. Last time I had seen him he was wearing Shannon as a belt at Devine's. After sampling the rest of the Triangle area, she had gone back for seconds. Charlie spilled his guts to Captain DesJardins, figuring getting busted for having sex in the bathroom beat everyone thinking he was some kind of rapist or pervert. Don told him to leave and not come back, which was pretty easy terms. Of course, Don was a guy who believed in cutting his losses.

Shortly before the Bulls put the final touches on their 6-3 win over Winston-Salem, Shannon followed her partner in crime out the door. Oh, how I would love to have been a fly on the wall in that meeting. I'll never know exactly how Don worded it, but the essence had to be something like, "Get your skanky ass out of my ballpark, and please don't show up for the good-bye lunch tomorrow." She defiantly marched out the gate in the top of the ninth, her mosquito-bite chest thrust out, chin high, reputation firmly in the gutter.

I debated whether it made me a bad human being to find joy in her expulsion, and decided in the end that it didn't. Which was good, because she was the primary topic of discussion long into the night. "I should have guessed," Jenna said, every time someone mentioned the incident. "Probably wasn't the first time," Rich speculated, and a murmuring chorus concurred. It was well past two by the time we'd fully exhausted the subject and headed home.

To mark the farewell of the two remaining students, Don treated the staff to a family-style lunch at Bullock's Barbecue on Friday. We were especially gluttonous; by savoring the hush puppies and barbecue we postponed the inevitable round of farewells that awaited back at the DAP. There were plenty of hugs and tears shared as we bid adieu to Peanut and Emma. With Saturday's trip to Lynchburg in my pocket, I kept my emotions in check, though I watched her Jetta disappear with a certain tinge of sadness that afternoon. Emma had grown from co-worker to sister to something more as the season wore on. I wasn't ready yet to reverse that progression.

Saturday morning I was haunted by a nagging fear she wouldn't show for the bus trip. I invented pretexts on which to call her and erase these doubts, but they each seemed so transparent upon further review that I left for the park without picking up the phone. Having never led a booster club outing, I wasn't entirely sure what to do, but the driver was an affable man in his sixties named Gus, who soon put me at ease. He asked if I had a passenger manifest, reminding me that I had printed out such a list the previous afternoon. Having borrowed Rich's keys, I let myself into the park and the office trailer, emerging with purpose and a clipboard. As Bulls fans embarked the Southern Tours motor coach, I checked their names off the list and handed them an envelope containing their tickets.

Every minute on the minute, I checked my watch. Emma had twenty-nine minutes left. Emma had twenty-eight minutes left. Damn, where was she? Would she really bail out on me? No. With three minutes to spare, her aunt's Audi barreled into the gravel lot, raising a cloud of dust as tiny stones pinged the undercarriage of the vehicle.

"Sorry, y'all," Emma cried as she rushed up to the bus, her camera flapping violently against her side. "My little cousin fell off the swing set and hadda get stitches. It took forever."

With a relieved heart, I waved her aboard, just ahead of Randy Munn and his mother, who were the last passengers to arrive. I plopped into the seat next to Emma and learned the lurid details of Hannah's backyard misadventures. Emma had originally planned to drive herself, but her aunt had talked her out of leaving her car in the DAP's unattended parking lot all evening, setting up her dramatic arrival. The three-hour drive up Route 501 through rural North Carolina into the foothills of the Blue Ridge Mountains in Central Virginia passed with nary a pause in our conversation—and nary a mention of Alton Hobgood, IV.

We were welcomed to Lynchburg's City Stadium by the Red Sox' general manager, Hank Castle, who met our bus out front. He led our group of thirty-seven, including Gus, on a tour of the park, then handed us off to Gordy McNulty and Roger Gale, who thanked everyone for their unwavering support, which meant so much to the team. Emma and I guided our charges to the concession stand and arranged for meals (one hotdog or a slice of pizza, and a drink) to be distributed to each guest. So supplied, we carved out our territory behind the visitor's dugout and made ourselves comfortable.

The park, while historic, derived the bulk of its character from the surrounding landscape. The view over the outfield fence made up for the plainness of the stadium itself. Spotting the old press box on the roof, I persuaded Emma to join me for an impromptu tour. She huffed up the ladder behind me, halting at the top to admire the scenery, which was twice as impressive from up there, especially behind the park. We introduced ourselves to Lynchburg's beat reporter, who was smoking a cigarette outside the press box as he waited for the game to start. Emma snapped half a roll of pictures of the park and the mountains in the distance, then he took one of us with the field in the background. We returned to our seats just in time for the national anthem.

The game quickly developed into a pitchers' duel, with J.T. Gaines posting goose eggs for the Bulls and a 5-foot-11, left-handed junkballer named Ed DelVecchio countering for the Sox. A pop foul into our section off the bat of Dain Gregson was the highlight of the early innings. Randy Munn corralled it on a couple of hops, raising the trophy above his head as his proud mother beamed in the seat next to him. Clinging to a 2-1 lead in the bottom of the eighth, Gordy called for Goose Grascyk, who bolted in from the bullpen, took a lap around the mound, and proceeded to serve up a gopher ball to the first Lynchburg hitter he faced. Three batters later the Sox held the lead, which they wouldn't relent.

Though the outcome was a disappointment to our fans, we boarded the bus in generally high spirits and Gus headed us south down darkened highways. Emma and I talked quietly for a while, but by the time we hit South Boston, Va., she was fading fast. She tilted her seat back and closed her eyes. I followed suit. I dozed off soon after, waking up forty minutes later with my face pressed against the window, Emma's head resting on my left shoulder. Careful not to disturb her, I watched her chest rise and fall, her breath mechanically exhaled through her nostrils every four and a half seconds. Her eyeballs twitched under their lids as she dreamed, and I wished Gus would slow down and draw the moment out.

He sped on, however, and the terrain grew more familiar as the miles passed under our wheels. Shortly after one, the bus pulled into the DAP lot. I shook Emma softly to wake her. She blinked a couple of times and wiped her eyes, then smiled at me, and I dreaded the moment that was now so near at hand. She pointed to her uncle's minivan in the middle of the gravel lot, indicating her ride was there waiting. With a sigh and a wheeze the bus door swung open and our guests began to file off. Emma and I were to the stairs when a ruckus from the back of the bus drew my attention. "My baseball!" Randy Munn whined. "I lost my baseball!"

Fighting my way up the stream of exiting passengers, I found him shaking and staring at his seat, as his mother tried to calm him down.

"Don't worry, don't worry," I said. "We'll find it."

Crawling on all fours I scanned under every bench in his row, eventually locating his prized possession lodged under Gus's seat, where it must have rolled after falling from Randy's hand when he drifted off to sleep. Mrs. Munn thanked me six times, finally disembarking when Randy had collected the rest of his belongings.

Good-bye was here at last.

I rehearsed it as I descended the steps, deciding a hug would indeed be appropriate despite our current status. But when my feet touched the gravel, I found no Emma to embrace. My eyes swept over the ground that had so recently been occupied by her uncle's van. She was gone.

CHAPTER TWENTY-SIX

Disheartened, I drove home through dark and deserted streets and found Rich lingering on the porch, leafing through the new *Baseball America*.

"Hey," he said. "How was the trip?"

I shrugged my shoulders and dropped into the papasan chair. "All right, I guess."

"Something bugging you?"

"Nah," I waved it off, not eager to relive Emma's vanishing act. "I'm just tired's all."

"This'll wake you up." He tossed the magazine aside and jumped to his feet. "We got two calls tonight. Which do you want to hear first? Good news or great news?"

"I dunno. Good news, I s'pose."

"Cole called. I told him about College Night. He's totally stoked."

"Really?" I grabbed the side of the chair and pulled myself up. "Is he back in Raleigh?"

"Not yet. He will be on Tuesday."

"Which would definitely work if we did it Thursday night. We'd have plenty of time to call all the radio stations, the schools, thc—"

"Yeah," he interrupted. "But there's more."

"What? Did they get signed?"

"Not yet. They've had some contact with a guy at Geffen. They're getting close, man."

"That is great news. Wow."

"Yes." Rich paused dramatically and stooped down to grab the *Baseball America*. "But it's not *the* great news."

"What? Is Paul in there?"

He flipped through the paper, turning the magazine around and thrusting it in my face as he tapped the page with his forefinger. I read through the agate print at the end of the South

Atlantic League notes, finally locating the two-sentence write-up on our friend. "Macon second sacker Paul Giordano, a 43rd-round pick last year, has hit .335 since June 1, with seven home runs and 46 RBIs. The UNC-Pembroke product was hitting .308-9-61 on the year."

"Way cool," I said after re-reading it a third time. "Someone finally noticed."

"That's not all," Rich said. "He's coming to Durham."

"Serious?"

"Juan Escarola broke his hand last night. They're moving Harcourt up to Greenville for the playoff run and Paul's coming here."

"We just saw Harcourt playing for the Bulls."

"Paul called around eleven-thirty. He had just found out. Martin probably got the call after the game."

I drove to the ballpark Sunday morning to prepare a couple of press releases. I sent the College Night one to the papers, every news crew in the Triangle, and about a dozen radio stations. The second one was about Paul, mixed with a healthy dose of Martin, who had really grown on me over the course of the season. Much like our buddy, he wasn't a guy who would catch the eye of the casual fan. But anyone who knew the game would appreciate the subtle qualities he brought—the defensive positioning, bat control, and base-running instincts that didn't show up on the stat sheet. I was happy for him to get his chance in Double-A.

Monday I followed up all of the press releases with phone calls. Normally I hated calling. People were like, "Who? I'm not sure we got that one. Can you send it again? Okay, I'll check. Yeah, it's here. I'll pass it along to the sports guy. Blah. Blah. Blah. I don't care." I'd found it was generally a waste of time to call anyone because they didn't give a mouse's teat what we were doing, but for Cole and for myself, I wanted this thing to be huge. The only radio stations that had a clue what I was talking about were the college stations, which all knew Disingenuity because they played their music.

After spending two hours on the phone my first instinct was to pat myself on the back and take a break. Unfortunately, the grounds crew was a man short and that didn't jibe with Sonny's expectations. I spent most of Monday afternoon baking in the sun, riding a mower back and forth across the outfield.

Tuesday was even crazier. I had four voicemails when I came up from morning field duty. Paul's mom and Nicole were both looking for tickets. Cole wanted to know if they could come out and walk through everything Wednesday so they'd know where to set up and what kind of space they had. And Aimee Lynn from WRAL news called about my press release. She actually remembered me from Opening Night, which shocked me down to my boxers, because we hadn't seen a trace of her since. I invited her to stop out Wednesday night and meet the guys from the band, figuring she'd blow me off, but she bit. I should so have been Cole's manager.

The game was such a blur that the only thing I remembered were Paul's at-bats. I loitered in the press box when he was due up in the bottom of the first so it would look like I was working. Maybe I should have found something else to do. He struck out on four pitches, and didn't look good doing it. Welcome home, buddy. He finished 1-for-4 with a gift single that the official scorer probably flipped a coin on. I was biased, and I would have scored it an error on the Salem third baseman. Paul said the same thing after the game.

I rose a notch in Don's eyes when Aimee Lynn walked in with a cameraman and asked for me Wednesday night. He was standing in the concourse chatting with Captain DesJardins at the time. I introduced the reporter to Cole and his bandmates and when she was done with them I led her around the park, subtly suggesting shots for her cameraman. They ran a minute and six seconds worth of Durham Bulls on the newscast that night, with a couple of Lane cameos mixed in. You can't buy publicity like that.

My mom called Thursday morning and said three people in her office told her they saw me on the news. I would have been excited if I hadn't been so nervous. What if no one showed up? That thought haunted me as the day wore on, nearly driving me to retch a couple of times. I literally felt my throat clinch up and tasted the vomit. Just before noon Rich checked into the office and found me hyperventilating.

"You alright, man?" he asked.

I took a deep breath and exhaled slowly through my nose. "Yeah."

"You all set for tonight?"

"I think so. I can't think of anything else I can do until late this afternoon."

"Well then, let's go grab some lunch and chill out for a little while."

"Nah. I really shouldn't."

"You really should. Come on. Let's go to Devine's. I have something to tell you."

Rich talked about anything but College Night on the drive over. He told me about his dentist appointment, his dad's new haircut, Burt's latest laundry mishap—anything to get me to relax. It helped. By the time we got there my stomach was no longer knotted up and I realized how hungry I was.

"What's your news?" I asked after we'd put in our order.

"I had a call from Turner Wyand this morning."

"From Burlington?"

"Yeah."

His smile could have powered a small submarine and I knew what he was going to say next.

"Matty's moving on."

"Where to?"

"Albany, Georgia."

"Albany?"

"Yup. The Sumter team is moving down there after the season. Kevin Klopak wants Matty to be his assistant."

"So Turner's moving up to GM, and you're taking his spot?"

"That's the plan."

"Damn."

"Don't say anything to anyone yet. I haven't told Don."

"Don't worry. I can keep a secret."

Cole showed up a little after four. My anxiety subsided once I actually had something to do. I got the band situated on the lawn in front of the ticket tower, just outside the front gate. I'll never forget the feeling I had when a couple in UNC t-shirts strolled over and unfolded a blanket in front of the makeshift stage. By six o'clock there were nearly a hundred kids on the lawn waiting for Disingenuity to kick it out. Dave smacked his drumsticks together four times and they busted into "Sneaking Home," which they played more up-tempo than they had at our house party. It sounded better this way.

They played for forty-five minutes as college students swarmed in from all directions. I floated through the crowd with a clipboard, signing up volunteers for the on-field competitions. When I had enough names, I took a break and became a spectator. All around me kids were dancing. Not a flop, not even close, I thought as I surveyed the rolling sea of heads.

After the band wrapped up its set with an extended version of "Lost It," Alex, the lead singer, summoned me back to the stage as we'd rehearsed. I took the microphone and thanked them for playing and announced they had copies of both of their albums for sale next to the main souvenir stand. Alex's girlfriend, who was selling the CDs, was swamped with customers a moment later.

The bleachers in both left and right field swelled with raucous revelers, lending the game a pep-rally flavor. The between-inning contestants received louder ovations than the ballplayers. In the seventh inning Nick announced UNC had turned out the most students. The Tar Heels immediately burst into their school fight song. The park was soon a cacophony of competitive singing, as the other schools tried to drown them out. The players on the field stared up into the stands, marveling at the energy of the fans, and I felt like I'd knocked one onto the roof of the Brame building.

Don handed me a slip of paper an hour after the game that read, "4,400, 5,316, +916."

"Nice job," he said. "We were almost a thousand over my target for the night."

"Thanks. I was so afraid no one would come."

He reached into his pocket and pulled out an envelope, which he pressed into my hand. "You earned this tonight."

After he retreated to his office, I lifted the flap and counted eight twenty-dollar bills. If that doesn't sound like much of a reward, remember, I was only making a thousand bucks a month.

CHAPTER TWENTY-SEVEN

The pandemonium meter held steady throughout the week. We crammed more than 5,000 fans in each night and the Bulls beat back Salem before welcoming hapless Peninsula to town. The Pilots scuffled into Saturday's contest having lost thirteen straight, but the fans streamed through the gate nonetheless, queuing up at the concession stands under Don's watchful gaze. The headman surveyed his domain, arms folded across his chest as he spoke with Captain DesJardins. Though both were on alert, they weren't familiar enough with Landon to recognize him when he clicked through the turnstile just before seven o'clock on the heels of a dolled-up Trina. A familiar pout etched on her face, she marched across the concourse without waiting for him. As he beelined for the beer stand, I knifed through the crowd to interrupt my boss.

"Landon Dowager's here," I said.

Don's eyes twinkled and he allowed himself half a smile. "Point him out for me."

He and the police captain followed my directions and spied their target as he lodged a pair of large beers into a cardboard tray.

"I know I don't need to tell you this," Don said, "but stay out of this one, Lane."

"Yes, sir."

He didn't say I couldn't watch. I zipped down to the press box and stationed myself by the door. Landon and Trina were once again seated four rows back, just down from the dugout. Good seats that must have been left by someone on the team. Landon sipped on his beer as Trina sat on the corner of her seat, her bag slung over her shoulder as a barrier separating the two of them. With a wave I caught Rich's attention on the field. I lifted my radio and flashed eight fingers. A moment later he buzzed in.

"What's up?"

"The eagle has landed."

"Suh-weet. Does Don know?"

"Oh yeah."

"What's he gonna do?"

"I don't know, but I've got a front-row seat."

I stood watch until the game started, breaking eye contact only briefly during the national anthem. Landon worked his charm and reengaged Trina in conversation, and they chatted blissfully unaware he was in anyone's crosshairs. Rich buzzed in twice during the first inning wanting updates. He couldn't see from the mouth of the tunnel and didn't want to raise suspicion by cruising past.

As Evan Wayne completed his warmup pitches in the top of the third I spotted Officer Pickett looming at the top of the stairs, talking into the radio on his shoulder. I scanned the bowl of the stadium and located two more policemen. They descended in unison, slowly tightening their radius.

"Richard."

"Now?"

"Yeah. Get up somewhere you can see this."

"I'm on my way."

Stretched casually in his seat, Landon pointed toward shortstop, motioning and explaining something to Trina. She was so engrossed in his Baseball 101 lesson that neither of them noticed when two Durham police officers approached on either side of their box.

"You seeing this, Rich?"

"Yup."

I raised my line of sight and found him loitering just the other side of thc Bulls dugout, his face lit up like Christmas morning.

Officer Pickett crouched down in the aisle next to Landon and the bookie stopped talking. He listened attentively to the cop as Trina spun in her seat, her mouth flapping open in disbelief when she found another policeman on her left. Their brief conversation concluded, Officer Pickett stood and motioned for Landon to do the same. He started up, then leaned over to embrace a hysterical Trina. As he hugged her, he palmed a black object from his waistband and plunged his hand into the side pocket of her purse. He then rose and held out his wrists. Officer Pickett shook his head and pointed up toward the exit. Landon mounted the stairs, flanked by two policemen.

"Did you see that?" I asked Rich.

"That was awesome. I wish they'd take Trina, too."

"No, not just him leaving. Did you see him stash something in her bag?"

"What was it?"

"I couldn't tell."

"You're the only man in this park without a badge who can find out."

"I'm on it."

I stowed the radio in my back pocket and made my way over to Trina, who stood staring after Landon as he disappeared from view. Assuming his seat, I motioned for her to retake hers.

"What's going on?" she demanded. "What do they want with him?"

"I don't know. But I'm sure everything's going to be fine."

"How do you know?" Her voice rose and she started to get up again. "Where are they taking him?"

"Maybe they just want to ask him some questions."

I grabbed at her wrist to pull her back into her seat. She wrenched it out of my fingers then swung it back toward me, her elbow grazing my ear as it flew past. Before she could take another shot I secured her forearm and with one hand around her waist coaxed her into a sitting position.

"Relax," I said. "Calm down."

"Relax? They just—did you have something to do with this?"

"No. How could I?"

"This is a fucking setup. What, are you jealous? You get your cop friends to harass Landon?"

Now her free hand came at me, nails first. I turned away and blocked it with my left elbow. Still clutching her right arm with one hand I snatched her left wrist and pinned it against the armrest.

"I had nothing to do with it, Trina. I swear."

"No? Where'd this all come from then? They said something about amphetamines. And gambling. Landon doesn't gamble."

"I'm sure he doesn't. Maybe it's all a mixup."

"Maybe it's all a joke." She glared at me.

"I don't think they're allowed to joke about stuff like this."

I released my grip and she withdrew her arms to adjust her tank top, which had been twisted beyond its PG-13 threshold. As she did I scouted her handbag. It had been knocked on its side as we skirmished, pushing a black address book up out of the side pocket.

"What are you doing over here anyway?" she asked.

"I was in the press box." I pointed across her seat toward the plexiglass window from which I'd witnessed Landon's exit. "Someone said there were cops out here, so I came out to see what was going on."

Trina bit down on her lip and looked from me to the press box, then back again.

"You know," she said. "You haven't changed a bit since I dumped you. You're still a horrible liar."

"What?"

"Most guys, when they stare at my chest, I figure they just like what they see. You, you look there when you lie."

"That's, no … that's not true."

"Yeah, it is. You always talked to my chest when you couldn't look me in the eye."

"Gimme a break."

"Spare me." She folded her arms in front of her tank top.

I looked past her covered chest, down to her purse. Landon's book hung like a loose tooth. I was no closer to securing it than I had been when I first sat down. Further away, really. As usual, I had stormed into battle with no plan. Trina stared out at the field, sneaking a peek at me out of the corner of her eye every ten seconds or so as I belatedly mulled my options. Pretending to be nice hadn't worked. Maybe I could somehow provoke her. Another minor scuffle should suffice. One well-placed kick would pop that book clear of her bag. I just had to make sure she wasn't looking down when I did it.

"Why are you still here?" she asked at last. "I thought they worked you nonstop."

"I just wanted to make sure you were okay—"

"I'm fine," she said without looking at me.

"With your boyfriend going to jail and all, I figured—"

"He'll be back."

"Wouldn't be so sure on that one. Those are some pretty serious charges and—"

"I thought you didn't know anything about it."

"About him selling drugs to the players?"

Trina stopped pretending to watch the game and turned her head toward me, her nostrils flaring as she drew air in through her nose.

"Of course I knew," I said. "How did you not know is the real question? Do you think all the players just like him because he's rich? You honestly didn't know the guy was a bookie? Does he even have—"

"God, I fucking hate you. Why the fuck did I ever go out with you? You're such an asshole."

"Maybe. But at least I'm not getting anally probed by the Durham PD right now."

"Would you please leave?"

"Why?"

"Because I hate you," she said slowly through her most sarcastic smile. "You know what? You stay. I'll leave. I don't want to see your fucking face anymore anyway."

She turned and leaned down to pick up her bag, her fingers now mere inches from Landon's book. Desperate to stall her, I placed my left hand on the exposed bare skin of her lower back. Trina snapped at me, her whitened teeth shining as she drew her lips into a snarl.

"You—don't touch me there. Or anywhere. Ever again."

"Oh come on, Trina. Let's at least part friends."

"Get your fucking hand off me, Lane."

She grabbed the strap of her purse and spun toward me, swinging her bag up at my face. I ducked out of its path and it crashed harmlessly into the back of my seat. For a moment it balanced on the armrest, so tantalizingly close. Before I could inspect the side pocket Trina yanked it away.

"Good-bye, asshole," she said.

She stood over me, glaring, almost daring me to respond as she readied her handbag for another strike. But I sat quietly, my teeth clamped around my bottom lip, focused on the ground beyond her. "Please don't look down, please don't look down," was all I was thinking. Finally she turned and strode away, stepping over a small, black leather book as she left.

In the dim light of Devine's front patio after the game Rich and I examined the spoils of my battle. A soft leather cover, monogrammed with the initials LJD, encased a couple hundred looseleaf pages, separated by alphabet tabs. I flipped to the V's and there we found "Verotto, Dominic," followed by a series of numbers: 400, 650, 330, 1,200, 800. All but the last had been crossed out.

"Damn," Rich whispered. "Dom was into him for a lot of money."

"And he was only here for two months."

I turned to the start of the alphabet and we paged through, letter by letter. Under C we found Ray Crocker, a sportscaster with one of the local news teams. His numbers had all been struck through. A folded sheet of paper was tucked in a few pages later. I recognized it immediately as I flattened it on the tablecloth. It was one of Blake's bet faxes, copied onto plain white paper.

"A hundred bucks Blake's name is in here somewhere," I said.

"No shit. Let's see what he owes."

I ran my finger down the M page and back up again, but didn't find him.

"Maybe 'cause of the faxes," Rich suggested.

"Yeah, I guess. Damn. I wanted to see his balance."

"Forget him," Rich said. "Look for something on his greenie trade. Where's Goose?"

We leafed through the rest of the listings without spotting the reliever or anyone else we recognized. Beyond the alphabet tabs there were about fifty blank sheets. I flipped through them quickly with my thumb.

"Stop." Rich jabbed his forefinger into the book. "I saw some writing."

On the second-to-last page there were three names listed. The third was Blake Mungo. After his name it said "Bulls," with our office phone number. The other two were "Josh Greene, Mudcats" and "Dirk Larriman, Hornets."

"Fuckin' A," Rich said. "Blake was his clubhouse guy."

"What do you mean?"

"Look, he's got a guy with the Mudcats, and a guy in Greensboro. What a setup. He's like the greenie Wal-Mart. He's got a branch in every town."

"So Blake took the stuff from him and delivered it to the players?"

"Exactly. Landon couldn't just walk into the locker room. Blake's his bag boy. Lemme see that fax again."

I pushed the sheet of paper toward him and he held it up in the soft light emanating from above in the awning.

"Oh, man." He shook his head. "We're stupid."

"What do you mean?"

"These aren't all bets. They're just what he says. 'This week's order.' This number one, with a five dozen, that's got to be greenies. Some guys probably go through a bunch of those in a week."

"What's the number two? Ten? Ten what?"

"Dunno. Steroids maybe? Could be anything. Didn't Landon tell J.T. he could get him anything?"

"Yeah, that's what he said."

"One stop shopping," Rich said. "Gambling, pills, maybe he was whoring Becca out on the side."

"Wonder what Blake's cut was."

"Not enough to be worth his job. Retard bitched about his salary so much. Guess he found a way to supplement his income."

"I wouldn't want to be him when Don finds out."

Rich cackled and took a pull on his beer. "Stupid fucker," he laughed.

"You going to blow him in?"

"You found the book. You get the honors. I say you lay it on Don's desk tomorrow morning."

"What do you think he'll do?"

"Whatever he said to Shannon, that was just a warmup."

I figured I wouldn't drift off easily that night with Landon's book resting on the nightstand and Trina's vicious diatribe looping through my head. I was wrong. I didn't just sleep, I hibernated. Rich pounded on the door for two minutes before I woke up Sunday morning. He was fired up.

I hovered outside Don's office, waiting for him to vacate it so I could steal in and drop the bomb on his desk. He never did. After lingering there for nearly an hour I finally moved on to Plan B and just marched in and handed it to him.

"What's this?"

"Landon Dowager dropped it last night."

"Oh?"

"I thought you should have it."

He flipped the cover open with his thumb and I exited. Blake, who was just reporting for work, passed me in the concourse and nodded hello. I returned his greeting with the pallid smile of a mob snitch. Blake deserved the door. He knew what he was doing. I'd been fired from the bank for oversleeping, so why should I feel bad for him? I don't know, but I did. I actually felt a little guilty for turning the guy in.

I never saw him again. Don summoned him to his office a short time later and the story goes he just laid the evidence out on his desk and asked Blake what he knew about it. Blake didn't say anything, and Don told him to leave. I'm not sure how reliable that version is, but it was the only one circulated. Maybe that was how Shannon's exit interview went as well.

Entering Monday we had drawn just over 292,000 fans on the season. Don placed ads in the Raleigh and Durham papers touting Monday's game as Fan Appreciation Night, Part I. Like a wacky TV pitchman who had lost his lease, he took an "everything must go" attitude toward team merchandise. I was pressed into full-time duty running stock from across the street down to Aaron in the souvenir stands, causing Rich to whine about having to rely on Batboy Eddie to groom the field before the game.

"He's fucking worthless, man," he fumed shortly before the gates opened. "You can't let him chalk the baselines or they look like a drunken blind man did them. He can't drive the tractor straight, so how's he gonna drag the infield? And he's too fucking lazy to do anything else."

"That's kangaroo," I said.

Rich laughed and turned back to the field, where Eddie had mounted the John Deere like a surfer riding a wave.

"Goddam Coño bastard!" Rich shouted. "Get off there and do some work!" He charged at Eddie, who tumbled off the tractor and collapsed in a laughing heap on the infield grass. He might not have had a clue what was going on, but he sure had a good time.

Moments after the gates swung open the souvenir stand was

inundated with bargain seekers. A throng of fans clutched at whatever they could reach, loading up on five-dollar t-shirts, half price caps, pennants, post cards, and everything else we didn't want to store all winter. As fast as we could open cartons of shirts, hands grasped for them. The only thing that mattered was size. I pulled out t-shirts I had never even seen before. Ugly brown ones with discolored logos disappeared in a flash. Don checked in every so often, monitoring sales and sending messages down to Nick to announce a special on can huggers or Bulls gym shorts and a new wave of shoppers would crash down upon us.

When the game ended our stand looked like a hurricane had struck. The ransacked cubbyholes were jammed with t-shirts or caps that had been flung aside when rejected by a potential purchaser. Packs of baseball cards, coated in a syrupy mess from a spilled Coke, littered the floor. Money that had been tossed toward the cash box in the frenzied storm of commerce lined the shelf under the counter. Aaron didn't even bother taking inventory; he handed Don the money and evacuated the area, vowing to come in early the next morning and clean up the mess.

Tuesday was a surreal rerun with the added dynamic of being the last hurrah of the year. The final home game. The team was three games behind Kinston, but despite a strong run in August they were gaining no ground, making a playoff bid unlikely even if they swept their upcoming road trip. This was it. I confess I got a little emotional a couple of times that afternoon, though I was ninety-eight percent glad the season was ending. Working all those hours over the past five months had worn on me.

Don toured the Ballpark Corner store with me and Aaron Tuesday afternoon, pointing out stuff he wanted gone. He planned to discontinue two of the t-shirt styles and one type of baseball cap. "I don't care what you get for them," he said. "They're not coming back up here."

When the game started we drafted Carson to help, which gave us an extra set of hands but almost no space to move. It took us an hour to work out a system so we weren't knocking into each other every time we turned around. By the sixth inning, things had settled down enough that we could hear Ron Anders' broadcast out of the speakers in the concession stand. I divided my attention between the customers and the radio when Paul's name was announced.

"What size do you need, ma'am?" *Weymouth's first pitch to Giordano looks like a slider. Broke outside and down. Count goes to one-and-oh. We've got one down in the bottom of the sixth, all knotted up at three.* "I'm out of mediums in that style. I can give you a large, or maybe you'd like the red one?" *Weymouth toes the rubber and picks up the sign from Bender.* "The back? It's got the big D logo on the back. Just like the blue one up there." *The kick and the wind, it's a hard strike that splits the plate. Giordano's shown a lot of patience tonight, but that looked like his pitch right there.* "No, it won't shrink much. I've got a couple of them. They've held up well." *Weymouth has been strong in his inning and a third of relief tonight. One of Peninsula's more impressive pitchers. Here's the one-one pitch to Giordano, swung on and hammered, deep to left...* "Carson, take over, man! I gotta see this."

I dashed out the door midsale and charged through the concourse into the seating area in time to see Paul rounding second base as the crowd serenaded him with a thunderous applause. *That's Giordano's first Durham home run and it couldn't have come at a better time. The Bulls take a 4-3 lead.* Paul continued his circuit in slow motion as the crowd roared its approval, clapping and stomping until he crossed the plate. He looked up behind the dugout and waved, probably to Nicole or his parents, and trotted to the bench. *Left fielder Luther Hudson steps to the plate as the crowd settles back down.*

"Sorry, man," I huffed, jumping back behind the counter. "I was really hoping to see that."

"Was that your friend?" Aaron asked.

"Yeah. I missed the hit, but I got out there in time to see him cross the plate."

Nick announced all remaining t-shirts were down to three bucks apiece and the tidal flood crested again. The crowd around the stand was so thick I couldn't see through it until half an hour after the game ended. We didn't quite sell every last item as Don had stipulated, but we came awful close. I reached under the counter for my cup and nearly gagged on a stray dollar bill floating in the warm, flat Cheerwine.

"Disgusting," Carson said, when I pulled the money out of my drink. "But you'll have a beer in a minute, anyway."

"Not soon enough," I said, collapsing onto a cushioned stool.

Aaron and Carson ran behind the ticket tower and secured the plywood window covers, which they jammed into place as I dumped my soda down the drain just outside the doorway. I pitched the cup in a trash barrel and hoisted the last board, grabbing it by the handle and lugging it through the door, where Aaron helped me lock it down.

"What a night," he said. "I'm beat."

"The fun part's just starting," I said. "You're sticking around tonight, right?"

"I don't know." He glanced from me to Carson, who like myself was overdue for a cold one. "I'm exhausted, guys."

"Suit yourself, man. You're gonna miss the best party of the year."

"What's his problem?" Carson asked, as we slipped out of the stand.

"Don't know. Don't care. Need a beer."

We marched purposefully across the concourse into the gathering mob concentrated around the nacho stand. Several of the players had joined the celebration. I looked around for Paul but didn't see him. Nick had appointed himself head bartender, and I twirled my hand in a small circle, signaling for him to step up the pace, which only made him go slower. Finally armed with a drink for myself and one for Carson, I emerged from the sweltering nacho shack and tracked down the ticket assistant, who was leaning against the wall, staring intently down the hill.

"You still want this?" I asked, when he failed to reach for his drink.

He ignored my question, answering instead with one of his own. "Is that who I think it is?"

"Where?" I turned to follow his gaze and spotted Rich and Paul amongst a jocose knot of people, laughing as they migrated up from the clubhouse. As they moved I picked out Sonny, Spanky, Jenna, and a dumpy, frumpy girl from Shallotte, and the most wondrous pain raced from my gut all the way up to my throat.

"It's Emma," Carson murmured.

I wanted to be aloof and just sip my beer in the concourse as I waited for them to arrive. I tried. I managed for about three seconds before I took off as fast as I could move, sloshing beer with every step. My cup was empty by the time I reached them.

"Hey, y'all," Emma called, breaking into a jog.

"When'd you get here?" I asked when we met midway down the ramp. Carson caught up with us a moment later.

"Fifth inning. I tried to come see you guys, but I couldn't get anywhere near you."

"Yeah, it was awful," Carson said, as if she were there to talk to him.

The rest of the group had caught up with us. I turned away from Emma for a moment to high five Paul and congratulate him on his dinger. When we started moving up the hill Emma grabbed my shirt sleeve and pulled me back. As the others passed on ahead of us she leaned against the wall and fidgeted with her watch.

"I never got to say good-bye last week," she said.

"Yeah," I laughed nervously. "By the time I found that damn baseball you were long gone."

"I'm sorry. My uncle had been waiting here since midnight. He wanted to go."

"Ohhhhh." I mentally kicked myself in the ass for imagining it could have been her fault.

"I felt horrible about it for two days. And then I realized it wasn't what was really bugging me."

"What was?"

She reddened slightly and averted her gaze. When she smiled up at me again the edges of her eyes glistened. "It wasn't good-bye I wanted to say."

"No?"

"I couldn't stop thinking about you. You were right. We should try this."

"What about Alton?"

"The hell with Alton. I want to be with you. I mean, if you're still in—"

I'd heard enough. I flung my plastic cup aside and pounced on her, my lips damming the words pouring forth from her open mouth. I pinned her against the brick wall, oblivious to the odd glances from up the hill, answering her with two weeks of warehoused kisses. She fought only long enough to earn herself a more comfortable position. I came up for air after a minute, and leaned against the wall next to her.

"I'll take that as a yes," she laughed, rubbing the back of her head.

"Absolutely."

"I wasn't sure what you'd say. I didn't even decide to come up until five o'clock tonight. I thought maybe you'd met someone else by now."

"It's only been a week," I laughed.

"Ten days. And they were ten long days, too."

"You ain't kidding."

Emma grabbed my hand and pulled away from the wall. "Come on. They're gonna wonder what happened to us."

"I think they've probably figured it out."

I didn't let go of her hand until I had to use the bathroom forty minutes later. We ground our clammy palms together as we drank and celebrated the end of a long season and the start of something even more exciting. With the exception of Aaron, every full-timer on the payroll—and a few dozen others out for a great party—stuck around. Don toasted our surpassing the 300,000 mark, temporarily besting Frederick, who had six home games remaining. Sonny pulled his truck in through the gate and cranked up his George Strait, which lasted for about three minutes before Gray reached in and replaced it with a James Brown CD.

Paul and his teammates left at midnight, citing an early morning departure for Salem. Every half hour the party lost mass, until only the diehards remained: Mike, Carson, Rich, Emma, and me, and I was on fumes.

"One last round," I called as I checked my watch. "It's almost three. Who's in for one more?" Three hands went up and I fetched drinks for Mike, Carson, Rich, and myself.

"You gonna sneak into Uncle Abe's tonight?" I asked Emma, who looked ready to go.

"That would sort of blow my cover, y'all. I'm supposed to be in school tomorrow."

"You mean today, right?" Rich asked.

"Today, tomorrow—I mean Wednesday, whatever."

"You're not driving back now are you?" I asked, checking my watch again.

"What kinda hospitality do y'all call that?" she replied. "Jeez,

I drive all the way up here to see you, and …"

"So you're staying with us?"

"If you can be trusted to behave yourself!"

"But of course. I'll even lend you a t-shirt."

"That's quite all right. I brought my flannel PJs. They cover *everything* up good."

"So you planned on staying the whole time?"

"I figured you boys would need a ride home tonight. And your taxi's ready to go."

We offered the sleeper sofa to Carson, easily convincing him not to drive all the way to Chapel Hill, and piled into Emma's Jetta after locking the gate. When we arrived home she pulled an overnight bag from the trunk and followed me upstairs.

"A twin bed?" she sniffed, when I turned the light on in my room.

"Don't worry. I'm too tired to try anything."

After freshening up in the bathroom and donning her pajamas—full tops and bottoms—she crawled under the covers. I cut the light and lay down with one cheek hanging over the edge of the mattress. I rustled in place for a couple of minutes, trying to get comfortable, but succeeded only in preventing Emma from drifting off to sleep.

"Lane," she said at last.

"Yeah."

"We can cuddle, you know. That's allowed."

I rolled over and pressed up against her, burying my nose in the tuft of blonde hair jutting up from my pillow. I thought I felt her heart beating, but soon realized it was only mine, reverberating off her breast. Her breathing steadied into a soft, regular pattern, exhaling every four and a half seconds, and I whispered in her ear. "Good night, Emma Leigh. I think I love you."

"I heard that," she mumbled into my neck. "You called me Emma Leigh."

ACKNOWLEDGMENTS

I had the privilege to work for the Durham Bulls for three years when I was in college, back in the early 1990s. Minor league baseball was different then. The boom that has swept the nation, gentrifying small towns with miniature versions of major league stadiums, hadn't yet occurred. Most teams were still owned by individuals instead of corporations, and life at the ballpark was certainly less formal than it is today, when many team employees look as though they just stepped away from their desk at an investment brokerage. Sure, the pay was lousy and the hours were long, but that was part of the bargain if you wanted to spend your days in a ballpark.

I set this story in old Durham Athletic Park, because to me it is the essence of what the minor leagues are all about. Several years ago, I stopped in to see the DAP on a visit to Durham and was saddened to find it in such a state of disrepair. Fortunately, over the past couple of years it has been fully refurbished and is once again regularly used for games, including one "heritage" contest each season by the Bulls.

In peopling *The Greatest Show on Dirt,* I borrowed some attributes from some of the larger than life characters I met while working for the Bulls and later while covering the minors for *Baseball America.* Rest assured, however, this is a work of fiction. While I strove to realistically reflect life of that era in the minor leagues, this is not a thinly disguised memoir. Lane Hamilton is not me.

I am fortunate to have kept in contact with some of the friends I met while working for the Bulls two decades ago, including Bill Miller and Dave Chase, who were both kind enough to read my manuscript and provide their feedback. I am grateful to them for helping me remember details about the DAP, which Bill knows better than any man alive.

I'm also heavily indebted to Dave Atias, Bill Ballew, Bruce Winkworth, and Andrew Zibuck, who each read the book twice and offered their brutally honest opinions of what worked and what didn't. Thanks also to Andrew Bernstein, Marylaine Block, Will Carroll, Matthew Eddy, Robbie Gurganus, Al Marshall, Rob Miller, and Ben Wittkowski for reading the manuscript and sharing their suggestions.

Valerie Holbert was the creative force behind the cover, which came out looking better than anything I could have dreamed up on my own. I appreciate her time and talent.

Finally, I owe a special thank you to my wife, Jill, who not only read multiple versions of the book as it progressed, but allowed me to indulge my creative need by working late into the night down in my office. I hope that it may prove worthy of the sacrifice in family time.

A NOTE ON THE AUTHOR

James Bailey worked for the Durham Bulls for three seasons, from 1990-92. He is a regular contributor to *Baseball America* magazine, for whom he spent six years covering minor league baseball. He lives in Rochester, N.Y., with his wife Jill and son Grant. *The Greatest Show on Dirt* is his first novel.

57579542R00152

Made in the USA
Columbia, SC
10 May 2019